Talk

to the

Hand

a novel by

Darrien Lee

Q-Boro Books
WWW.QBOROBOOKS.COM

An Urban Entertainment Company

Published by Q-Boro Books
Copyright © 2006 by Darrien Lee

ISBN-13: 978-1-933967-61-5
ISBN-10: 1-933967-61-7
First Printing October 2006
Mass Market Edition November 2008

10 9 8 7 6 5 4 3 2

This is a work of fiction. It is not meant to depict, portray or represent any particular real persons. All the characters, incidents and dialogues are the products of the author's imagination and are not to be construed as real. Any references or similarities to actual events, entities, real people, living or dead, or to real locales are intended to give the novel a sense of reality. Any similarity in other names, characters, entities, places and incidents is entirely coincidental.

Cover Copyright © 2006 by **Q-BORO BOOKS** all rights reserved
Cover Layout & Design—Candace K. Cottrell
Photo by Ted Mebane
Editors—Melissa Forbes, Candace K. Cottrell

Q-BORO BOOKS
Jamaica, Queens NY 11431
WWW.QBOROBOOKS.COM

Acknowledgments

I would like to thank my entire family for your support. It's been a difficult year, and I couldn't have made it without your love. I want to send out words of gratitude to Pastor Vincent Windrow and First Lady Stacy Windrow of Olive Branch Missionary Baptist Church for your prayers, spiritual guidance, and encouragement.

To The Ties That Bind Book Club in Murfreesboro, TN and Sistahs Keeping It Read Book Club and Fade 2 Black African American Book Club in Nashville, TN as well as the Women of Color Book Club of LaVergne, TN. I appreciate your continued encouragement and support. Many thanks also go out to Terryl Manning and the Circle of Friends Book Club in Atlanta, GA for your willingness to promote me in my efforts.

I send a sincere thanks to Melissa Forbes for her editing services. Melissa, you are a gem and your expertise is invaluable and I'm so glad we were brought together.

To Candace Cottrell, I have mad love for you! We've known each other for a long time, and your professionalism, friendliness, and support is greatly priceless. I also love the "fierce" book cover image you designed for my novel.

A special thanks goes out to Cory and Heather Buford of Gateway Marketing Online who designed my flyers and maintain my website. Your creative ability and friendship is precious, and I thank you for your efforts.

I would like to send out a heartfelt thanks to the members of RAWSISTAZ.com for your support. A special thanks go out to Martina "Tee" Royal of RAWSISTAZ for showcasing authors like myself every day. I love you and I thank you for all that you do. Kiss Joy for me!

To my dear friends and fellow authors, V. Anthony Rivers and J. Daniels, we go way back and words can't express how priceless our friendship is. To authors Allison Hobbs, Tina Brooks-McKinney, Shelley Halima, and Harold Turley II, need I say more? Our inner circle has shared a lot over the years, and I know there are even better things on the horizon for all of us. Keep up the great writing. I can't go on without thanking authors Carmen Green, Deirdre Savoy, Gayle Sloan, and Margaret Johnson-Hodge, who I look up to as sisters. To author Laurinda Brown, much love goes out to you for motivating me to keep on keeping on.

I would also like to honor and remember a dear friend and fellow author, James "Jimmy" Hurd Jr., who passed away in April. Jimmy, your smile and winning spirit will never be forgotten and neither will your novels. I'm so happy you were able to fulfill your dream.

Many thanks and devotion go out to Mark Anthony and the entire staff at Q-Boro Books for your hard work and dedication to this novel and for welcoming me in with open arms. Additional appreciation goes out to Carl Weber and Urban Books for your vision.

To my special friends, Brenda Thomas, Tracy Dandridge, Sharon Nowlin, Buanita Ray, Robin Ridley, and Monica Baker, thank you for giving me plenty of juicy material to write about. Remember, I'm always listening.

A special thanks goes out to Ms. Judy Sharp and the staff at the Hadley Park Library, Yusef Harris of Alkebu Lan Images Bookstore in Nashville, TN, the staff at the Bordeaux Library, the Antioch Library, and the Nashville Public Library for your support.

Lastly, to my husband, Wayne, and daughters, Alyvia and Marisa, I want to let you know that I love you with all my heart. None of this would be possible without you. You make me proud every second of every day.

Prologue

How Did I Get Here?

Nedra couldn't believe a man could punch a woman like she was just hit. When her body hit the floor, her head struck it hard, dazing her. Before she could gather her senses, he was on top of her, squeezing the life out of her as he screamed at the top of his lungs.

"This relationship is over when I say it's over!"

Nedra tried again to loosen his grip, but he only tightened it more. She realized the man she once cared deeply for was finally going to make good on his threats. She would never have the opportunity to get married, have children, or do anything else with her life. She was too young to die, especially like this. She was her parents' only child, and they were going to be heartbroken to know that she had stayed in such an abusive relationship and kept it hidden from them.

As she started to black out, she wondered how

she let herself get into this situation. Looking up at his enraged eyes, she heard a loud pop as she fought for one last breath just before the room went dark.

Chapter One

Five Years Earlier . . .

Nedra Harris was about to begin her freshman year in college at East Georgia University, and she was happy to finally be out on her own. She loved her parents, but she was ready to say her good-byes to them so she could settle into campus life and her newfound independence. She was going to be a long way from her home in Biloxi, Mississippi, and as their only child, her parents were a little apprehensive about her leaving.

"Mom, don't cry. I'll be fine," Nedra assured her.

"I know, but you're our baby," her mom replied while wiping her tears.

Her father stepped in with a big hug.

"What your mother is saying is, we're going to miss you, sweetheart. We're going to miss you very much."

"I know, Daddy, and I'm going to miss you guys too."

In the courtyard in front of the dorm, other parents were going through a similar ritual with their loved ones. After finally convincing them she would be okay, Nedra walked them to their awaiting car and bid them good-bye. She watched them drive off, then turned around on her heels and headed back to her room to relax.

The following morning classes began, and Nedra woke up realizing she had overslept. She quickly jumped up and hurried into the shower. After dressing, she grabbed her book bag and rushed out the door to class. Her first class was English literature, which was on the second floor of the Language Arts building. As she ran down the hallway and turned the corner, she ran into a tall, hard body, which knocked her to the floor. Slightly disoriented, she shook her head and looked up into one of the most handsome faces she'd seen since arriving on campus.

The stranger extended his hand to help her up from the floor.

"I'm sorry. Are you hurt?"

Embarrassed, Nedra took his hand and smiled.

"I don't think so. Did I hurt you?"

He laughed. "I'll live. What's your hurry anyway?"

"I'm late to class," she explained as she brushed dust from her jeans.

He leaned down and picked up her book bag.

"What's your name, Roadrunner?"

She tilted her head and looked up at him curiously.

"Roadrunner? I see you're a comedian. My name is Nedra. What's yours?"

"Donovon," he said as he handed her the book bag.

He was gorgeous, all six feet, four inches of him. He had all the assets a woman would love in a man. Tall, dark, and handsome, and built like an Adonis. The best thing was he seemed to have a very nice personality. Dressed in faded jeans and a red button-down shirt, his smile captivated her immediately.

"Well, it was nice to meet you, Donovon, but I really have to get to class," she said as she glanced at her watch. "I'll see you around."

"I hope so. See you later."

"Good-bye, Donovon."

Walking away, she looked back over her shoulder and smiled. He waved at her before turning the corner to go on his way.

Nedra finally made it to class with only seconds to spare. As Donovon made his way into his classroom he was still spellbound by his encounter with Nedra. Her dimples and beautiful smile immediately stole his heart, leaving him spellbound. Her skin had a cinnamon hue and it appeared to be as smooth as silk, which complemented her shimmering, shoulder length, auburn hair. Her dark, brown eyes were bright and friendly, and her curvaceous body left his mind spiraling out of control. Nedra had basically knocked him off his feet, physically and emotionally, and he couldn't wait to see her again.

Nedra's next class was biology. When she walked into the classroom, she saw an unexpected but familiar face smiling, and he was waving at her. She shook her head, walked over to a seat next to him, and sat down.

"Well, well, well, Donovon, we meet again."

"Isn't this great? I was hoping we might have a class together."

She sat down and blushed at his enthusiasm.

"You are going to be my lab partner, right?" he whispered.

"You sure are presumptuous, aren't you?"

He leaned closer and continued to whisper.

"Come on, Nedra. It's not like we don't already know each other."

"We don't! All I did was run into you!"

They laughed together.

"I know, but I hope you'll give us a chance to get to know each other better. I believe it was fate that we met today. You'll see."

Surprised, she pulled her biology book out of her book bag.

"Why do you say that?"

"I just know, Nedra. I'm good at stuff like this. We're going to make a good team."

She giggled.

"A comedian and a psychic too? I am impressed."

The professor walked in and started calling roll. She looked over at Donovon and he nodded and winked at her. He was able to make her laugh, and that was important in a relationship, but what kind of relationship was in store for them? Only time would tell.

Nedra sat there rewinding the events of the morning in her head. She was excited to finally be at college. She just hoped her experiences would come to last a lifetime.

*   *   *

After class was over, Nedra headed toward the student center. Donovon ran to catch up with her. Outside, he called out to her.

"Nedra! Wait up!"

She turned to see him running toward her.

This guy is becoming my shadow.

"Where are you headed, Roadrunner?" he asked once he caught up to her.

"Well, if you must know, I'm going to grab some lunch," she answered as she continued to walk toward the student center.

"Do you mind if I join you?"

"No, I guess you have to eat too."

He rubbed his stomach playfully.

"Thanks, my stomach was growling all during class. Did you hear it?"

She smiled and shook her head. "No, I didn't hear it. You didn't eat breakfast?"

"Nah, I didn't have time."

They walked into the dining area and joined other students in the food line. As she continued to talk to Donovon, she noticed a group of girls staring at her.

She turned to Donovon.

"Why are those girls staring at me? You're not going to get me stabbed by any of your girlfriends, are you?"

He looked over at a table full of girls and laughed.

"No way! They're just envious of you, and for your information, I don't have any girlfriends."

Thinking he was being arrogant, she rolled her eyes.

"Now why would they be envious of me? Is it because you're some type of jock or something?"

With sincerity in his eyes he looked down at her.

"No! They're staring because you're so beautiful."

She looked up into his eyes and saw a true friend.

"Ah, that was sweet, Donovon. Thank you."

Sliding down the food line, he continued to point out his selections.

"You're very welcome, Nedra, and it's true. You're beautiful from the inside out. It's so obvious, and I just met you."

She smiled again and playfully bumped him with her hips.

"You sure know how to flatter a girl."

"I try."

At the end of their line, Donovon paid for her lunch.

"Donovon, you didn't have to do that."

"I wanted to."

"Thank you."

He looked around the room and then asked, "Where do you want to sit?"

"It doesn't matter to me."

He nodded to the right and said, "Follow me."

Nedra followed Donovon through the room and they found a table in the area where the girls who were staring at them were sitting. The pair sat down with their food and began eating. It was here their friendship was born as they got to know each other.

Chapter Two

Someone To Watch Over Me . . .

Weeks passed and Donovon and Nedra were spending as much time together as possible. She was impressed by how he never acted conceited, even though he possessed a sexy allure from head to toe. His dark, wavy hair perfectly fit his cinnamon complexion and the cutest pair of dimples. They shared a unique friendship and were inseparable.

The debutante Donovon had started dating hated Nedra in more ways than one. There was no love lost by Nedra either. In fact, they couldn't stand to be around each other, which put Donovon in the middle. He didn't like that the two women he cared most about actually hated each other. Nedra, on the other hand, was dating a young man on the baseball team. As expected, Donovon had his issues with him; however, he had good reasons not to like the boyfriend.

In the library one night, while studying together,

out of nowhere Nedra sat her book down and folded her arms.

"Why don't you like Kevin?"

Without looking up from his book, Donovon mumbled.

"I just don't. He's a punk!"

"Don't you think that's kind of harsh?"

"No, I don't," he answered without making eye contact.

She leaned forward and whispered her concerns to him.

"You must have a reason, Donovon. Kevin's nice to you every time we run into you. Is there something you're not telling me?"

Still looking at his book, he sighed.

"I just don't like him Nedra, OK?"

Nedra closed her book in frustration.

"That's crazy. You don't like him, but you can't tell me why?"

Donovon got up out of his seat without acknowledging her and disappeared between the bookshelves. Nedra leaned back in her chair and sighed. Within minutes, he returned with two books. She sat there staring at him as he thumbed through the pages of the books.

"Donovon!"

He looked up, surprised at her outburst.

"Nedra, be quiet before you get us thrown out of here."

"Well, tell me!"

"Nedra, leave it alone! OK? I have a right to my opinion about that pinhead fool you're wasting your time on," he answered angrily as he pushed his books away.

"Oh, and what about Miss I'm Better Than

Everyone Else who you're going out with? Why are you wasting your time on her?"

He picked up his book again and tried to study.

"Now you're tripping."

"The truth hurts, doesn't it, my dear?" She laughed.

Frowning, he looked back down at his books.

"Whatever you say, Nedra."

They continued studying in silence. Nedra was having trouble accepting Donovon's mysterious hate for her boyfriend, so she pushed the envelope even more.

"If you were really my friend you would be honest with me and tell me why you don't like my boyfriend."

He looked up and saw the sadness in her eyes, and it made his heart melt.

"Damn, girl! Come with me!"

Donovon grabbed her by the hand and pulled her out of her chair and toward the stairs. They walked up to the third floor toward the study booths in the back of the room.

"Where are we going?"

"Just be quiet and follow me," he ordered her as they walked down several aisles.

Once they reached the back of the room, he pointed to a study booth and Nedra's eyes widened in shock. Inside the booth were her boyfriend and an unknown female. They were locked in an embrace, kissing. Donovon watched Nedra's facial expressions change, and he could almost see her heart break. He didn't want to see her hurt, but he had no choice but to let her see the deception for herself. She turned to walk away, but Donovon stopped her.

"Aren't you going to confront him?"

"What's the point?"

Donovon put his arm around her shoulder.

"I'm sorry, Nedra. I knew you had to see it for yourself before you would believe it."

They walked slowly back to their table and sat down.

She sat there stunned as tears dropped from her eyes. Her tears caused anger to boil over in Donovon's heart.

"How long have you known?"

"I've seen them together a couple of times around campus."

Streams of tears ran down her face, which hurt him even more.

"Why didn't you tell me about them?"

He took her hand into his and caressed it.

"This is the reason I didn't tell you. I didn't want to see you hurt."

"I can't believe he's made a fool out of me."

Donovon released her hand and leaned back in his chair.

"He's the fool, Nedra, not you."

She stood up and started gathering her books in silence.

"Where are you going?"

She zipped up her backpack and threw it across her shoulder.

"I'm tired. I don't feel like studying anymore. I'm going back to my room to go to bed."

He stood and gathered his belongings as well.

"Wait up so I can walk you back."

*   *   *

Back at her dorm, they took the stairs to her room instead of the elevator. Once they arrived at her door she knocked to alert her roommate.

"Ashley, it's Nedra. Are you decent?"

She swung the door open.

"Yes! Why?"

Nedra walked through the door.

"Because Donovon is out here with me. That's why."

Donovon followed Nedra inside the room, hugging Ashley upon entering.

"With that bit of information, I wish I wasn't decent. Hey, baby!"

Donovon shook his head and sat down in a nearby chair. Ashley flirted with Donovon every chance she got.

"What are you guys up to?"

Donovon sat his book bag on the table.

"Not much. What are you doing?"

Walking on her heels back over to her bed she sat down and propped her foot up on the bed. She wiggled her toes at him playfully.

"As you can see, I'm painting my toes."

He laughed.

"I forgot that's a requirement to graduate for you females."

Ashley giggled and looked over at Nedra, who was detached from their conversation.

"Nedra, why are you so quiet? Are you feeling OK?"

Nedra opened her dresser drawer and pulled out her pajamas. Without making eye contact with Ashley she announced, "If Kevin calls, tell him I don't live here anymore."

Ashley replaced the top on the nail polish and became very concerned about Nedra's comment. She knew for a fact that Nedra really liked Kevin, so this let her know something big must've happened.

"What's wrong? What did he do?"

Nedra disappeared into the bathroom without answering.

Ashley looked over at Donovon and whispered, "What happened between Kevin and Nedra?"

He grabbed the remote and leaned back in the chair. "She caught him kissing on some girl over in the library."

Ashley jumped up off the bed and put her hands on her hips.

"What? I hope she dropkicked his ass!"

Scanning the channels on the TV, he revealed more information about what had happened in the library.

"He doesn't even know we saw him."

Nedra returned to the room, dressed in her pajamas. She sat on the side of her bed and started wrapping her hair. Ashley crossed the room and sat down next to her.

"I'm sorry about Kevin. He's an idiot and doesn't deserve you anyway."

Ashley took the comb out of Nedra's hand and finished wrapping her hair.

"Thanks."

Nedra climbed under the covers of her bed and sighed.

"I think I'm the one who's been the idiot. I'm tired now and I just want to go to bed. OK?"

Donovon looked over at her before he stood

and grabbed his book bag. He shoved his hands inside his pockets.

"Are you mad at me for showing them to you?"

She found the strength to smile.

"No, I'm not mad at you, Donovon. I just wish you would've told me sooner."

Donovon sat on the edge of her bed and hugged her. He caressed her back gently and kissed her forehead.

"You never were around when I saw them, and I knew you would have to see it for yourself in order to believe it."

She lay down on her pillow and hugged it.

"I trust you, Donovon"

Donovon swung his book bag up on his shoulder and sighed.

"Let me get out of you ladies' way. Can I do anything for either one of you before I leave?"

Nedra reached up and grabbed his hand lovingly.

"Don't go. I want you to stay until I fall asleep. Please?"

Ashley smiled, knowing they were the best of friends. She sat in silence as they spoke softly to each other. He kissed her hand and sat back down.

"If that's what you want. I'm sure I can talk Ashley into a game of poker or something."

Ashley jumped up, clapping her hands.

"Strip poker it is!!"

"I don't think so," he said, laughing as he pulled his chair up to the table.

Nedra turned over and also laughed.

"Give it up, Ashley. You know Donovon's spoken for."

She pulled out a deck of cards and started shuffling them.

"We'll see how long that will last. Donovon's too sweet for her."

"Just deal the cards," he instructed her as he pulled out a handful of change.

They started playing cards, and an hour later, Nedra was sound asleep. Even though Ashley wanted Donovon to stay longer, he felt it was time for him to leave. He kissed her on the cheek, picked up his book bag, and walked out the door. There was something he had to do before returning to his dorm.

Ashley walked him downstairs. Before he walked out into the night, he turned back to Ashley.

"Take care of Nedra for me," he said.

"I will. Thanks for being such a good friend to her."

"You too. Good night."

Donovon returned to the library to find Kevin still cuddled up with the large breasted female in the study booth. He burst into the room and pulled Kevin up out of his seat by his collar.

"What the hell is wrong with you, Donovon?" he yelled.

Donovon shoved him against the wall.

"What do you think is wrong with me? Nedra saw you in here getting your freak on!"

His eyes widened with shock.

"Wait! She saw me? Damn! Where is she?"

Donovon released his collar and shoved him backward, causing him to stumble and fall on the floor.

"You don't have to worry about Nedra anymore,

so stay away from her. If you don't, I *will* kick your ass! Do you understand?"

"You can't tell me what to do! Nedra is *my* woman, not yours!"

The girl he was with jumped up and swung her weave over her shoulder. She put her hands on her hips and pointed her finger at Kevin.

"Hold up! Who the hell is Nedra?"

Donovon turned to her and proudly revealed Kevin's secret.

"She *was* his girlfriend until she saw the two of you in here getting busy."

"Girlfriend? I thought I was your girlfriend!"

Kevin turned to her and tried to explain.

"Baby, don't worry, this is just a little misunderstanding."

"Whatever!" she yelled as she grabbed her purse and stormed out of the room.

"Wait! Let me explain," he begged as he started after her. His pleas fell on deaf ears.

He turned to Donovon and said, "Thanks a lot, bro."

Donovon pushed past him. Before walking away he looked down at him.

"You're lucky all I did was grab you this time. You need to stop treating women like this."

On his way back to the dorm, Donovon felt better that he had confronted Kevin when Nedra wouldn't. That was the last boyfriend who ever disrespected Nedra. All the others knew they had to walk a straight line because Donovon was always watching over her.

Chapter Three

Confessions

Freshman year for Nedra and Donovon was uneventful. It wasn't until they visited each other's families during the holidays of their sophomore year that Donovon realized Nedra was much more than a friend to him. He always knew she had a special place in his heart, but it didn't take long for him to fall deeply in love with her. He didn't know if Nedra felt the same way about him, so he struggled with the decision of telling her his true feelings.

He visited Nedra's family for Thanksgiving, and as soon as Nedra's aunt laid eyes on him, she threw up her hands and screamed.

"Welcome to the family, Donovon!"

He was a little surprised by her outburst, but he accepted the invitation. There was nothing he wanted more than to be a part of Nedra's family. They were warm, loving, and welcomed him with open arms. They were just like Nedra—special. Nedra's grandmother, Leona Foster, was especially nice as she talked about when she was a young woman in college and how those were some of the best times of her life. She also told both of them to savor their moments and not to take any of them for granted.

Later that evening, Nedra's Aunt Tina pulled her aside.

"Nedra, Donovon is wonderful. He's a keeper, so don't act a fool and let him get away."

"What are you talking about, Auntie?"

Nedra's Aunt Tina was known to have some psychic abilities and had a pretty good record of being accurate with her visions.

She pulled Nedra into a nearby room and shut the door for privacy.

"Nedra, unless you're blind, I don't see how you don't see it. Donovon's in love with you, girl!"

"Shhhhh!! What are you talking about? Donovon is my best friend—period."

Tina smiled and switched her hips as she walked across the room to the window.

"I'm never wrong, Nedra. That man has it bad for you, and I'm sensing you have it just as bad for him."

The color left Nedra's face. She couldn't believe what she was hearing.

"Auntie, stop that," she begged. "Donovon is my best friend. Yes, he's wonderful, but he has a girlfriend. I don't know what makes you think he's in love with me."

"I have eyes, I have the gift, and I'm never wrong. Donovon may have a girlfriend, but his heart is with you."

Sighing, Nedra sat down in a chair and put her hands over her eyes.

"Look, Auntie, don't be going around telling people this nonsense. Donovon is my boy and nothing else. I'll see you out in the family room."

When Nedra walked out of the room and back to the kitchen, Tina laughed because she knew she was right, and so did Nedra.

Later that evening when everyone was gone, Nedra, Donovon, and her parents shared hot apple cider around the fireplace. Nedra couldn't get the things her aunt had told her out of her head. She stared at Donovon as he held a conversation with her parents. He seemed so relaxed and comfortable, even with this being his first time there. He looked over at her and smiled, sending chills down her body. She took a deep breath and smiled back at him. She had to admit to herself that Donovon did have a special place in her heart, but just where, she would have to sort out later.

Weeks later, Nedra visited Donovon's family a few days after Christmas. His parents were just as smitten with Nedra as Nedra's parents were with Donovon. They had met his girlfriend on a previous visit, but she was no match for Nedra. Donovon felt the same way, but he didn't want to ruin their friendship by expressing his true feelings.

Donovon was from a small town near Chicago, and they were thankful to have a white Christmas.

Donovon was an only child just like Nedra, so having her around during the holidays felt great. His girlfriend wasn't happy with the arrangement, but Donovon told her to get over it because Nedra was his friend a long time before he met her, and there was nothing she could do about that.

One evening, Nedra was sitting in the family room watching a Lifetime movie when Donovon walked in with a mischievous grin on his face.

"Hey, Roadrunner, do you feel like challenging me in a snowball fight?"

She looked up at him and her smile said it all. He was already decked out in his coat, hat, and boots. She didn't get to enjoy this type of weather while growing up in the South. Her eyes widened as she sprinted for her coat and boots. Donovon's mom heard all the giggling and walked into the foyer to see what all the commotion was about.

"What are you two up to?"

Donovon kissed his mom on the cheek.

"We're going out to throw snowballs. Do you want to come?"

Waving them off, she backed away. "No way! You guys go on and don't stay out there too long. Nedra, I don't want you going back home with a cold."

"Ah, Mom! She'll be fine. She has on her long johns."

Nedra playfully punched him in the arm.

"Oh, you're really going to get it now, Donovon."

Nedra pulled her knit hat down on her head and giggled some more.

"Come on, Mrs. McNeil, so you can watch me beat up on your son."

Turning toward the kitchen, Mrs. McNeil blew a kiss to them. "I'll take a rain check," she said.

Donovon opened the door and put his arm around Nedra's neck.

"All right, Momma. Come on, Nedra, so I can show you how to make a real snowball."

Before they walked out the door, his mom yelled, "Don't you hurt her, Donovon!"

He rolled his eyes.

"What about me? Aren't you going to tell Nedra not to hurt me?"

"I mean it, Donovon!"

He winked at Nedra and pushed her out onto the porch. As he closed the door he yelled one last time at his mother.

"I'll handle her like a china doll, so don't worry, Momma."

He closed the door and said, "You are in so much trouble, young lady."

Nedra screamed and ran out into the snow. They immediately started bombarding each other with snowballs. Mrs. McNeil could hear Nedra screaming and laughing. Donovon was also laughing as they chased each other all over the yard. Mrs. McNeil returned to the kitchen and watched from the window as her son and Nedra played like little children in the snow. It was a beautiful sight, and she loved Nedra. If her prayers were answered, Nedra would eventually be a part of their family.

Nedra laughed as Donovon caught up with her in the backyard. He had a huge snowball in his hand and he threatened to smash it across her head.

Laughing, she warned him off as she backed away.

"Donovon, don't you dare!"

"Please, after what you just did to me? You deserve this, Nedra."

"I'm sorry. I didn't mean to put that snow down your back."

Nedra had jumped on his back earlier, allowing her to stuff a large snowball down his back.

"It's too late! Now take it like a woman!"

Nedra screamed as Donovon brought the snowball closer to her. She turned to run, but she lost her balance. They hit the ground and started throwing snow at each other.

"You win! I give up!" He stopped bombarding her for a moment.

"You promise?"

"Yes, I promise."

He stood and pulled her up off the cold, wet snow. They dusted the snow from their clothes and face. Nedra looked around at just how beautiful it was outside.

"It's so beautiful here. I love everything about your home."

He blushed and thanked her.

"We'd better get inside so I can make you some hot chocolate. Your face is getting red," he said. She playfully pushed him.

"No thanks to you."

"You asked for it."

She threw her arms around his neck and jumped into his arms. It surprised him and immediately caused him to become aroused.

"Thank you, Donovon. This was the most fun I've had in years."

He leaned down and kissed her softly on the lips, causing her eyes to widen. The kiss was for lovers instead of friends. It was hot, wet, and very sensual. He flicked his tongue quickly against hers and she savored the taste of him like she'd never done before. They kissed for several seconds before Nedra pulled away and looked into his eyes. His kiss caused her stomach to flutter and her lower region began to throb. Donovon had never kissed her like that before, and it felt wonderful. He released her so she could stand, but he still had her in his arms.

"Wow! What was that?" she asked.

He gently wiped the remnants of snow off her cheek.

"For being who you are. I love you, Nedra. You're important to me."

She stood on her tiptoes and kissed his chin.

"I love you too, Donovon, and I'm glad you're my best friend."

They stared at each other for a moment as their confessions sank in. It was sort of awkward for both of them, and Donovon realized one of them needed to say something.

"I think we'd better go get that hot chocolate," he said.

She linked her arm with his and held on tight.

"With whipped cream?"

"Whatever you want, Nedra."

They entered the house and never talked about that tender moment ever again, even though it never left either of their minds.

Chapter Four

Senior Year, The Party's Over

The years flew by before Donovon and Nedra realized their time together was almost over. Senior year was upon them and their fun was coming to an end. Their friendship had blossomed into an unbreakable bond. Both had experienced their share of joy and heartache over the past few years, but they were always there for each other.

Nedra pledged the sorority of her choice and even became a sweetheart of Donovon's fraternity. He welcomed her with open arms, but he wasn't happy when she agreed to pose in swimwear for their homecoming calendar. It was a fundraiser, and Nedra couldn't understand why Donovon felt the way he did about the calendar. She tried to justify it as his big brother protectiveness kicking in, but she knew deep down there was more to it.

Donovon's issue was that he didn't want any man to see just how perfect she was, inside or out. Not only was she physically fit, but she was also the sweetest and most trusting woman he'd ever known, and he was very much in love with her.

On one particular afternoon, Donovon and Nedra sat on a bench in the campus plaza eating lunch.

"I still can't believe you're going to pose for that calendar," he whined.

Nedra laughed and put her arm around his shoulder, kissing him on the cheek.

"Ah, come on, Donovon. It's not like it's *Playboy*. I do think it's sweet that you're trying to defend my honor, though."

Donovon playfully pushed away from her.

"Sure you do."

"Lighten up, McNeil! No one's going to see any more than they see in my majorette uniforms."

"I don't like that either," he admitted as he sipped his water and watched other students as they walked by. She studied his expression and saw just how serious he was.

"I bet you'd like to look if it wasn't me out there."

He frowned. "Whatever!"

She laughed out loud.

"You're a man, Donovon, and I know you like watching half-naked women just like all the other men around here."

"I'm not going to argue with you there, but we're talking about you."

"You'd better be nice to me, McNeil. You know I'm leaving next week to start my internship in Nashville."

"Don't remind me," he said with a sad look on his face.

Nedra was going to miss him, too, and she tried not to think about the distance that would be between them.

"I already know I'm going to have a huge phone bill," he said. He looked over at Nedra with a very serious expression.

"I don't know how I'm going to survive without you."

Even though she knew he was serious, she took his hand into hers and replied, "Sure you do. You have Miss Tracy to keep you company."

He pulled his hand out of her grasp and nudged her playfully.

"I don't know about that. What about Tyree? How are you going to handle being away from him for so long?"

Tyree was the man in Nedra's life and one of the most sought after running backs in the country. It was a given that he would be drafted into the NFL, which left Nedra a little nervous about the transition their lives were getting ready to take. Tyree loved Nedra dearly, and he assured her that his love for her was undying. She took a sip of her drink and thought for a moment.

"I don't know. I'm trying not to think about it right now. It's going to be hard."

"Why? Don't you trust him?"

"I think I do, but I'm not totally sure. I'll just have to take it one day at a time."

"I understand, but I think Tyree will be cool. If not, he knows he'll have me to deal with, and I'll be watching him."

"Are you going to be able to get permission from Tracy to visit me? My Dad's renting me a nice two-bedroom condo near my office, so I have your room waiting on you."

He cursed under his breath. "Tracy doesn't own me!"

Nedra giggled. She loved getting Donovon's blood pressure up about his latest love interest.

"We'll see about that! Seriously, though, you have to visit me. I'm going to be so lost and lonely up there with all those strangers."

"They'll love you the moment they see you, so don't worry. And yes, I'm coming to visit."

"You'd better! I keep telling myself this internship is necessary to cushion my resume."

"You know it, and who knows, you might get a job offer out of it."

He was doing his best to help her see the benefit of her sacrifice.

"I guess you're right."

He leaned over and hugged her tightly. His heart started pounding loudly in his chest.

"Damn! I'm going to miss you."

"Right back at you, my love. Look, I have something for you so we can stay in touch while I'm away."

Donovon watched curiously as Nedra reached inside her book bag.

She turned to him with a big smile on her face. "Ta da!"

He smiled and took the box out of her hand so he could inspect it. "You got me a webcam!"

Pleased with his reaction, she pulled another one out of her book bag and showed it to him. "Isn't it great? Now we can see each other when we chat online. It'll make me feel like I'm not that far away from you if I can see your face."

He thanked her and gave her a loving hug before tucking his gift into his book bag.

She kissed his cheek, causing him to blush. He stared at her as she wiped her lipstick off his cheek. Over his shoulder she saw his girlfriend approaching, and she didn't look happy. Nedra assumed she had witnessed their loving exchange, but she didn't care. She took a bite out of her sandwich.

"Don't look now, but here comes Cruella DeVille."

He turned around and noticed Tracy walking their way.

"That was cold, Nedra. You and Ashley need to stop doing that. I don't call your man names," he said while trying to keep from laughing.

"Yes, you do! You call Tyree 'Mighty Mouse' all the time." She giggled.

Tracy walked up, and without acknowledging Nedra's presence, she kissed Donovon hard on the lips.

"Hey, baby."

Nedra rolled her eyes and took another bite of her sandwich. She knew Tracy only did this as a territorial stance, but Nedra wouldn't lose any sleep over it. Nedra figured she did it only because she had just seen Nedra kiss Donovon on the cheek.

Donovon casually greeted her.

"Hey, Trace."

That was the nickname he'd given her. She let out a loud breath, leaned over, and surprisingly greeted Nedra.

"Oh, hey, Nedra. I didn't see you sitting over there."

Nedra mumbled under her breath before returning a greeting. She held out an extra sandwich and tried to be nice.

"Would you like to join us for lunch?"

Tracy turned her nose up at the chicken salad sandwich.

"No, thank you. I'm dieting. I don't want my baby dumping me because I put on a few pounds."

Now it was Nedra's turn to mumble curse words under her breath.

"You don't need to lose any weight, Trace," Donovon said.

Nedra turned away from them and stuck her finger in her mouth as if she was gagging herself. Donovon saw Nedra's theatrics and he had to stifle his laughter so Tracy wouldn't catch on. He was stroking Tracy's ego when it didn't need any help.

"Oh, thank you, baby."

Sitting down, she snuggled closer to Donovon. He looked over at her and asked, "Rough day?"

Tracy hugged his neck and said, "It was, but I'm cool now that we're together."

"Good," he said as he winked at Nedra.

Donovon continued to eat in silence.

"Are you almost done, baby? I need you to help me with something."

"What? I was getting ready to hang out with Nedra for a while."

"It's personal."

Nedra stood. "Don't worry about it, Donovon. We can hook up some other time."

He stood and gave her a peck on the lips.

"Are you sure? I know we already had plans and I don't like breaking—"

She pulled her purse up on her shoulder and interrupted him.

"No, it's OK. I'll holler at you later. I have to meet Tyree anyway. See you around, Tracy." Tracy waved Nedra off victoriously.

"Bye, bye."

Donovon sat back down and sighed with disappointment.

"I can't believe you kissed her right in front of me. Don't you have any respect for me at all?"

"Leave it alone, Tracy. What's so important that you need it done right now anyway? I hate canceling plans at the last minute."

"Don't change the subject! Why did you kiss her like that?"

"Nedra's like family to me."

"But she's not family, Donovon!"

Tracy had struck a nerve with him.

"Nedra's family as far as I'm concerned," he said without hesitating.

This bit of information really pissed Tracy off.

"What is it about her? Are you in love with her?"

Donovon was angry now. Tracy was about to walk into territory she had no business being in.

"Don't start with me, Tracy. I told you, Nedra is my friend and you need to stop treating her funky every time you come around. She hasn't done anything to you."

Picking up her book bag she yelled, not caring who heard her.

"I don't like her! People think she's your girl, and not me!"

He calmly walked over to a garbage can and threw his leftover lunch away. Tracy stood watching him in silence, clearly agitated.

"You're overreacting as usual."

"No, I'm not! She's always with you or over at your apartment. It doesn't look right," she argued. "I don't see how her man allows her to hang around you as much as she does."

Donovon's irritation was obvious now.

"Maybe Tyree's not as insecure as you are, Tracy!"

They were silent for a moment. Tracy stood there with her arms folded and bottom lip poking out.

"It just doesn't look right," she whispered.

"It doesn't look right to whom? Damn, Tracy, what are you so worried about?"

"You know exactly what I'm worried about!" she yelled. "She's a freaking majorette, Donovon! You can't sit there and pretend you're not attracted to her!"

Other students were starting to enjoy the show Tracy was putting on for them. Students breaking-up and making-up was a normal occurrence in the plaza, and at the moment, no one knew which way this pair was going to end up.

Tracy was an attractive woman, but her temper tantrums didn't help her personality. She was slender, yet curvaceous, with a light complexion. Her light brown eyes and honey blonde hair made her resemble actress and former Miss America, Vanessa Williams.

Not wanting to fuel Tracy's fire any more, Donovon tried to calm the situation.

"For the last time, I told you where Nedra and I stand. Now leave it alone!"

Tracy threw up her hands in defeat.

"Forget it! You didn't hear a word I said, and it's obvious who you really care about."

As she tried to walk away, Donovon grabbed her arm, pulling her back.

"Trace, this is silly. Nedra is with Tyree and she's leaving next week to do her internship. Why are you so threatened by her?"

"That doesn't mean anything."

"Maybe not to you."

Her eyes filled with tears, and the students could tell the public show was starting to wind down. She sniffed.

"I don't want to be made a fool of. Now, turn me loose!"

He shoved his hands into his pockets and watched her angrily grab her purse. He toyed with her hair, but she pulled away.

"Tracy, you really need to calm down. You've given everybody a pretty good show out here today, and for nothing."

She looked around at the students watching them and lowered her head.

"Donovon, if you love me you would stay away from her."

He picked up his books and laughed out loud.

"Oh, now you're really tripping!"

"I mean it, Donovon. It's either her or me."

He put his arm around her shoulder and looked directly into her eyes.

"Sweetheart, ultimatums don't work with me. My relationship with Nedra is something you're going to have to get over because she's my friend, and no one picks my friends for me. If you can't accept it, then I'm sorry. Do what you need to do."

Tracy rolled her eyes and mumbled something under her breath. Donovon found himself in another relationship where the woman felt threatened by his relationship with Nedra, and if he was honest with himself, he knew she had a right to be.

They stood there staring at each other before he took her book bag from her hand and they walked in the direction of her dorm. Tracy realized Donovon couldn't be bullied, not even by her.

Chapter Five

New Beginnings

Two weeks into her internship, Nedra was beginning to settle into her new position alongside three other interns. As she sat in her cubicle, she reminisced about her first day on the job. They spent most of the day in meetings and touring the office. This was a small, but prestigious advertising firm, and Nedra was impressed with their history, accomplishments, and growth.

Her telephone rang, snapping her back to reality. Nedra's team leader was calling to inform her that the United Negro College Fund fundraiser was being held at the downtown convention center at the end of the week. It was an after-five affair, and all the interns were required to attend. She smiled as she envisioned herself in the black, beaded gown she had spotted in a boutique a few days earlier. Nedra e-mailed Donovon as she finished up the conversation with her team leader. She hoped he would be able to fly in to go with her. Almost immediately, he e-mailed her back that he had a major exam the following Monday and was going to be studying all weekend. Sad, she sent him a reply that she understood and that she missed him terribly. Within seconds, her telephone rang again.

"Nedra Harris. How may I help you?"

"Hey, Roadrunner," Donovon whispered through the telephone.

A huge smiled appeared on her face.

She giggled. "You're so silly."

"I know, and I'm really sorry I can't go to the fundraiser with you. I know they're going to set it out."

Nedra continued to work on her computer as she talked to her best friend.

"I don't know about all that, Donovon. It's going to be weird going to something like this without a date."

"Too bad Tyree can't get away. Playing college sports doesn't leave much time for a social life."

She sighed with disappointment. "Don't remind me. I'll be all right, though."

"I know you will and I want to hear all about it. Take your camera in case there are some celebrities there."

"OK. I guess I'd better get back to work."

"I miss you, Nedra," he softly whispered.

"Same here. I'll talk to you later."

"Will do. Now get back to work," he ordered.

"Bye, Donovon." She giggled once more as she hung up the telephone.

Friday night rolled around quickly for Nedra. When she arrived at the fundraiser, it was in full swing. There were limos lining the avenue as hundreds of people, adorned in tuxedos and ball gowns, filed into the building. Nedra looked splendid in her black, beaded gown as she wandered gracefully through the room. The dress was backless and fit snugly to her shapely figure.

As she scanned the crowd looking for her co-workers, she felt the heat of someone's glare. She turned to look over her shoulder and noticed a very attractive gentleman smiling at her. He held his champagne glass up to her in salute before taking a sip. She shyly turned away when she noticed him approaching. Within seconds, he was standing next to her.

"Excuse me. I wanted to come over and apologize to you for staring, but I couldn't help myself. You are stunning."

Nedra lowered her eyes shyly before thanking him. He held his hand out to her to introduce himself.

"Hello, my name is Simeon Mathews. And yours is?"

She shook his hand and smiled.

"It's nice to meet you, Mr. Mathews."

He laughed out loud.

"Please, it's Simeon and I'm still waiting to find out what name goes with your beautiful smile."

Nedra nervously fidgeted with her hair. She was having trouble making eye contact with the stranger because he was so handsome.

"Nedra Harris," she answered as she shook his hand. He took another sip of champagne.

"Nedra. That's a pretty name."

She blushed and said, "Thank you."

Looking around the room, he pried into her personal life.

"Where is your date?"

"I'm here on business, but I can't seem to find any of my coworkers."

"What kind of work do you do?"

"I'm with a local advertising firm."

He couldn't take his eyes off her. She was breathtaking.

"Would you like to join me at my table until you find your friends? I wouldn't feel comfortable letting an attractive woman like yourself wander around alone in this crowd, looking so stunning."

Nedra didn't know what to think of this stranger's advances.

"I'm sure I'll find them. I just need to check the other side of the room."

He looked at his watch and then reached down and took her hand in his.

"Please, join me at my table. I would love the company, and it'll give us a chance to get to know each other. Besides, dinner won't be served for another fifteen minutes."

Reluctant at first, she looked into his eyes and decided to join him after all. He looked like he had stepped off the cover of a male fashion magazine. He was tall with broad shoulders, smooth, dark brown skin, and a smile that lit up the room. He spoke with intelligence, confidence, and raw magnetism. This man was the poster boy for sexy.

Simeon kept Nedra company for the next several minutes before her team leader found her. During their shared time, she found out that he was a thirty-year-old lawyer whom everyone in the building seemed to know. He was single and originally from New Orleans.

Before leaving his table, he reached inside his jacket and pulled out a card.

"Nedra, if you ever need anything, and I mean anything, please call."

Taking the card, she glanced down at it and then smiled before shaking his hand once again.

"Thank you, Simeon. Hopefully I won't need your services, but just in case, thank you."

"You're very welcome, Nedra Harris."

As she started to walk off, she turned back to him.

"Simeon, I really want to thank you for being so nice to me tonight. I would like to do lunch or dinner or something to thank you, so I'll give you a call. "

Pleased, he smiled back at her.

"You don't owe me anything, but it will be nice to see you again. You've made this evening most enjoyable, Nedra."

It was very noisy in the room because the band was playing and people were talking all around them. Nedra walked even closer to him.

"You have made my evening enjoyable also, Simeon."

He took her hand into his and kissed the back of it. Startled at the electrical sensation, she jumped. She had a boyfriend, but at the moment, she wasn't thinking about Tyree, which made her feel very guilty. The casual contact she was having with Simeon was causing her temperature to rise slightly. Simeon noticed Nedra's reaction to his kiss and smiled mischievously.

"I'm sorry, I couldn't help myself. Please forgive me."

"It's OK. Once again, I had a nice time. Enjoy the rest of your evening."

"You too," he happily responded as he watched her walk away.

"Who are you, Nedra Harris?" he whispered to himself.

Later that night, Nedra couldn't sleep. She couldn't get Simeon Mathews off her mind and he caused her to toss and turn in her bed. He was mysterious and mesmerizing, but there was no way she could get involved with another man. She loved Tyree and there was no way she could risk messing things up between them. She rolled over onto her back and stared at the ceiling. She realized she was long overdue for some sexual healing, and it would be weeks before Tyree could come up for a visit. Sighing, she picked up the telephone and called Donovon.

"Hello?"

"Hey, Donovon. Did I wake you?"

He chuckled. "Of course not. I told you I was going to be studying all weekend. What's up?"

"I don't know. I met this guy tonight at the fundraiser and he's . . . he's . . . "

Donovon's heart almost stopped beating.

"What? Are you thinking about stepping out on Tyree?"

Nedra couldn't help but laugh.

"I just met the man and no, I'm not stepping out on Tyree, but damn this guy was fione! He's nice, sexy, educated, handsome, yadda, yadda, yadda."

"Listen to you. What's this guy's name?"

"Simeon Mathews and he's a lawyer. Everyone in the room seemed to know and respect him."

Donovon poured himself a glass of apple juice and said, "A lawyer, huh?"

"I know, I know. I'll be careful. I plan to do some investigating on my own tomorrow. I want to find out the mystery behind the man."

Not happy with her news, he questioned her more about Simeon.

"How old is he?"

Nedra hesitated a moment.

"He's thirty, but he looks like he's still in his mid twenties."

"Thirty!"

"I know, I know," Nedra said as she covered her face.

He walked over to the window and looked out onto campus.

"Slow your roll. A thirty-year-old lawyer is not someone I think you need to get involved with. Number one, he's too old, and number two, lawyers can't be trusted."

"I'll be careful. I promise."

Donovon shook his head in frustration. In his gut he was worried that Nedra was about to get in over her head. He just prayed she would stay safe. Nedra didn't like it when Donovon got quiet on her, so she decided to change the subject.

"So, where's Miss Thang?"

Donovon quickly drank his juice. His mood had changed because he was worried about her.

"I'm in isolation this weekend, remember? I told her I couldn't hang out with her this weekend, so I guess she's off somewhere pissed at me."

"Well, she'll just have to get over it. You're studying and she can't blame me this time."

"That's the truth."

With sadness in her voice, Nedra sighed and said, "Well, get back to your books. I just wanted to tell you about my new friend."

"I'm glad you called. It's not the same around here without you."

"I miss you, too. I can't wait until you come up for a visit."

"Me too. I love you, Nedra, and be careful."

"I will, and I love you too. Good night."

Chapter Six

Playing With Fire

The following Monday, Nedra walked into her office and was shocked to find two dozen yellow roses on her desk. She sat her purse down and opened the card attached to them.

> *Nedra,*
>   *I couldn't get you off my mind all weekend. I'm so glad we met and I hope to see you again very soon.*
>
>   *Affectionately,*
>   *Simeon*

Smiling, she leaned down to smell the roses. Her heart was beating wildly as she pulled Simeon's business card from her wallet and dialed his number. Her hands were trembling as she waited for him to answer. When he did, his voice radiated power.

"Simeon Mathews."

"The roses are beautiful. Thank you, Simeon."

He twirled around in his chair and looked out

over the skyline. He was excited to hear from her, but he made sure he kept his cool.

"That was nothing; however, I am glad you liked them."

"A girl would have to be a fool not to," she replied as she caressed the rose petals.

She could tell he was smiling on the other end.

"Well, you deserved them. You really made my night at the fundraiser."

She took a deep breath. "Can I ask you something?"

"Sure," he said.

"How did you find out where I worked?"

He laughed, sensing her apprehension.

"I saw the name of your company on the table. The rest was easy."

"Oh, yeah, I'm sorry."

She was clearly embarrassed. He laughed again and it comforted her.

"Don't tell me you thought I was stalking you?"

She turned on her computer and sat down. "A girl can never be too careful these days."

He was totally fascinated with her.

"You're right about that. Look, Nedra, I would love it if you had dinner with me tonight. I know it's short notice, but I really would love to see you again."

Biting her nail, Nedra contemplated her response. She wanted so much to see him again, but she was afraid it was too soon. Most people talked over the telephone a while before actually going out on a date. Tyree was her man, and she loved him. She didn't want to do anything to jeopardize her relationship with him. But she was definitely intrigued by Simeon. He was nothing like the college men she was used to dating.

"I don't know, Simeon. We just met and I like to get to know people first before going out on date."

Persistent, he pushed her. "Then it's not a date. I'm just a friend taking you out to dinner. You have to eat, don't you?"

Nedra felt reckless. She'd had men pursue her like this, but never a man of Simeon's stature.

"I guess I could break my rule this one time. Thank you."

Victorious, he softly replied, "Wonderful. What time shall I pick you up?"

Stuttering, she didn't want to seem inexperienced, but she had to let her common sense kick in.

"I'd rather meet you if that's OK with you."

"That's no problem, Nedra. How does six o'-clock sound at Versalles?"

"It sounds great. I'll see you there, and thanks for the invite."

"You're welcome. Don't work too hard."

"I won't. Good-bye."

"Good-bye, Nedra."

Nedra hung up the telephone and went into a slight panic. She was traveling in uncharted territory and was beginning to think that Simeon might be more than she could handle. In any case, she would at least gain a friend and get a nice dinner at an expensive restaurant.

Later that evening, she tried on three different outfits before deciding on a short, navy skirt and an ivory, silk blouse. She chose a pair of three-inch leather sandals to accent the outfit. Checking her watch, she grabbed her purse and hurried out the door.

At Versalles, she found Simeon waiting for her in the lobby. He greeted her with a huge smile and a kiss on the cheek. His cologne smelled expensive, and he looked very sophisticated. It was obvious his designer suit was tailored, and his jewelry was subtle and classy.

"Nedra, you look beautiful."

"Thank you. You look nice also."

Simeon looked sinful and it excited her. He took her by her hand and pulled her in front of him.

"Our table is all set. Ready?"

"As ready as I'm going to be," she answered after taking a deep breath.

They followed the hostess to their table and took their seats.

Over dinner, Simeon was spellbound as Nedra spoke. He was drawn to her lips and he hung on her every word. During their conversation he found out that she was a senior in college doing her internship. She was ambitious and educated, and it made him want her even more. He noticed that in her innocence, she didn't realize she had a powerful sex appeal.

"I'm sorry, Simeon. I didn't realize I was talking so much."

He took a sip of wine and spoke tenderly to her.

"I love watching you talk. You have very beautiful lips."

She blushed and looked away, embarrassed. Nedra was so taken by him that she struggled not to fidget in her seat or play nervously with her hair.

"Don't be embarrassed. However, I should warn you that I always say what's on my mind, and Nedra Harris, you have me mesmerized. I know we just met a few days ago, but there's something about you that has me captivated."

"I don't know what to say."

She looked away bashfully because his eyes revealed that he wanted more than just a friendship with her. He covered her hand with his and caressed it with his thumb.

"Say you'll go out with me again and again and again."

All the air left her lungs as she found it hard to breathe or swallow. She quickly picked up a glass of water and tried to wash the lump out of her throat.

He released her hand and smiled.

"Are you OK?"

She nodded as she continued to drink the last of her water. Simeon was a master of seduction, and she had unknowingly become his latest victim. She sat the glass down and cleared her throat.

"Simeon, I've really enjoyed being with you tonight, but, huh, I have . . . "

"But what, Nedra?" he asked, interrupting her.

She sighed. "Simeon, I have to be honest with you too."

"I wouldn't want it any other way. What do you have on your mind?"

"I have a boyfriend, and I don't want to mislead you in any way."

"I appreciate your honesty, but I'm not interested in your boyfriend. I'm interested in you," he whispered with seriousness in his voice.

Chills shot from her head to her toes. Her admission didn't even shake him. She sat there amazed at his cool, calm demeanor, so much so that she didn't know how to respond.

"If that's the case, I need to know what your intentions are, Mr. Mathews."

His eyes met hers without blinking and once again he took her hand into his, caressing it. When he spoke, his voice was barely above a whisper.

"First of all, Mr. Mathews is my father. Secondly, I have every intention of making your stay here as uninhibited and electrifying as you'll allow me to. I like you, Nedra. I like you very much, and I hope you're open to some exciting experiences while you're here. I guarantee you won't be disappointed."

Nedra had no idea what exciting experiences Simeon had in mind, but whatever they were had her body trembling.

"I don't know what I'm ready for, Simeon, but I do enjoy your company. I'll just have to take it one day at a time and see what happens."

The waiter approached their table with the check and to remove their plates. Simeon signed the slip. Once the waiter was gone, he winked at her.

"Are you ready to get out of here?"

Wiping her mouth with the dinner napkin, she nodded in agreement. He helped her from her chair and held her hand as they walked out of the restaurant and into the night air.

Outside, the air had slightly chilled, causing her to fold her arms across her chest.

"It's getting a little cool out here."

Without skipping a beat, Simeon took off his jacket and politely wrapped it around her shoulders. She graciously pulled it up on her shoulders and thanked him.

He handed the valet his keys and they watched him run off to retrieve Simeon's vehicle. Nedra was about to do the same until Simeon stopped her.

"How would you like a tour of Nashville?"

It wasn't what he said. It was how he said it. Once again, she shivered at the tone of his voice.

"What about my car?"

"It'll be safe here with the valet until we get back."

Nedra had forgotten all about the fact that Simeon was still a total stranger to her. After a relaxing dinner and great conversation, she felt at ease with him.

"In that case, I'd love a tour. Thank you."

Within minutes the valet returned in a shiny, black, Cadillac Escalade. Nedra's eyes widened as the valet opened the door for her to climb in. Simeon tipped the young man and then climbed in on the driver's side.

"Your truck is beautiful."

"Thank you. Let's ride, Miss Harris," he announced with a twinkle in his eye.

Nedra buckled her seatbelt and relaxed as Simeon pulled out into traffic.

An hour into the tour, Simeon stopped at a local coffee house for coffee and pastries. There they shared in more joyful conversation. Hours later, after a complete tour of the city, Simeon returned to the restaurant. Nedra was totally relaxed and thoroughly pleased with the gentleman sitting beside her. She didn't want the night to end, but knew it had to. He waited for the valet to return with Nedra's car. When he did, Simeon walked around and opened the car door for her. He extended his hand to help her out of his car.

"I'll follow you home so I know you made it safely."

"That's not necessary. I don't live that far away. I'll be fine."

He motioned for her to buckle her seatbelt.

"This is not up for discussion, Nedra. I'm going to make sure you get home. OK?"

She tried not to go into panic mode, but she did. The way Simeon spoke to her was firm, yet made her feel that he was genuinely concerned over her safety. She decided not to make a big deal out of it, and agreed to let him follow her.

When they pulled into her complex, Simeon realized Nedra was serious when she said she lived only ten minutes from downtown. She pulled into the parking space and turned off her engine. Simeon pulled in beside her and climbed out of the truck so he could walk her to the door.

"You weren't kidding when you said you lived close."

"I told you," she answered as she unlocked the door to her building.

She turned to him and leaned against the door. He shoved his hands inside his pockets and took a step closer to her.

"I really had a good time tonight, Nedra."

This was always the awkward moment. Saying good night could mean a hug, a handshake, or a kiss.

"I'll ditto that statement. Would you like to come in for some coffee?"

"Maybe next time. You need to get some rest. I've kept you out long enough."

They stood there for a moment in silence. Nedra reached inside her purse and pulled out a pen. She took his hand and jotted down her cell phone number in his palm. He smiled and then leaned down and kissed her on the cheek.

"I'd love to go out with you again, Simeon," she said as she closed his hand.

A huge grin graced his face as he backed away.

"I'll definitely call you. Good night, Nedra."

"Good night and drive safely."

Walking back to his truck he answered, "I will."

She entered her house, closed the door, and watched as he drove off. After closing the door she nearly collapsed with excitement. Simeon Mathews was as raw and sexy as any man should be, and he definitely knew how to dress. Her skin was tingling where he had kissed her cheek. She rubbed the area as she made her way upstairs to get ready for bed. She quickly showered and climbed into bed. As she reached over to turn out the light, her telephone rang.

"Hello?"

"Where have you been? I've been calling you all night," an angry voice greeted her.

It was Tyree.

Trying not to give her deception away, she lied.

"I hung out with my coworkers after work."

"Do you have any idea what time it is? You couldn't call?"

"I didn't mean to worry you, Tyree. You're right; I should've called to let you know where I was."

"Where's your cell phone?"

"It went dead on me while I was out. It's charging up now."

He was silent.

"Tyree?"

"I'm here," he answered after hesitating briefly.

She sat up in bed, worried that he had picked up on her lie.

"I'm sorry I worried you, baby. I promise I won't let it happen again."

He cleared his throat. "I thought something had happened to you."

"Ah, babe. I'm fine and I think it's sweet that you were worried about me."

He was still somewhat silent.

"I love you, Tyree."

"I love you too, Nedra. Get some sleep. I'll holler at you tomorrow."

"OK, baby. Good night. "

She hung up the telephone, feeling disgusted with herself. Looking over at the clock, she knew it was late, but she needed to talk to someone. She wasn't ready to talk to Donovon about this, but she did need some guidance. Her Aunt Tina was the one she always talked to when it came to men. She was her father's youngest sister and they were very close. She was only thirty-five-years-old, and now was a better time than any to see if her psychic abilities were on target. Nedra dialed her number and Tina quickly picked up the telephone.

"Hello?"

"Hi, Auntie."

"Nedra? Girl, what are you doing calling me so late?"

"Don't even go there." Nedra laughed. "I know you don't go to bed before two a.m. most nights."

"I beg your pardon," she playfully answered. "Now, tell me about this new man you've met."

"Dang, Auntie, you didn't give me a chance to tell you." Nedra sat there amazed with Tina's unique ability. "I can't believe you already know about him. Anyway, he is wonderful and the man is fione! His name is Simeon and the man can wear a suit!"

Tina laughed.

"He sounds yummy. As soon as you get a chance, take his picture and email it to me. So, what are you going to do about Tyree?"

"I don't know. I had to lie to him tonight."

"Why?"

"I went out with Simeon, but I told Tyree I was out with coworkers. He left me several messages on my cell, and I didn't know what to do or say."

"He was worried about you, huh?"

"Yes," she solemnly admitted.

"Tyree's cool and I like him. I have a feeling that you're about to get in over your head. This man is older, right?"

"How do you do that?" Nedra asked.

"I told you I have the gift!" They laughed together.

"He's thirty."

"Thirty! What does he do for a living?"

"You mean you don't already know?"

"Come on, tell me," Tina pleaded.

"He's a lawyer."

"Uh oh."

"What?"

"Honey, lawyers have very intense personalities. They're usually under a lot of stress, they don't like to lose, and they don't take rejection well. They can be arrogant, too, which is not good."

"Simeon doesn't seem like that," Nedra said as she rolled over in bed and sighed.

"Exactly! They have to be deceptive in their profession, and their personal life is usually no different. All I'm going to say is watch your back. He's older and I'm sure more experienced."

Nedra started laughing. "You don't even know how experienced I am."

Tina laughed even louder. "Don't make me go there with you. Go to bed and keep me posted on this Simeon character. How's Donovon?"

"He's great as usual. I miss hanging out with him."

"You do know that man has been yearning for you for a long time, don't you?"

"You know Donovon and I are just friends."

"If you say so. Don't say I didn't tell you so."

"Whatever."

"I'm not wrong on many things, Nedra. I like Tyree, but Donovon is the one."

"On that note, I'm going to bed, Auntie," Nedra announced as she lay back on her pillow.

"You need to listen to me, Nedra. I'm serious."

"I will. Thanks, Auntie."

"You're welcome, and Nedra?"

"Yes?"

"Playing around with a person's heart is never a good thang. Remember that, OK?"

"I will. Good night."

They hung up, and Nedra turned out the lights and went to sleep.

Chapter Seven

No Turning Back Now

At work the next day, Nedra called Tyree to apologize again for worrying him the night before. He was still upset with her, but eventually he accepted her apology. Donovon called later that day and blasted her for being so careless. It was obvious to Nedra that he had talked to Tyree. He also told her if she ever did anything like that again, there would be hell to pay from him.

"Dang! Everybody's mad at me."

"Everybody has a right to be! Nedra, believe it or not, there are some people around here who love you and don't want to see you hurt. Where were you anyway?"

"I was out with Simeon."

Donovon wanted to come through the telephone and choke her.

"Out with him where? You don't even know this dude and you're going out with him already? What the hell is wrong with you, Nedra? You're acting like you're sixteen-years-old. Don't you know if something had happened to you we wouldn't have known a damn thing? What is it about this guy that has you tripping? Damn!"

Tears welled up in her eyes and she choked them back. Donovon had never yelled at her like he was doing right now

"I said I was sorry."

Saying he was angry was an understatement. He finally calmed himself before speaking. "Nedra, do me a favor. The rest of the time you're there, could you please act like you have some common sense?"

"Yes."

"Don't let this happen again, and stay away from that dude! He's too old for you anyway."

"I'm sorry, Donovon. I'll talk to you later."

"OK. Good-bye, Nedra."

"Good-bye.

She hung up and wiped her eyes. Turning to her computer, she got back to work.

A couple weeks passed and Nedra was trying not to let guilt consume her. She had not only upset Tyree, but Donovon too. During phone conversations with Simeon, he picked up on her solemn demeanor and tried to find out why. He had invited her to lunch on more than one occasion, but she declined all his invitations until they could get to know each other better. Simeon tried to convince her otherwise, but she wasn't budging. Nedra was trying her best to be faithful to Tyree and follow her own rules regarding dating someone new.

On one particular evening, Simeon showed up

at her house unexpectedly. When she opened the door she froze in shock. He was casually dressed in jeans and a white starched shirt, but he still radiated power and sex appeal.

"Nedra, I'm sorry for showing up on your doorstep like this, but I couldn't help myself. You've been avoiding me and I want to know why. I thought we hit it off great. Have I done something to offend you?"

Still shaken by his presence, she forced herself to lie.

"I haven't been avoiding you, Simeon."

He was clouding her thoughts with the sensual scent of his cologne. Taking a step toward her, he tilted her chin upward.

"Then why won't you go out with me?"

"I've been out with you, Simeon."

He folded his arms and took a stance. "Once."

She lowered her eyes. "Look, can we please talk about this inside?"

She moved to the side, giving him room to enter. He walked in and waited for her to invite him to sit.

She closed the door and softly said, "Have a seat."

"Thank you," he answered.

Nedra sat down across from him. Simeon studied her and noticed her nervousness.

"What's going on, Nedra?"

Running her fingers through her hair, she took a deep breath.

"This is not working for me, Simeon. I have a boyfriend and going out with you is wrong."

"And I told you I'm not interested in your boyfriend."

She looked at him and her heart thumped against

her ribs. He was doing a number on her, and she didn't know how much longer she could resist him.

"Why are you putting the full court press on me, Simeon?"

"That's cute, Nedra. I told you—I like you, I enjoy your company, and I thought you enjoyed mine."

She stood, walked nervously to the window, and looked out.

"I do like your company. I'm just worried about where this might lead and what going out with you could do to my relationship with my boyfriend."

He joined her at the window.

"Like I told you before, I just want to show you a good time while you're here. Anything more will be your call. OK?"

She turned and looked up into his warm eyes. "Promise?"

"Promise," he said before hugging her.

She leaned into him and exhaled. "I just don't want any misunderstandings."

"There won't be. Now get your jacket so I can take you out."

"I'd like that."

She gathered her purse and left with Simeon for a day of fun.

That day was the first of many dates with Simeon. They took trips to the mountains, casinos, ball-games, and other relaxing locations. Nedra was getting even more comfortable with Simeon and the expensive lifestyle he lived. He was always showering her with gifts and he even tried to give her money; however, she refused to accept it. The pair shared some normal evenings as well when Nedra would cook dinner and afterward they watched a movie together. It was in these intimate settings that the first of many sweltering kisses were shared, and they were better than she had imagined. Lying to Tyree was getting easier as each day went by, and as each kiss was shared. It was time for her to admit to herself that she was getting pulled deeper and deeper into a relationship with Simeon. His attentiveness was no comparison to that of any other man she'd dated.

During the upcoming weekend, Simeon was having a get-together at his house for a few friends, and Nedra was a little nervous about it. Little did she know, Simeon was looking forward to showing off the woman who had stolen his heart.

Simeon's home was a beautiful stucco-styled house with an in-ground pool. Simeon had arranged to have the caterers set up all the food around the pool. There were candles and magnolia blossoms floating in the pool. When Nedra saw the setting, she was in awe.

"Everything is so beautiful, Simeon."

He smiled proudly.

"I'm glad you approve."

"I'm a little nervous about meeting your friends tonight," she admitted while wringing her hands.

He pulled her against his chest and caressed her back. "Don't be, sweetheart. They're going to love you."

"I hope so," she said as she straightened his collar.

They stared at each other for several seconds.

"You look beautiful tonight."

She twirled around to showcase her outfit.

"I'm glad you like."

She was wearing black linen pants with a mauve silk blouse. Black high-heeled sandals adorned her freshly manicured feet.

"I like very much," he whispered before kissing her on the lips.

Nedra melted as his hands rested on her backside. She moaned slightly as he deepened the kiss. At that moment, the doorbell chimed, startling them. Simeon continued to kiss her, ignoring the doorbell. Nedra tried to pull away, but he wouldn't let her.

"Simeon, don't you think you should get the door?"

"Let them wait," he said without hesitating.

He pushed her against the wall and kissed her breathlessly. The subtle contact of his mouth on her neck set both of their bodies on fire. The doorbell chimed again as Simeon kissed her even more aggressively.

"Come on, baby, you're going to have some upset guests if you don't answer the door."

He finally stopped kissing her and pulled a handkerchief out of his pocket so he could wipe her lipstick off his mouth.

"OK, now come with me. I want you to help me greet everyone."

Holding his hand, Nedra fanned herself as she walked with him to greet the guests.

Nedra was a hit with Simeon's friends. They were so friendly and welcomed her with open arms. Nedra sat around the pool chatting with some of the ladies, while Simeon and the guys were on the other side sipping their drinks. Simeon's friend, Chris, pointed over to Nedra and questioned Simeon.

"Simeon, where did you meet her? She's very attractive and we won't talk about that body."

"We met at the United Negro College Fund fundraiser," Simeon proudly informed them.

Chris smiled and saluted Simeon.

"You're my hero." The men laughed together.

"She's genuine too," Simeon continued. "As sweet as they come, and I'll stomp any of you punks in the neck if you try to step up to her."

They all laughed again playfully, but Simeon was dead serious.

Later that night, after all the guests were gone, Nedra and Simeon shared a chaise lounge by the pool. It had gotten much cooler, so Simeon pulled a throw over their bodies for warmth.

"I had a great time," she whispered as she nuzzled his neck.

"I told you, you would," he whispered back as he caressed her arm.

She yawned.

"It's late, Simeon. I'd better be getting home."

Still caressing her arm, he made a suggestion.

"Why don't you stay over?"

She looked up into his yearning eyes.

"I don't think that would be a good idea."

"I'll be a good boy. It's not like I don't have an extra room for you to sleep in."

She swallowed hard as she contemplated his

suggestion. Simeon was relaxed as he sat there sipping his wine, waiting for her answer. She thought about Tyree momentarily, but decided it was too late for her to drive home.

"I'll need something to sleep in," she whispered softly.

He smiled and kissed her on the forehead.

"That won't be a problem. Come on, let's get you settled into your room."

Nedra and Simeon blew out the candles and went inside for the night. She called Tyree when she got in the bathroom so she could tell him good night. He had called her earlier as she was dressing for the party. Tyree didn't suspect anything out of the ordinary, so he wished her a good night. After hanging up, she showered and climbed into the large bed across the hallway from Simeon.

In the middle of the night, Nedra was awakened by an unusual noise. Startled, she forgot where she was for a moment. She heard the noise again and eased out of bed. She walked over to the window and looked out. Below she noticed Simeon cleaning up around the pool. She slipped into a pair of Simeon's slippers and made her way outside to join him.

Within minutes she was outside on the pool deck observing him. He looked up.

"Did I wake you?"

"Not really. Can I help you?" she asked as she walked farther out into the cool night air.

"No, you're my guest. Besides, I'm almost finished."

The pajama pants he wore accented his physique and caused Nedra's body to start simmering. She watched him as he moved around the tables, throwing away leftover paper products. He tied the garbage bags and stacked them in the corner.

"See? I told you I was almost done."

He walked over to her and put his arm around her waist.

"Did you really have a good time tonight?" he asked as he looked into her eyes.

"Oh, yes! Everyone was so nice."

"Hmmm, Nedra, can I ask you something?"

"Sure."

He had a concerned look on his face as he spoke.

"I noticed you and my friend, Raymond, had a long conversation. What were you guys talking about for so long?"

She thought for a moment.

"Which one was Raymond?"

"The bald-headed guy."

"OK! I think we talked about college, where I was from, stuff like that. Why?"

"I didn't like it," he responded.

"Are you serious?" she asked, thinking he was kidding.

"I'm dead serious." He stood over her and stared directly at her. "I don't trust any man around you."

"But he's your friend," she reminded him. "You have nothing to worry about, because all of your friends were perfect gentlemen."

"Exactly! Keep your distance from those clowns. I know them too well."

He's jealous.

"It's cool out here. Come inside so I can get you something warm to drink," he said.

Walking next to him, she told him that she didn't need anything to drink. Arriving at her assigned bedroom, she turned to face him.

"Well, good night again, Simeon."

He cupped her face and planted a sultry kiss on her lips. Nedra kissed him, wrapping her arms around his neck. Their kiss became even more heated and Nedra felt herself spiraling out of control. He trailed kisses along the side of her neck and ran his hands under the dress shirt he'd given her to sleep in.

"Damn, Nedra," he whispered as he explored her soft body.

"Simeon?"

He looked into her eyes and saw her desire to be with him. "Are you sure about this?"

"Yes," she said without hesitation.

It had been a couple of months since she'd been intimate with Tyree, and the distance between them had taken a toll on her emotionally and physically. Having Simeon's hands and lips on her body broke down the last of any resistance she had. He led her into his room and that night was a night full of indescribable passion. It was the first night of many passionate nights she would spend in his bed and in his arms. Maybe her aunt was right. Simeon Mathews just might be more than she could handle. That idea became even more realistic when he showed up the next night to take her to dinner.

They walked out into the parking lot and Nedra started looking around for Simeon's vehicle.

"Where's your truck?"

He grinned at her and continued to walk through the parking lot. She watched him as he stopped next to a champagne colored Lexus. She walked over and inspected the car.

"Very nice!" He held out the keys to her.

"I thought you would like it. It's yours."

Nedra felt her head spin as she looked at him.

"What did you say?"

He kissed her and repeated himself.

"I said it's yours. I want my lady riding around in style. Have a seat," he said as he opened the driver's side door.

"Simeon, I can't accept this."

"Why not?"

"Because there's nothing wrong with my car."

He closed the door, walked around to the passenger side, and climbed in. Nedra felt her body melt into the leather seat. It felt wonderful.

"Look, Nedra, I know there's nothing wrong with your car. I just wanted you to have something extra nice to drive in while you're here. It's a lease, so it's no big deal."

Nedra caressed the steering wheel in silence. She turned to him and smiled.

"This is very sweet, Simeon, but it is too extravagant."

He held her hand and caressed it.

"You've turned down all my other gifts. It would mean the world to me if you would accept the car as a token of my affection."

"I don't know about this," she said, shaking her head.

"Well, I can't take it back for three months, so you might as well drive it."

"You're not making this easy for me."

"Nedra, let me pamper you this one time. OK?"

"If you insist," she whispered.

Chapter Eight

Make It Last Forever

A couple of weekends later, Nedra was glad it was Friday and she was able to get off work a little early. She'd been spending a lot time between the sheets with Simeon and she needed a break. It'd been several days since she'd seen him, and she told him she had plans for the weekend, hoping to extend her alone time. She wanted to relax, read a hot romance novel, and just pamper herself. Simeon was a very intense lover, and after a week with him, a woman needed to let her body rest.

It had been three days since she'd slept with him, but he'd called and dropped by her office to check on her. They'd even managed to have lunch one day, and, of course, he tried to talk her into slipping away to a nearby hotel. It was hard for him to stay away from her, but he did his best to abide by her wishes.

While vacuuming her living room, she was interrupted by the sound of her doorbell. She peeped out the window, hoping it wasn't Simeon dropping by unexpectedly. She didn't see his car, so she opened the door. There stood Tyree. Nedra screamed and jumped into his arms.

"Oh my God! Hey, baby, why didn't you tell me you were coming?"

He picked up his bag and carried Nedra into the house, closing the door behind him. She openly cried as she held onto him.

"I wanted to surprise you, baby," he softly said as he caressed her body. "Since I'm going to be out of town for your birthday, I thought we could celebrate early. Have you missed me?"

Tyree sat down on the floor and pulled her down into his lap. He kissed her greedily. She buried her face into his warm neck.

"Of course I've missed you. How did you get away?"

"We didn't have a game this weekend."

"I'm glad."

"You look tired, baby," he said as he stroked her face. "Have you been getting enough rest?"

"I'm fine, sweetheart. Are you hungry? Do you want to go get something to eat?"

"All I want is you."

"I think I can arrange that. Come on upstairs so you can put your things away."

Tyree picked up his luggage and followed her upstairs to her bedroom.

Not for one second did she think about Simeon, but Nedra was definitely heavy on Simeon's mind. He was still in court and planned to call her as soon as he could. He had a special night planned for them, full of champagne and a lot of sweating. Yes, she told him she had plans for the weekend, but he was confident that he would be able to change her mind.

Hours later, Nedra and Tyree lay in tangled sheets after making love. She kissed his chest and ran her hand up his thigh.

"I hope you're ready to eat, baby, because I am starving, thanks to you," she said.

He rolled onto his side and teased her.

"I've really missed hearing those little noises you make when you do what you do."

She giggled.

"You're so silly. What do you want to eat?" she asked.

He raised her comforter and looked under the sheets.

"Do you really want to know?"

"You're so bad."

"I love you, Nedra," he said as he pulled a strand of her hair out of her eyes.

"I love you too."

They stared at each other for a moment. He leaned over and kissed her tenderly.

"Don't move. I have something for your birthday."

Tyree jumped out of bed and opened his bag. He walked back over to the bed with a small velvet box in his hand. He climbed back into bed next to her and she looked at him with gleaming eyes.

"What's that?"

"Close your eyes," he whispered.

Nedra closed her eyes and waited anxiously. He opened the small box.

"You can open them now."

Nedra opened her eyes and screamed.

"You like it?"

"I love it."

Tears fell out of her eyes as he pulled the ring out of the box and slid it on her finger.

"It's not the one I wanted to get you, but as soon as I get drafted, I'm going to get you the kind of ring you deserve."

Nedra was speechless. The ring he put on her finger was exquisite and perfect. She cupped his face and kissed him before gazing at her hand.

"You don't have to get me another ring, Tyree."

"I know I don't have to, baby, but I want to. So, this is your pre-engagement ring. OK?"

More tears fell out of her eyes and a huge lump formed in her throat.

"Are you saying you want to marry me, Tyree?"

He looked at her with a smirk on his face.

"Of course I do, but I don't want to make it official until after we graduate. I want to propose to you the right way, baby."

She nodded in agreement and then straddled him. He ran his hands over the length of her body and covered her breasts with his mouth. Nedra shivered as he nibbled on her greedily. She kissed her way down his chiseled body, causing him to groan and pant loudly when she began to pleasure him orally. Watching her mouth move slowly over his body caused him to verbally praise her efforts.

Seconds later, he flipped her onto her back and happily returned the favor. Tyree placed her legs over his shoulders and gripped her hips as his mouth danced against her hot, throbbing flesh. Her body sizzled as he flicked his tongue against her moist center. He watched as her body trembled out of control. It was music to his ears to hear her whimper and feel her wiggle in agony. She screamed for mercy even though she knew he would never give her any. He loved to torture her this way and could devour her for hours. Her reaction to him was never the same, which really turned him on. Nedra screamed out as waves of passion overtook her. It was then, and only then, that he pressed his rigid body into her wet center and professed his need and undying love to her.

Nearly an hour had passed before either of them could move. Nedra was on cloud nine and never wanted the moment to end. Lying there in each other's arms, listening to the rhythm of each other's hearts was familiar to them, and they wanted to savor the moment as long as they possibly could. Unfortunately, their stomachs had other plans. They couldn't tell which one of them was the loudest, but one thing they did know was that they needed to eat.

"I guess we can't ignore it any longer, huh?"

They laughed together.

"Do you want to order in or go somewhere?" He nibbled on her earlobe.

"It doesn't matter to me."

Nedra closed her eyes and moaned.

"Hmmm, why don't I show you around town a little, then we can come back here and do some more of this."

Throwing back the sheets, he agreed. "Let me take a shower first, then I'm all yours."

She sat up on the side of the bed and ran her fingers through her tousled hair. "You'll find everything you need in the linen closet."

Smiling devilishly, he turned to her.

"Don't you want to join me?"

She stood and folded her arms.

"Tyree, you and I both know that if I get in the shower with you, we'll never get any food. They'll find our bodies satisfied, but dead from starvation."

He gave her a loving pat on her bare backside.

"I guess you're right, but can I at least get a rain check?"

She ran her hand down his body and rested it on his midsection.

"Without a doubt. Now go and save me some hot water."

He laughed and closed the door behind him. Seconds later, he was singing in the shower. Smiling, Nedra walked over to her closet to search for something to wear. Her telephone rang almost immediately, startling her. She hurriedly picked up the phone without checking the ID.

"Hello?"

"Hey, sexy. Pack a bag because I have a cabin reserved for us that you have got to see."

She nervously looked at the bathroom door and then walked out into the hallway so she could talk privately.

"Simeon, I told you I had plans this weekend."

"Cancel them. You've kept me at arm's length for nearly a week now, and I want to see you."

Simeon's tone was clearly agitated.

"I'm sorry, Simeon, but I can't this weekend.

Look, I'll give you a call Sunday, OK? I have to go now because I'm running late."

He was silent on the phone, then from out of nowhere he asked her the unthinkable.

"Are you giving my stuff up to someone else?"

His stuff?

"Your stuff? I don't like the way this conversation is going, Simeon. I can't talk to you right now. I have to go. Good-bye."

She hung up the telephone and started trembling. She closed her eyes and prayed Simeon didn't show up at her doorstep while Tyree was in town. The way he was talking left her uncertain, so she had to make sure she kept him at bay.

After hearing Tyree turn off the shower, she quickly grabbed an outfit from her closet and laid it on the bed. Tyree re-entered the bedroom with a towel wrapped around his waist.

"Did you save me some hot water?"

"Just enough. Now hurry up, because I may pass out from hunger."

Nedra grabbed her undergarments and entered the bathroom. She discreetly took her telephone with her in case Simeon decided to call back. Turning it off wasn't a good idea because he would surely come over if he didn't get an answer. All Nedra wanted to do was hurry up and get out of the house. She prayed he didn't show up on her doorstep. She took a quick shower and hustled Tyree out the door.

A secluded restaurant outside of town was the setting for dinner. Nedra didn't want to risk any chance of running into Simeon. If they did, she knew the scene would quickly turn ugly and she would lose Tyree forever.

After dinner they stopped to play several games of pool at a nearby sports bar. On the way back to the condo, Tyree picked up a bottle of wine and something to snack on. When they finally made it back to the condo, it was well after midnight. Nedra was so anxious to get Tyree back into bed that she kept putting the wrong key in the door. As she struggled to open her door, Tyree kissed and caressed her body. She giggled as she finally swung the door open and practically fell inside the condo. They peeled each other's clothes off, beginning at the front door and leading to the upstairs bedroom. It wasn't until the lights in the condo went totally dark that Simeon, who had staked out Nedra's condo, had seen enough. The proof was there. Nedra's busy weekend was spending time with another man, and it sickened him. He started the engine of his truck and peeled off.

Simeon staked out Nedra's condo the following night as well, but there was no sign of her and the mysterious man he'd seen her with the day before. Every time he called, he got her voicemail. He gripped the steering wheel of his truck in anger. Just the thought of another man putting his hands on her made him furious.

It wasn't until Sunday morning that her door finally opened and the man exited her condo. Simeon watched as the man put his bag in the trunk of his car before giving Nedra an eternal hug and kiss. Whether this man was the boyfriend she told him about was unclear, so he jotted down the license plate just in case he had some local competition. Nedra was dressed in her bathrobe, which all but told him what they'd been doing all weekend. Simeon was exhausted from sleeping in his vehicle, but it was worth it to get a look at this mysterious man. Whoever he was, he had an athlete's build, but these days, anyone could work out and get a defined body like his.

"Who are you?" Simeon mumbled to himself.

Using his binoculars, he got a close-up view of the kiss they shared, and he was also able to see just how intimate the kiss was. It was obvious Nedra was tearful as the man climbed into the car and pulled out onto the street. Simeon watched as she blew the man a kiss before going back inside her condo.

After locking the door, Nedra lay down on the sofa in tears. Her heart ached at the sight of Tyree driving away. All she had left was the ring he'd put on her finger two days ago. Just as she was about to go upstairs to take a shower, her doorbell rang. She wiped away her tears and opened the door without looking out to see who it was. As soon as she did, Simeon hurried past her without saying a word. His forwardness startled her, and it was then that she realized Simeon must have seen Tyree leave.

"What are you doing here, Simeon?"

"I need to have an invitation now before visiting you?"

He looked stressed and fatigued. His clothes were slightly wrinkled and he was unshaven. Nedra had never seen him looking so unraveled or in such an agitated state. She pulled the belt on her robe tighter and folded her arms across her chest.

"What do you want, Simeon? I was just getting ready to get in the shower."

"I bet you are."

"What's going on with you?"

He walked over to her and grabbed her upper arm, pulling her to him. He pressed his face against her neck and sniffed. He frowned and gently pushed her away from him. She noticed a weird look in his eyes, and for the first time since she'd met him, she felt uneasy.

"Who was he?"

Nedra didn't know whether to lie or tell the truth. The realization that Simeon had seen Tyree leave had come to light. She started feeling like the room was closing in on her, so she chose her words carefully and tried to play dumb.

"What did you say?"

He walked over to her, backing her against the wall. He was calm as he spoke, but his body language told a different story.

"I just saw a man leaving here. I saw him kissing you. Who was he?"

She had no escape route and Simeon's face was within inches of hers.

"Simeon, what is wrong with you? You don't have a right to ask me about who comes and goes from my house."

He ran his finger down the side of her face before placing his hand on her neck. Nedra shuddered as he leaned down and kissed her hard on the lips. Next he pulled open her robe and covered her breasts with his large hands. Nedra tried to ease out of the spot she was in, but he had her pinned against the wall with his aroused body.

"Simeon, please!"

He stared down at her and shook his head. He stepped back and made fists with his hands. Simeon spoke softly, but his demeanor was still off key.

"What's wrong? I can't touch you now?"

As she closed her robe, Simeon noticed the ring on her finger. He grabbed her hand and questioned her.

"What is this? Did he give you this ring?"

Still concerned, she pulled her hand out of his grasp and walked across the room so she wouldn't get cornered again.

"Simeon, calm down. I told you I had a boyfriend. It just so happens that he decided to pay me a surprise visit this weekend for my birthday. I haven't seen him in a long time, so we hung out. You can understand that, can't you?"

"Why didn't you just tell me?"

Nedra couldn't answer that question herself. Maybe it was because she knew she should've slowed things down with Simeon when she noticed he was getting attached to her, and telling him Tyree was in town might have angered him.

"I didn't tell you because I didn't want to hurt your feelings. You told me you would let me decide which way our relationship would go, but you're not, Simeon. You're making me feel like I did something wrong by spending the weekend with my boyfriend."

Simeon ran his hands over his face because she was right, and in a way it flattered him that she wanted to spare his feelings. He walked over to her and extended his hand to her. She looked up into his eyes before reluctantly taking his hand. Pulling her into his arms, he hugged her.

"I'm sorry, Nedra. Everything you said is true. I care about you so much, and I guess I let things get out of hand. I let jealously consume me, and I shouldn't have. Please forgive me. I never meant to scare you or cause a scene."

"It's all my fault. I never should've let things get this far," she said. "I care about you too, Simeon, but I'm only here for a few more weeks. Things between us have been great and I don't want us to leave each other on a sour note. You've taken me places I've never been before, both intimately and physically. Your generosity has been unbelievable and I'm so glad we met. I'll always appreciate you for making my stay here bearable."

He tilted her face upward and covered her lips with his. He was gentle and loving as he kissed and teased her mouth. Nedra had shared an incredible sexual relationship with Simeon, and it had taken her mind and body to places she'd never dreamed possible. Walking away from someone who was full of so much passion and vigor wasn't going to be easy, but she knew she had no choice.

"Simeon?"

"Yes?" he answered while still holding her in his arms.

"Are we still friends?"

He looked down at her and smiled.

"We're beyond friends, sweetheart. You are my lover and I'll never, ever forget you. Again, I'm sorry for overreacting. It just shows how special you are to me."

She walked him to the door.

"I understand, Simeon, and I'm overwhelmed that you care about me so much."

He chuckled and kissed her once more before stepping out onto her porch.

"Get some rest and call me sometime."

"I will. Good-bye."

Nedra watched him as he walked out to his truck. She closed the door and immediately locked it. She was so glad her internship would soon be over soon so she could go home. Having a jealous lover wasn't something she had dealt with before. Hopefully, Simeon now had everything in perspective so they could eventually go their separate ways.

Chapter Nine

Just Like Old Times

The week after the incident with Simeon and her unbelievable weekend with Tyree, Nedra needed to regroup, so at the urging of Ashley and Donovon, she decided to take a trip back to campus and hang out with her friends for her birthday. Little did she know, Donovon had purchased the beautiful gold bracelet she had been eyeing for a couple of years in the jewelry store at the mall. Every time they went there she tried it on and admired it. Her plan was to purchase it with some of her graduation money, so he was excited to be the one to purchase it for her birthday instead.

Nedra had talked to Simeon a couple of times since that crazy day, and he seemed to be just fine. He told her he was going to back off a little and give her some much needed space, because the last thing he wanted to do was have her upset with him. This pleased Nedra and let her know he was more than a friend to her because he put her needs before his own.

While in town, her friends decided to give her a surprise birthday party. Her roommate, Ashley, was given the job to bring her to Donovon's apartment for the party. Nedra was under the impression they were all going out on the town for her birthday. Ashley lied and told her that Donovon called to say he wasn't feeling well and couldn't go. She knew Nedra would be concerned and would want to stop by the apartment to check on him. Unbeknownst to Nedra, this was the plot to get her to her surprise birthday party. Nedra and Ashley walked up the stairs and knocked on Donovon's door.

"Come in."

Nedra walked through the door and heard a thunderous, "Surprise!"

She was shocked and the tears immediately fell from her eyes. Nedra made her way into the room, hugging all her friends as she went along. Donovon walked up and kissed her on the lips.

"Happy Birthday, Nedra."

"I'm going to get you for this. Seriously though, thank you."

"You're welcome, Roadrunner."

Tracy watched closely from across the room as she sipped a wine cooler. Donovon's former roommate cranked up the music and they got their dance on. Donovon had sandwiches, hot wings, Rotel dip, and plenty of beverages. The most important thing on the menu was a huge birthday cake. They partied until way past midnight. Things finally slowed down so Nedra could open her birthday gifts. She cried as she read each card out loud to her friends. Even Tracy got her a gift, which was a bath set complete with scented gels and lotions. Nedra thanked her in spite of the way she had treated her in the past.

Later, as the guests were beginning to depart, Nedra stacked up her gifts.

"Thank all of you for coming and for the presents. I love you all."

Ashley ran over and hugged her roommate once more.

"Nedra, I would help you get your things back to the room, but Andre is waiting for me to pick him up from work."

"Traitor."

"I'm sorry."

"It's OK, Ashley. I'll drive her back to the dorm," Donovon said.

Tracy interjected. "I can take you, Nedra."

"No, it's late, Trace. You wait here and I'll be back in a few."

Nedra walked over to Tracy and gave her an unexpected hug. "Thanks again for my gift. It was very thoughtful of you."

Tracy curled up on the sofa.

"You're welcome. Hurry back, Donovon, so we can tuck each other in. I'm so sleepy."

Nedra turned on her heels and rolled her eyes so only Donovon could see her.

"Go on to bed if you're so tired, Tracy. I'll clean up when I get back."

"No, I'll wait up for if you're not going to be gone long."

He picked up Nedra's stack of gifts and walked toward the door.

"See you in a little bit. Let's go, Nedra."

She walked out ahead of him and down the stairs.

Tracy walked over so she could lock the door.

"I'm getting sick of your nasty attitude toward Nedra."

She sighed and closed the door without responding.

Down at Donovon's car, he put the gifts in the trunk and then opened the car door for Nedra. He climbed in next to her, rested his head against the steering wheel, and let out a breath.

She looked over at him curiously.

"Donovon, what's wrong? Are you OK?"

"Tracy is really starting to get on my nerves."

Nedra lowered her eyes.

"It's because of me, isn't it?"

He sat up and started the ignition.

"Don't worry about it, because her days are numbered anyway. Let me get you back to campus so you can get some rest."

"Rest? I'm trying to find out where the party is," she said while dancing in her seat.

They laughed together, then Nedra's cell phone interrupted them.

"Hello?"

"Happy Birthday."

She smiled. "Thank you, Simeon."

Donovon rolled his eyes at the mention of Simeon's name.

"Are you having a good time?"

"I am. Thanks for asking." He let out a breath.

"I have something special planned for your birthday when you get back."

Nedra blushed.

"Sounds nice. I really appreciate you calling to wish me a happy birthday."

"You're welcome. Be safe and call me when you get back in town, OK?"

"OK. Good-bye."

She hung up the telephone and looked over at Donovon.

"Was that your Cake Daddy?"

She looked out the window.

"He was just calling to wish me a happy birth-day."

"Whatever, Nedra."

"I don't want to hear it tonight, Donovon. It's my birthday and I don't want to fight."

Donovon pulled the car into a parking space and turned off the engine.

"Nedra, I'm worried about you with this lawyer. You told me how upset he got when he saw Tyree leaving your house last week. What's going on? Are things getting serious between you guys?"

She closed her eyes and laid her head back on the seat.

"No, but it's complicated. He's so nice and at-tentive to me. The sex is off da hook and I like him. He's dignified, respected, and so handsome. It's not so easy to just cut off all ties with him. He's been good to me while I've been living there."

"What about the jealous fit he threw on you about Tyree? Doesn't that tell you something?"

"I think he's in love with me, but there's noth-ing I can do about that. He understood in the beginning that I had a boyfriend and he understood that I was only going to be in town for a few months. We're cool."

"Are you sure?"

"He's just a little jealous. That's all."

Donovon opened his car door and climbed out. He popped open his trunk and walked around the car to open her door.

"Nedra, you should've known that would happen after you started sleeping with him."

"I guess you're right. I'll be glad when this internship is over. That, I do know."

They gathered all the packages out of the car and walked quietly to her room. After entering, he sat her gifts on the table and let out a breath.

Nedra smiled and took off her jacket.

"Have a seat, Donovon."

Instead of sitting, he smiled and motioned for her to come to him.

"Come over here for a second." She looked at him curiously.

"For what?"

Donovon took her by the hand and repeated himself.

"I said, come here. I haven't given you my present yet."

They sat down on her bed and he reached inside his pocket and pulled out a small gift-wrapped box. Nedra's eyes widened with surprise because she recognized the signature wrapping paper.

"What's this? You know you didn't have to get me a gift, Donovon. The party was more than enough."

"No, it wasn't. Go ahead, open it," Donovon proudly suggested.

Nedra tore into the small box and opened it. She gasped and immediately started sobbing. Inside was the gold bracelet she had been admiring for over two years.

"Oh! Donovon! I can't believe you did this!"

He took the bracelet out of the box and snapped it on her wrist.

"There! It looks great on you. Now you can stop drooling over it every time you go to the mall. Happy Birthday, Nedra."

Nedra hugged him tightly, burying her face in his warm neck. Her tears flowed steadily as they sat there holding each other. She had no idea what she was doing to him, but he was dying a slow death. Witnessing her fall in love with Tyree was one thing, but to watch her get involved with an older man on the side was even worse.

They embraced each other for about five minutes, until Nedra looked up into his eyes.

"I'm glad you like the bracelet. I know it doesn't compare to Tyree's gift, but I knew it was something you wanted."

She looked at him curiously, because she would never expect him to get her a gift like Tyree's, since it was an engagement ring.

"Donovon, you could've given me a card and I would be just as excited. You've always been there for me and I'll always love you for that."

She leaned in and kissed him on the lips. They looked deep into each other's eyes before kissing again, this time deeper. Nedra hadn't received a kiss from Donovon like this since their freshman year, and it caught her off guard. A soft moan escaped her lips, shocking both of them. She jumped up and moved away from him. Donovon stood and tried his best to collect his thoughts. Nedra rubbed the goose bumps from her arms as they stood staring each other down.

Embarrassed over her response, she cleared her throat and lowered her eyes.

"Donovon, it's late. Thank you so much for the bracelet."

He stared at her.

"You're very welcome."

"Maybe you should be heading back to your place. I'm sure Tracy's wondering what's taking you so long."

"I'm not concerned about what Tracy's thinking right now," he answered as he moved toward her.

Nedra's body tensed when he embraced her, which caused her heart to beat wildly in her chest.

"Maybe Tracy gives you grief about me because you don't give her enough attention. As a woman, I can understand why she would be jealous of me. I love Tyree, but since he's playing football he doesn't have a lot of time for me, so when Simeon came along it was only natural for me to be attracted to him. He gives me everything I'm missing in my relationship with Tyree, and then some. It's powerful, Donovon, so if you really care about Tracy, then be there for her."

"You really know how to flatter a guy," he said teasingly.

"I'm serious, Donovon," she replied as she released him and looked at the bracelet dangling on her arm.

He sighed and shoved his hands inside his pockets.

"Don't worry about Tracy. She actually gets too much attention from me."

They were silent a minute as both searched for something else to say.

"I do love you, Nedra."

She held his hand. "I love you too. You know you're my dawg."

Donovon shook his head, realizing Nedra wasn't hearing him, or she was avoiding the issue. Maybe the love triangle with Simeon and Tyree was all she could deal with at the moment. Not wanting to upset her, he decided to call it a night.

"Well good night, babe. Sweet dreams and happy birthday again," he said as he hugged and kissed her once more.

"Good night, Donovon," she said as she walked him to the door. "Thanks again for the surprise party and this beautiful bracelet. Don't forget to call me when you get home so I'll know you made it safely."

"You're welcome and I'll call," he answered as he walked down the hallway.

She closed the door and leaned against it. Her lips still tingled from the unexpected kiss from Donovon. She felt his love for her, but she couldn't let him know she did. Could her aunt be right? Could Donovon really be the one for her? She couldn't afford to bring a third man into her drama, but he was very special to her. Love him? Yes. But in love with him? She never really thought about it or gave it a chance. They'd always been just close friends. Simeon was already having a problem accepting their relationship as strictly casual. She couldn't allow herself to complicate her life further. Besides, Tyree was her fiancé.

She walked over to her closet and made room for her gifts. She would go through them again tomorrow. Tonight she would put them away so Tyree could look at them with her. He couldn't be with her tonight because he was at an out-of-town football game. She hoped to see him as soon as he got back to campus, even though it would be way into the night.

Donovon pulled up to his apartment and shut off the engine. He entered his apartment and found that Tracy had cleaned up while he was gone. He dropped his keys on the table and walked into the bedroom where he found her sound asleep. He stared down at her and realized just how empty their relationship was. Outside of the bedroom, he felt hollow, and that's not what he wanted in life. He sighed and sat down so he could remove his shoes. Before entering the bathroom, he picked up the phone and called Nedra.

"Hello?"

"Hey. I'm home."

"Good, because I wasn't going to bed until I heard from you." He laughed quietly.

"Has Tyree made it back from his game yet?"

"I don't know. He'll be tired when he comes back, so he'll probably just wait and see me tomorrow. I think the game ended around ten. Adding in their travel time, there's no telling when the team will get back to campus. I still can't believe he made the basketball team too."

"Don't hate on the man, Nedra. He's an all around athlete, and that'll make him more valuable to the pros."

"I guess you're right. I still wished he could've been here tonight."

"I know, but at least he came to see you last week."

She yawned and looked at the clock. "Well, it's not my birthday anymore. It's after midnight."

"I guess you're right."

They both held the phone in silence. Both wanted to say something, but they weren't sure what to say. Nedra broke the awkward silence.

"Is Tracy still there?"

He looked over at her. "Yeah."

"You'd better go. Good night."

"Good night. I'll see you tomorrow."

He placed the phone back on the cradle and entered the bathroom. He prayed he could get Nedra off his mind because the last thing he wanted to do was whisper the wrong name.

Nedra tossed and turned in bed as she experienced a stressful dream. Waking up in a sweat, she sat up in bed and hugged her knees. Looking over at the clock, she realized it was almost four a.m. She climbed out of bed and opened some bottled water. She drank it down in less than thirty seconds and it temporarily cooled off her body. She had so much tension in her neck and she knew exactly what was causing it. The stress of being away from Tyree and her friends was taking a toll on her.

After saying a short prayer, she cuddled back up with Tyree. When he arrived back on campus, he came straight to her dorm and picked her up. Their reunion was explosive, leaving her exhausted and in tears. Tyree himself was overwhelmed with emotion as he made love to her with every ounce of passion in his body. He expressed the sadness he felt because he was unable to spend more time with her during her birthday weekend. Even though he'd given her the ring the previous weekend, he wouldn't have felt right if he didn't give her a gift on the day of her birthday too. He surprised her with a sexy, red lingerie ensemble, which she quickly put on.

She lay across Tyree's chest and thought about Donovon's kiss. Maybe it was the moment. Maybe it was because they missed each other. Whatever it was, she couldn't let it happen again. They were best friends who cared deeply for each other. Her feelings for Donovon were strong, but she never thought about taking their relationship to another level. It was Tyree she was in love with, and her thoughts had never been cloudy to that fact. One thing was clear—she already had one man too many in the equation, and one would definitely have to go. She hoped Simeon wouldn't be a handful when the day came for them to say their good-byes. She also prayed they would be able to part on good terms and maintain their friendship.

Chapter Ten

All Good Times Must Come To An End

A few weeks later, Nedra's internship finally came to an end and she was going to be leaving in three days. To celebrate, she was going to spend her last days with Simeon at his house. On this night, she shared a going-away dinner with Simeon. He leaned back in his chair and shook his head.

"I can't believe you're leaving."

"I have to, you know that," she said softly.

He reached over and touched her hand lovingly.

"It's going to be hard for me to let you go. You're in my system, Nedra Harris."

She covered his hand with hers. "That is so sweet of you to say that."

He stared at her.

"I want you, Nedra," he announced as he finished off a glass of wine. "I want you bad."

"That's impossible, and you know it. I'm engaged and will be getting married a few months after graduation."

He laughed out loud.

"What does that have to do with me wanting you?"

"Come on, Simeon, don't start."

He kissed her hand. "It can't be helped. I get aroused just by smelling your perfume."

She blushed and looked away from him.

"You'll make sure I get an invitation to your graduation, won't you?"

"I don't know if that would be a good idea. It might be a little awkward."

"Why? Because you've been sleeping with me for the past four months?"

She lowered her head with guilt. He stood and took her by the hand. Nedra could see he had a lot on his mind, and she realized she was going to miss him.

"Are you upset with me?"

He pulled her out of her chair and into his arms. He kissed her deeply, not caring that they were in the middle of a crowded restaurant. Nedra was a little embarrassed and surprised at his public show of affection, but Simeon was in a league of his own. He was handsome, full of excitement and passion, and she was going to miss him. Simeon broke the kiss and breathlessly answered.

"No, sweetheart, I'm not upset with you. I'm upset with me. Now, why don't we get out of here so we can really celebrate?"

Nedra blushed because she had an idea of the kind of celebration Simeon had in store for them, and to be honest, she was looking forward to it.

"I'm going to miss you."

Simeon paid the check and placed his arm at the small of her back.

"Are you ready? My Jacuzzi is waiting on us."

"I'm ready." She giggled.

Three days later Nedra flew back to campus. As she sat on the plane, she thought about the last few days she had shared with Simeon. They didn't get much sleep the first night, and she could still feel his hands, lips, and everything else on her body.

Their evening started with a relaxing soak in his Jacuzzi, and it was there that they made love to start the evening off right. Simeon made sure his deck was decorated with candles, music, champagne, and strawberries. He wanted her to feel the full power of his seduction, and then hopefully he would win her heart. Nedra, on the other hand, felt like her heart was going to burst through her chest with each thrust of his body. He knew her spot, and he had no trouble hitting it every time. Simeon was so overcome with emotions that Nedra was afraid his neighbors might hear him and call the police. How embarrassing that would be. However, at that moment, neither of them were too concerned with the volume of their moans. Steam was rising off the water of the Jacuzzi, as well as off their bodies. Simeon was like the Energizer Bunny. He had been making love to her in various positions nonstop for over thirty minutes. He'd guided her through multiple orgasms, but he was still going strong with no end in sight.

She held onto him and gasped for air.

"Simeon, baby, what are you doing to me?"

Without missing a beat or losing his rhythm, he cursed and said, "Loving you, baby! I'm just loving you!"

Nedra kissed Simeon and mated her tongue with his. When his mouth came in contact with her breasts, she felt another wave building in her lower region. She didn't know how much more of him she could take, but she would hang in there with him as long as her body would allow her.

Snapping out of her daze, Nedra smiled at the thought of Simeon. She reached inside her purse and pulled out the small box he'd given her as a going away present. He gave her specific instructions not to open it until she was on the plane. Nedra curiously opened it, but she read the card first.

Nedra,

I miss you already. You will always have a special place in my heart and for what it's worth, I really do love you, but I also wish you the best with your new life. This ring is a token of my affection, and I hope you wear it as a reminder of the passion shared between us. I also pray that one day God will allow our paths to cross once again.

With Love Always,
Simeon

She pulled a beautiful platinum diamond band out of the box and placed it on her right hand. The diamonds glistened as she admired it before falling asleep. She would just explain to Tyree that it was a graduation gift from a dear friend, and hopefully he wouldn't question her further about it. Simeon Mathews was gone, but he would never be forgotten.

Chapter Eleven

One Door Closes As Another One Opens

Weeks later, graduation day had arrived. Donovon was happy Nedra was back on campus and he was excited about having a joint graduation party with her. Over the years their parents and family members had become very close, and the day felt like one big family reunion. The day was going to be bittersweet because they would finally be going their separate ways to begin their lives.

Nedra got the best job offer, financially, from the company she interned with, which would put her back in the city with Simeon. They also provided her with a house to live in while she worked there. She wasn't sure what this would mean for her relationship with Tyree, whom she was sure was going to be drafted and sent God knew where. After the dust settled, they would have a wedding to plan, and Nedra wasn't sure how long she was going to be able to stay in her position before joining Tyree. Donovon obtained a junior executive level position with a company in Dallas, Texas. He was looking forward to his new career, but not being separated from Nedra.

As Donovon socialized with family and friends, he stole a private moment to reminisce about the past four years. As he glanced around the room, he temporarily made eye contact with Nedra and smiled. She blew him a kiss and smiled back lovingly as she posed for pictures with friends. Donovon's heart thumped in his chest as he stood there and watched her with a heavy heart. He remembered why she was so important to him and why he loved her so much. She was his best friend, but he wanted her for much, much more. Unfortunately, she was engaged and his life was going to have a void in it without her.

He continued reminiscing back to their junior year when he was feeling a little left out of her life. That's when Nedra met and started dating Tyree. Nedra began spending more time with Tyree and less time with him, but he couldn't complain because he was dating someone too. He was glad she finally found someone who seemed to really care about her and that he approved of.

It wasn't until their senior year that Tyree caught the eye of almost every NFL team in the nation. He was one of the most sought after collegiate players in the country, and somehow, he still remained humble with his popularity. He remembered Nedra coming to him with her concerns because she had started to worry about the women coming from all directions, trying to seduce Tyree. Tyree only had eyes for Nedra, and Donovon did his best to reassure her. She was the one who kept

Tyree focused on his studies, which allowed him to maintain a 3.5 grade point average even during football season. It was right before graduation that Tyree was selected as a first round draft pick for the Oakland Raiders, instantly making him a millionaire.

While Donovon was standing there watching all the important people in his life, his mother, Olivia McNeil, came over and gave him a loving hug. She looked beautiful in her beige pantsuit, and she couldn't be more proud of her son.

"Donovon, are you OK? I came over here because you looked like you were a million miles away." He kissed his mother on the cheek.

"I'm fine, Momma. I was just thinking."

She knew her son better than he knew himself.

"I know you're going to miss her, sweetheart. If you feel that strongly about her, you need to tell her how you feel."

"Thanks for the advice, Momma, but Nedra and I have gotten along fine just the way we are."

"I know you don't honestly believe that, but I'll stay out of it. You do what you feel is best. Now come on, because it's time for you two to take the floor."

"Thanks, Momma."

She looked at her son with pride. "You're welcome, my love. You are every mother's dream, and I want you to know that you have made me and your father very proud. We love you."

"I know, Momma, and I love you guys too." He escorted her through the crowd and up to the stage.

* * *

The room was filled with over two hundred family members and friends. Their parents went through the formality of making toasts, and then opened the floor for family and friends to follow. Tracy stood nearby as the toasts continued. Tyree held Nedra's hand in support because he could feel her trembling.

Minutes later, it was time for the honorees to say a few words. Nedra could feel the lump in her throat as she went first. Trying to form her words, she took a deep breath.

"First, I would like to thank all of you for coming here to be a part of our graduation. I know I wouldn't have been able to make it without all of your love, support, and especially the care packages. Momma, Daddy, I want you to know that I appreciate everything you've done to help me get where I am today."

The crowd sighed and wiped away tears.

Next, she turned to Tyree. "Tyree, I want to thank you for loving me and for keeping me motivated when I was feeling down. I'm also looking forward to sharing your dreams and your life with you. I love you, baby."

Tyree kissed her and whispered something intimate in her ear, causing her to blush.

Lastly she turned to face Donovon and she let out a deep breath. "Wow! Donovon, there's so much I can say about you, but I'll try to keep it brief. For one, I know I wouldn't have made it to this day without you in my life. I didn't believe you then, but the day we met, you told me it was fate for us to meet each other. I nearly knocked you down when I bumped into you on my way to class, and I actually thought you were going to be a nuisance because you were so talkative and persistent. Instead, I got the best friend I could ever have. I love you with all my heart and I wish you success, love, and happiness. I'll never forget you for as long as I live."

They hugged and kissed each over lovingly. Nedra wiped away her tears, and now it was Donovon's turn to speak. He took the microphone out of her hand and scratched his head.

"Dang! It's kind of hard to follow a speech like that, but I'll try."

He hesitated and took a moment to form his words.

"I also would like to thank everyone for coming to see us graduate. To Mom and Dad, you guys have no idea how important you are to me."

He took Nedra's hand into his and gave it a squeeze before continuing.

"Yes, Nedra and I met in an unusual way, and I believe it was destiny that brought us together, and friendship and love that have kept us together. We've been through a lot over the years and not all of it has been pleasant, but we have always been there for each other. Nedra, I never doubted you or your dreams. I'm happy to know that you will be my friend for life, and I wish you nothing but the best life has to offer. I love you and I know you will be successful with anything you do. With that said, hit the lights so we can get this party started!"

More tears fell from Nedra's eyes as thunderous applause came from the crowd. The music was cranked up, the lights were dimmed, and everyone started dancing. Donovon and Nedra's parents called them over to the side so they could talk in private. Before walking off, Donovon whispered something in Tracy's ear and she nodded in agreement. She wiped away a tear and joined the other guests.

In dim light near the back of the room Simeon watched as Nedra and a group of people walked out of the room. He spotted Tyree and couldn't help but stare at him. That was the man who had lured *his woman* away from him. No woman walked away from Simeon Mathews, and he would see that Nedra was his once again, one way or another.

Before leaving he decided to mingle a little. He especially wanted to meet Tyree up close and personal to see just what Nedra saw in him. It couldn't be money because he had plenty of that, and she never asked or accepted it even when he offered it. He kept his eyes on Tyree as he moved around the room. He eventually got close enough to approach him.

"Excuse me, aren't you Tyree Williams, the All-American?"

"Yes I am, and you are?" Tyree answered while shaking the man's hand.

Using an alias, he said, "Byron Edwards. I'm a friend of Nedra's."

Tyree noticed this stranger looked a lot older than Nedra and he wondered why Nedra had never mentioned him.

"I'm sure Nedra is glad you were able to come to her graduation. How do you know her?"

Simeon laughed mischievously.

"Oh, we go way back. She's good people."

Tyree immediately took a dislike to the man standing next to him in the thousand-dollar suit. The stranger's demeanor insinuated something Tyree didn't want to think about. Tyree looked around the room.

"I see. So, did you and Nedra work together?"

"No, but we did take care of a lot of business together. Nedra's very intelligent and she's not hard on the eyes either. I wouldn't have missed Nedra's graduation for anything. Congratulations to you as well on your graduation. I understand you've had a great career here, both academically and athletically. What's next for you?"

"I was drafted by the Raiders."

Patting him on the shoulder, Simeon congratulated him.

"That's great! They could use a good running back."

Tyree extended his hand to Simeon before walking off.

"Thank you, sir. It was nice meeting you. Enjoy the party."

Simeon reached inside his jacket pocket and pulled out an envelope.

"Unfortunately, I can't. I have a plane to catch, so I would appreciate it if you could do me a favor and give this to Nedra."

Tyree took the envelope out of his hand and inspected it curiously. He looked at Simeon.

"Sure, but I'm sure she would rather receive it from you." Simeon looked at his watch.

"I wish I could, but I can't stay. Please give her my love."

Love?

Before Tyree could respond, Simeon had disappeared into the crowd, leaving him with more questions than answers. Looking down at the card, he was anxious to ask Nedra about this Byron Edwards character and why she'd never mentioned him before.

Chapter Twelve

Giving Out The Goodies

While the party continued in the next room, the Harris and McNeil families gathered privately so they could talk to the graduates. It was then that they presented Donovon and Nedra with their graduation gifts. Nedra's grandmother, Leona Foster, joined them as well, looking as feisty as ever and not a day over fifty. She sat down at the table and crossed her legs.

"I'm going first if nobody has any objections."

In unison, the groups nodded in agreement. Leona stood and pulled an envelope out of her purse.

"Donovon, you are a wonderful young man and I want to thank you for being such a great friend to my granddaughter. You became a part of this family the first time Nedra brought you home for the holidays. You're welcome in my home any time."

He smiled. "Thank you, Mrs. Leona."

She held the envelope out to him and continued.

"With that said, I want you to take this gift to help you furnish that new bachelor pad or whatever you young people call it these days. Good luck on your new job in Dallas."

Donovon opened the envelope and gasped at the amount on the check. He kissed Leona on the cheek and hugged her lovingly.

"Thank you, but this is too much, Mrs. Leona."

She cupped his face. "There's no amount of money that can equal the value you are to Nedra. You will accept this gift with my love."

"You're one of a kind, Mrs. Leona."

She snapped her fingers. "Now that, I know."

Donovon sat down as Mrs. Leona turned to Nedra. She held her hand out for her to take and Nedra quickly did so.

"Nedra, ever since you were a little girl, your grandfather and I knew you were going to do great things with your life. You proved us right every day, and I'm just sorry he didn't live to witness this day. As you enter the work force there are going to be times in your life when you're going to want to get away to regroup. Having a career can be demanding and stressful. I know that for a fact. I just hope this gift will help make things easy for you and your children and so forth. I've made arrangements to ensure that this gift will remain in this family for generations to come. Accept it with all my love."

Nedra opened the envelope and read the paperwork enclosed. Leona had purchased a three bedroom, beachfront home in Miami. Nedra's eyes filled with tears. She was so overwhelmed.

Leona was very wealthy and because she and her late husband, Cecil, were smart business people; they made their money work for them, which paid off in their golden years. Leona had a successful career in education and served as dean of the local university for over twenty years. Cecil, on the other hand, made a comfortable living as a stockbroker, which allowed him to operate his own brokerage company. The beach house was what Nedra's grandparents had been planning for her for years. Unfortunately, Cecil died before the gift could be presented. He succumbed to prostate cancer when Nedra was in the ninth grade. It devastated the entire family, but especially Nedra because she was his little angel. Over time she was able to overcome her grief and get on with her life.

As she hugged her grandmother, she wept openly.

Leona patted her on the back to soothe her. "You're welcome. I love you, baby."

The McNeil and Harris families had become close over the years, so much so that they had even started taking vacations together. Cameron and Olivia McNeil waited their turn, then happily presented their gifts to the graduates. They gave Nedra a beautiful gold nameplate for her future desk and some money. Donovon was given money and keys to a new SUV. With this welcomed turn of events, he decided he would give his five-year-old vehicle to his sixteen-year-old cousin, DeMario. All in all, the pair came away with money, designer briefcases, and other goodies, and there was more to come.

Before returning to the ballroom Nedra took

Donovon's hand into hers and smiled with excitement.

"Are you ready for my gift?"

He blushed and caressed her hand lovingly. "Only if you're ready for mine."

Their parents gave them some privacy as they walked over to a nearby table and picked up two gift-wrapped packages.

"Ladies first, Nedra."

She sat down and swallowed hard before speaking.

"Donovon, you know how much you mean to me, right?"

"Of course I do."

She held the box out to him and continued.

"This is just a little something so you won't forget about me and our fabulous college days."

He started tearing away the wrapping paper and when he opened the box he froze. Inside the box was a framed collage of various snapshots they had taken together throughout their four years of college. The snapshots ranged from pep rallies, parties, and football games to spring break trips. Donovon stared at the pictures as they visually took him down memory lane.

"This is awesome, Nedra." He leaned over and kissed her softly on the lips.

"I knew you would like it."

"I love it, and I can't wait to hang it on my wall. Now it's my turn."

Nedra sat there with anticipation as Donovon handed her the small box. She opened it and pulled out a gold, heart-shaped locket.

"Oh, Donovon. It's beautiful."

He smiled and whispered, "Open it."

She opened it and found her baby picture on one side and her graduation picture on the other side.

"Where did you get these?"

"Your Mom gave me a copy of your baby picture, and as you know I already had the other one."

He helped her put on the necklace and they both sat in silence admiring their gift."

"I guess we'd better join the others before they start looking for us."

Nedra stood up and nodded as she held the necklace against her heart.

They had yet to open the gifts from other family members and friends. After all was said and done, they rejoined the guests in the main ballroom.

Later, as they slow danced together, Nedra questioned Donovon about his relationship with Tracy.

"So, are you going to have one of those long distance relationships with Tracy?"

"Nah, we broke up a few weeks ago. We're going to just be friends."

"Why didn't you tell me?" He cringed.

"I didn't want to bother you with my issues. She actually took it well. I guess because she knew we would be going in opposite directions after graduation anyway."

Donovon was surprised to see Nedra looking sad about his breakup with Tracy. He actually thought she would happy about the information. He smiled.

"Why are you looking so sad?"

"I want you to have someone to love, Donovon."

He kissed her cheek. "I do—you. So don't worry about me, OK?"

She looked up into his handsome eyes. "I'm really going to miss you."

"No, you're not. You're going to be an old, married woman soon and then you guys are going to have a house full of kids running around. You know, that happily-ever-after stuff."

Nedra felt like she was losing Donovon right before her eyes. "You make everything sound so final, Donovon."

"I don't mean to, but you have to admit, you're going to be pretty busy as an NFL wife."

She hadn't thought about all the glitz and publicity around the players and their wives. Leaning her head against his chest she sighed. "You're going to have to visit me as much as you can because my days of being around a crowd are over."

Donovon laughed out loud as he playfully twirled Nedra around on the dance floor, causing her to giggle out loud.

"Are you planning on hooking back up with that playa, Simeon?"

"No. He's in my past now. I probably won't even see him when I move back. We had a good time, but that's all it was. Besides, he knew I was dating Tyree."

"I see. So does he know about you and Tyree getting married?"

"No way! Can you believe he wanted to come to my graduation? You know that would've been a disaster. He's got it going on, but I couldn't have him messing up my life with Tyree. What he and I had was more like a booty call."

Donovon frowned.

"Nah, that wouldn't have been pretty at all. You'd better be careful if he's into you like you say he is. He just might show up."

"Don't say that, Donovon. I wouldn't know what to say to Tyree if Simeon showed up. He really did want to come to graduation, but I had to convince him it wasn't a good idea. I never lied to him about Tyree, and I don't need any drama."

They continued to dance together in silence until Donovon noticed Tyree watching them from his seat.

"I know you don't want any drama, Nedra, but you need to face the fact that messing around with Simeon behind Tyree's back could come back to haunt you one day."

"You sound like Aunt Tina."

"I'm just speaking the truth, and you know it."

"Tyree's leaving tomorrow. I don't know about this long distance relationship stuff. I mean, I love Tyree, but I don't know if I can trust him out there in California."

"Tyree might be feeling the same way about you."

She pushed him playfully. "Come on, Donovon, I'm being serious."

"So am I."

"He's the wealthy one who will be in the lime-light. You saw how the women threw themselves at him when he became a prospect. How do I know he'll be able to fight the same temptations thousands of miles away from me?"

Donovon frowned and defended Tyree. "I guess he'll resist temptation just like you did when you were doing your internship."

She looked up at him and knew he was speaking

the truth. If Tyree did cheat on her, she deserved it after messing around with Simeon.

"I'm sorry, Nedra. I shouldn't have said that."

"No, I needed to hear it," she said while shaking her head.

"Look, Nedra, if you guys are really in love, then you should be able to trust each other, right?"

Nedra looked over at Tyree and winked. His expression was unreadable at first, but then he smiled, relaxing her.

"You're right, Donovon. I'm worrying for nothing. See, that's why I love you so much. You always know the right thing to say and at just the right time."

They stopped dancing for a moment.

"I do what I can. Now go dance with your fiancé. I'll holler at you later."

Nedra stood on her tiptoes and kissed Donovon tenderly on the lips.

"You go have some fun too. I'll catch up with you later."

Nedra walked over to Tyree and pulled him up out of his chair.

"Hey, babe, would you please dance with me?"

He wrapped his arms around her waist and held her close. He looked into her eyes.

"Who's Byron Edwards?" he asked.

Confused, she shook her head. "I don't know anyone by that name."

Towering over her, he leaned down close to her ears because the music was so loud.

"Well he seems to know you very well."

Nedra thought and thought but couldn't remember crossing paths with anyone by that name.

"Byron, Byron. No, I've never known anyone by that name."

Nedra could tell Tyree was getting angry with her. "Stop lying, Nedra, and tell me who he is!"

"I told you I don't know anyone by that name," she pleaded.

Pulling the card out of his pocket, Tyree gave the envelope to her.

"Well he told me to make sure you got this gift from him for graduation."

Nedra took the card out of his hand and inspected it. The first thing she recognized was the scent of the familiar cologne and it caused her hands to shake. The handwriting on the outside of the card was the second clue. She couldn't believe Simeon would come to her party and do something to make Tyree suspicious of her.

"Well, are you going to open it?"

Her knees became weak. She was afraid to open the envelope in front of Tyree because there was no telling what Simeon had put on the inside.

"I'd rather wait to open all my gifts, baby. Come on and dance with me."

Tyree took the envelope out of her hand and ripped open the card. Nedra became sick to her stomach as she watched him pull out what looked like a gift certificate. Tyree showed her the certificate and quizzed her.

"You mean to tell me that you don't know a man who gave you a five-hundred dollar gift certificate to Victoria's Secret?"

She swallowed nervously. "I don't know what to say, Tyree. I don't know anyone named Byron Edwards." He folded his arms.

"Do you think I'm a fool, Nedra?"

"No, baby, I don't, but I'm telling you the truth. I don't know anyone named Byron Edwards."

"Maybe he didn't tell me his real name, but he was about six feet, two, brown-skinned, mustache, wavy hair, and he wore an expensive suit, and I think he had on a Rolex."

Nedra's heart was about to burst out of her chest. Tyree had described Simeon perfectly, down to his accessories.

She shook her head without responding. Tyree reached up and grabbed her upper arm.

"Have you been messing around on me, Nedra?"

"Just because some strange man gave me a gift, you're accusing me of cheating on you?"

"Yes! Victoria's Secret is as intimate as you can get! Now answer my question!"

Nedra looked around the room to see if anyone had noticed their altercation. Before she could say anything, Donovon walked over. He reached up and removed Tyree's hand from Nedra's arm. Tyree's grip had left an imprint on her skin. Donovon frowned at him.

"What the hell are you doing, Tyree? Look what you did to her arm."

"I'm OK," Nedra whispered.

Tyree was clearly emotional. "Ask Nedra what's going on!"

Donovon turned to Nedra. "What's going on with you two?"

Nedra wiped away a tear. Tyree held the envelope out to Donovon.

"This is the problem! An older guy in a Versace suit handed it to me and told me to make sure Nedra got it. His tone insinuated something was going on between them. He left because he said he had a plane to catch. Nobody gives someone a gift like this unless they know them in a most personal way."

Donovon glanced over at Nedra as he inspected the envelope. His eyes widened when he saw what it was, and the amount. He also immediately knew Simeon was responsible. He had tried to warn Nedra that he would come back to haunt her.

"Wow! I see what you mean, Tyree. Nedra, can you explain this?"

Nedra rubbed the place on her arm that Tyree had grabbed. "I told you, I don't know anyone named Byron Edwards. Look, it's graduation! If this man wants to spend his money on a stranger, there's nothing I can do about it! I'm not going to let you guys gang up on me! I'm leaving and I don't care what you do with that gift certificate!"

Her outburst drew the attention of Nedra's Aunt Tina. She walked over and noticed Nedra's tears.

"What the hell is going on over here? Nedra, why are you crying?"

Nedra wiped away her tears and shook her head. Tina looked at Tyree angrily.

"What did you do to her? If you hurt her, Tyree, I swear . . ."

Donovon stopped Tina from threatening Tyree. "Everybody calm down. Tina, Nedra and Tyree just had a little disagreement, but everything's straight now. Right?"

Neither Tyree nor Nedra responded. Tina folded her arms and gave them a look that could kill. Tyree took Nedra's hand into his and pulled her into his arms.

"I'm sorry, Nedra. I didn't mean to upset you, especially on graduation. I love you and that guy pissed me off with the way he was talking about you. If you say you don't know him, I believe you."

Nedra had never felt as low as she was feeling right now. She was guilty of all charges and loved Tyree too much to confess.

"I love you too, Tyree. Today starts our new lives. Don't let some stranger come between us to try to bring us down."

Even though Donovon knew the truth, he felt like he needed to somehow help Nedra out of a tight spot.

"Tyree, you're going to have to realize there are a lot of people out there who are jealous of you, and will try to keep you distracted from the ball field as much as possible. If they can invade your personal life by using Nedra, they will. Just don't be so quick to jump to conclusions. If this guy looked as expensive as you say, he could be anybody."

Tyree kissed Nedra to comfort her.

"I didn't think about that, Donovon."

Donovon shook Tyree's hand. "I know. Just keep your cool because you're one of the hottest rookies in the country, and the media is going to be in your face, trying to dig up any kind of dirt they can."

Tyree nodded, and then kissed Tina on the cheek. "I'm sorry, guys." He turned to Nedra. "Sweetheart, you know I would never hurt you."

"I know, and you can tear up that certificate as far as I'm concerned."

Tina stepped forward and took the certificate out of Donovon's hand.

"What kind of certificate is it?"

He looked at her with a smirk on his face.

"You mean you don't already know?" She smiled.

"No. Now let me see it."

Tina looked at it and was very impressed.

"Hmmm, Victoria's Secret. Nice! It would be a shame to let it go to waste." Donovon put it in her hands.

"Knock yourself out, because Nedra doesn't want any part of it," he said.

Tina tucked it in her purse. "Don't mind if I do."

She looked at Tyree and Nedra and sighed. "Seriously, don't start your lives out not trusting each other. You're getting ready to be separated for a while, which is going to be stressful enough. Nedra, Tyree needs to stay focused on running the ball. Worrying about what you're doing in Tennessee could get him hurt, so don't give him any reason to be suspicious. Tyree, there are going to be cameras in your face every time you turn around. They're going to try to use your personal life to distract you. Nedra loves you, period, and that's all you need to know. Now can we please get back to the party?"

The couple smiled and kissed again before finally walking out onto the dance floor.

Nedra couldn't help but scan the room to see if Simeon was lurking in a corner watching them. If he was, she didn't see him, but Simeon was smooth and could be anywhere. Donovon had just helped Nedra defuse an explosive situation. But that's what friends were for.

* * *

The next day Nedra placed a call to Victoria's Secret to confirm that Simeon was behind the gift. But since it was purchased with cash, there was no way to verify the transaction.

Two weeks later, Nedra and Donovon started their prospective jobs and new lives. Three months after that, Nedra and Tyree finalized their wedding date for the following spring. This gave them about ten months to plan. This bit of information completely broke Donovon's heart. He loved Nedra and truly wanted to be with her. Now the question was if he would let her say "I do" without sharing his true feelings with her.

Chapter Thirteen

A Whole New World

A few months later, Nedra was thankful Simeon hadn't tried to contact her or show up in her life. All she cared about was planning her wedding so she could marry the man she loved. Donovon, on the other hand, had to pretend to be excited for her even though he was emotionally devastated.

On this night, Nedra called Donovon and asked his opinion regarding the wedding. "So, what do you think about being my best man?"

"What?"

Laughing, she asked him again. "What do you think about being my best man?"

"Nedra, there's no such thing as a best man for the bride."

"There could be. You're my best friend, so I want you to be my best man, and that's final."

Donovon laughed. "I'll be a groomsman, but that's where I draw the line."

"Don't be silly, Donovon. You'll still be standing with the groomsmen, but you'll be listed on the program as my best man."

He sighed. "Fine, Nedra, whatever makes you happy."

She was silent on the phone for a minute. She wasn't sure what was wrong, but she had to try to find out.

"What's wrong, Donovon?"

"Nothing."

"Tell that to someone who doesn't know you. What's wrong?"

"I said nothing, Nedra, damn!"

When Donovon cursed, it was confirmed that something was going on with him.

"If I'm boring you with my wedding plans, just tell me." He cleared his throat. "It's not that . . . it's just . . . never mind."

"What is it? Have I done something to make you mad, or is it Julie?"

"Nah, I'm not with her anymore," he admitted.

"Why do you always not tell me when things are over? What happened?" she asked, surprised.

"She cheated."

That hit close to home with Nedra and brought the memories of her cheating on Tyree with Simeon flooding back. "I'm so sorry, Donovon."

"I'll be OK. Look, I have to go. I'll talk to you to-morrow."

"Are you sure you're going to be OK?"

"I'll be fine. I promise. Good-bye."

Donovon hung up the telephone before he made a fool of himself. He'd come so close to telling her that he was in love with her. His biggest mistake was not telling her a long time ago. Now he would have to suffer the consequences, sit back, and painfully watch her marry another man.

Nedra sat there on the bed, hurting for Donovon. Here she was going on and on about her wedding, and he had just had his heart broken by his girlfriend. He must've really cared about Julie, because he seemed distracted during their conversation. She dialed his number again and listened as the phone rang.

"Hello?" Donovon answered.

"I'm worried about you."

He chuckled. "I'll be fine, Nedra, and it's sweet of you to be concerned. It's been a long day, and I'm tired, that's all. If I don't seem enthusiastic tonight, I'm sorry."

"I understand, and I'm sorry for going on and on about my wedding."

"Don't worry about it. You have a reason to be excited, and you didn't know what happened between me and Julie, so stop worrying."

"I'll try. Oh! I've been meaning to tell you something."

"What is it?"

"I received an express letter the other day at my office. It had an all-inclusive, seven-day trip to Hawaii in it."

"Was there a note or anything?"

"No. It was an open ticket."

"Maybe Tyree gave it to you," he suggested.

"He wouldn't do that without telling me."

"Simeon?" he asked.

"Who else? Every now and then I'll get flowers delivered to me."

"Maybe you should have a talk with him. He's crazy if he thinks you're going to risk your marriage with Tyree to mess around with him."

Nedra closed her eyes. "Nah, I think I'll just ignore it because if I call him that will just fuel the situation. No contact is the best contact as far as I'm concerned. I'm just glad he's staying away. I returned the tickets to the travel agency though."

"Maybe you're right. I'm glad he doesn't know where you live and hasn't showed up at your office. At least he's doing the right thing in regards to that."

"I don't know if I could handle it if he did that," she whined. "He's very persistent when he wants something, but he's perfect in all other categories."

"What did you do to him to make him so crazy about you anyway?"

"I didn't do anything to him."

"If you say so."

"Well, I'll let you go so you can get some rest. Good night."

"Good night."

Nedra hung up the phone, feeling somewhat sad for Donovon. Until he was over losing Julie, she would choose her words carefully when talking to him about her wedding.

Chapter Fourteen

When All Hell Breaks Loose

A month before the wedding, Nedra was thankful that Simeon had finally stopped pursuing her so she could go on with her life in peace. The ticket he sent her to Hawaii several months earlier had been his last attempt to lure her away from Tyree. It seemed that he had finally given up on her and was respecting her wishes by leaving her alone.

Nedra was hurrying out the door to catch a plane to California to see Tyree when the telephone rang. They had to sign the contract on their new house and she was anxious to move to California permanently. Other NFL wives thought she was crazy for trying to have a career when she was about to be the wife of a millionaire, but she was very independent and wanted to establish herself in the corporate world. Tyree tried to get her to interview for some California positions, but Nedra believed that working a year with the company she was familiar with would help put her further up the corporate ladder, so that when she did switch companies she wouldn't have to start all over at the bottom. Besides, she was able to see Tyree every other weekend when he wasn't out of town playing football. Everything was falling into place perfectly, and in one month she would be Mrs. Nedra Williams.

Nedra picked up the telephone. "Hello?"

"Hey, baby. I'm glad I caught you."

"I was just on my way to the airport," she said, smiling.

"Nedra, I need to talk to you about something."

Worried that Simeon might've struck again, she went into a slight panic.

"About what?"

"Sit down, baby."

Nedra sat down and listened as Tyree spoke. Within seconds, her body went numb and the room started spinning.

Hours later, Donovon had dialed Nedra's cell and house phone a dozen times. He'd left her several voice messages, but she had yet to call him back. Saying he was worried was an understatement. When he tried to reach Tyree, he got the same thing—voicemail. It was nearly nine o'clock when he finally got up the nerve to call Nedra's parents. He dialed their number and her father answered.

"Hello?"

"Mr. Harris, this is Donovon."

Cutting him off, he said, "Donovon, I'm glad you called. I was just getting ready to pick up the telephone and dial your number."

"I can't seem to get in touch with Nedra. I left her several messages but she hasn't returned any of my calls. I'm getting a little worried about her."

Mr. Harris sighed. "Donovon, we have some bad news."

Donovon's heart nearly stopped beating. If Nedra had been hurt or worse, he would literally die.

"What's wrong?" he asked.

"Nedra told us that Tyree called off the wedding."

"He what!"

"I know. She said it had something to do with another woman, but that's all we know."

Donovon swallowed hard. "Where's Nedra?"

"She wouldn't come home, Donovon, and she won't let any of us near her right now. She flew down to Miami to her beach house last night. I have no idea what's going on, but whatever Tyree told her, he shouldn't have told her over the telephone."

Donovon felt his blood pressure rising. Once again, Nedra's heart had been ripped from her chest. He knew she was probably feeling hurt and embarrassed, and didn't want to face anyone, but he wasn't just anyone.

"Donovon? Are you still there?"

"Yes, sir."

"We're going to take care of sending out cancellation notices to all the guests in a couple of days. We want to wait to see if whatever's going on can be worked out first, but the way she was talking, it's over. We just mailed out the wedding invitations last week. This is a shame, and if I ever see Tyree, he's going to wish he never met my daughter."

Donovon pulled his suitcase from the closet and started pulling clothes out of his dresser.

"Mr. Harris, I'm going down there. Nedra doesn't need to be alone right now."

"I was hoping you would say that. We're so worried about her."

"I understand. Don't tell her I'm coming," he said as he packed his clothes.

"We won't. Call me as soon as you get there. Thank you, Donovon."

"No problem. I'll keep you posted."

Donovon hung up and hurriedly packed. Even though he didn't want Nedra to get married, he didn't want her to be hurt like this either. He dialed the airlines and caught a late flight out to Miami. It would be early morning before he would arrive at the beach house and find out what had happened.

The cab driver dropped Donovon off at the beach house around seven a.m. He was delayed in the Atlanta airport due to a thunderstorm, which added some anxiety to his already nervous state of mind. Stepping out of the cab, he retrieved his luggage from the trunk and headed to the front door of the beach house. Not wanting to startle her, he decided to ring the doorbell instead of using the key Nedra had given him. He rang the doorbell a couple times before becoming concerned. Only then did he use his key to let himself in.

"Nedra! It's Donovon! Where are you?"

He called out to her as he walked through the living room and up the stairs. When he entered her bedroom, he knew she was there because he could see her shoes and clothes on the bed. He called out to her again, but he still got no answer. Looking out the bedroom window, he saw her standing alone on the beach, watching the waves. The sunlight made her look like a silhouette and he could tell she was in a fragile state by her stance. He hurried downstairs and out onto the deck. She looked so lost, watching the waves as they rolled in toward her. He didn't know what he was going to say to her, because he knew she was devastated. He took a moment to take off his shoes before walking out on the hot sand toward her. When he got within twenty feet of her, she turned around slowly.

"I thought you might like a little company down here."

She walked slowly toward him. He could see the hurt on her face as well as her tears. When she reached him, she basically fell into his arms.

"Why can't I be happy with anyone? What am I doing wrong?"

He hugged her tightly. "You're not doing anything wrong, Nedra."

She burst into tears. Her tears rocked her body hard and Donovon held her as securely as he could. It tore his heart open, seeing her so defeated, while inside he was overjoyed with relief. The waves crashed against the surf around them as Nedra continued to unload her emotions on Donovon's shoulder. He cupped her face and wiped her tears away.

"It's going to be OK, Nedra, you'll see. Let's go inside so I can fix you some breakfast."

She nodded and they walked arm in arm back toward the beach house. Inside, Nedra sat down at the table and put her head down. Donovon opened the refrigerator and pulled out some eggs and bacon. He worked in silence as he turned on the coffee pot and the stove. Nedra sat up when Donovon sat a mug of coffee in front of her.

"Thank you," she whispered.

He smiled at her as he watched the bacon crackle in the skillet. He poured himself a cup of coffee, sat opposite her, and touched her hand.

"How did you know I was here?"

He sipped his coffee and sat the cup down on the table. "Your father told me."

"Thanks for coming, Donovon. I'm sorry I didn't return your calls. I just didn't feel like talking to anyone."

"I'm not anyone, and you know it. Besides, I'm here now. That's all that matters."

She smiled. "You're right. Do you need any help with breakfast?"

He stood up so he could check on the bacon. "I got it this time, so just sit back and relax."

She pulled a napkin out of the napkin holder and wiped her eyes.

"You need to call your parents and let them know you're OK. They're really worried about you."

She lay her head back down on the table. "I don't feel like talking to them right now."

He frowned and pointed at her with the fork. "They're your parents! They love you and they're worried about you. Call them!"

"I will. Daddy was so upset, and because I was crying Momma started crying."

He placed the bacon and eggs on a plate and sat it in front of her. "Here. Eat. You don't look like you've had anything to eat lately. I'll call your parents to let them know I'm here, but before the sun sets today, they need to hear your voice. Cool?"

She nodded, picked up a piece of bacon, and put it in her mouth.

After cleaning the kitchen, Donovon and Nedra took a long walk down the beach. He decided that he wasn't going to pry into her business. He was there to support and comfort her—that's all. If she wanted to talk about what happened, he would listen. If she wanted to scream, he would let her do that also. They continued to walk in silence, occasionally walking past others who lived on the beach.

"You're not jeopardizing your job by coming down here are you?" she asked while taking his hand in hers.

"I told them I had a family emergency. Don't worry about it. Everything's cool."

"I'm sorry, Donovon."

"Why are you apologizing to me?"

"You have your own life and relationship to worry about. You shouldn't be here babysitting me. I'm sure Vivica wasn't too happy when you told her you were coming."

He laughed loudly. "She doesn't know I'm here."

Vivica was Donovon's significant other at the moment, and like all the past women in his life, they never could hold a candle to Nedra. They started walking again.

"You're going to tell her, right?"

"I'll call her later."

"Good, because I don't want your relationship to end up like mine."

They were both silent for a while as they stood on the beach. The sound of the waves were mesmerizing and soothing in their own way.

"Are you ready to turn back?"

"Yeah, it's getting a little hot out here," she said as she wiped a small amount of sweat off her brow.

They turned and headed back toward the beach house.

"Are you going to be OK?"

She sighed and shook her head. "I can't say. I mean I feel numb, like it's a dream. You know?"

"I don't know what to say, Nedra. I'm sorry you're hurting."

She blew her nose with a Kleenex.

"I understand. I guess it's true when they say what goes around comes around, huh?"

He put his arm around her shoulder and pulled her close. "Feeling guilty about your relationship with Simeon is not going to help this situation."

"I can't help it. Somehow I feel like this is my punishment or something."

"You'll be OK, Nedra," he said to comfort her.

They spent the rest of the afternoon talking and enjoying the warm sunlight.

Chapter Fifteen

A Storm Is Brewing

Nedra's spirits were uplifted just by having Donovon there with her. She cooked them a delicious dinner, complete with conch fritters, avocado salad, and a spicy rice dish. They ate by candlelight out on the deck. The sounds of the crashing waves continued to set a relaxing mood as they took in the scents and beauty of their surroundings.

Picking up the bottle of wine, he held it up to her.

"Would you like some more?"

Nedra held out her glass and nodded. "I haven't drank this much in a long time."

"Maybe you'd better slow down then," he suggested.

"I'll be fine. At least I'll get a good night's sleep."

Nedra sat her glass down and wrapped her arms around herself. "So how are you and Vivica doing?"

"She's all right, I guess. For some reason, the women I hook up with seem to change after we've been together for a while. Some of them are money hungry, while others just can't commit to a monogamous relationship. KaNeisha was the only woman who was cool to me. You know that."

Nedra drank down the rest of her wine. "Why don't you call her?"

"Oh, I didn't tell you?"

"Tell me what?" she asked, surprised.

"She got married last year and now she's expecting a baby."

"At least she made it to the altar," Nedra solemnly responded.

"I'm sorry for bringing that up," he said sadly.

"Don't worry about it. I'm going to have to get used to hearing about other people and weddings."

"I guess you're right. So, you wanna go for a swim?"

"Are you crazy? It's dark and there's no telling what's in that water."

He teased her, hoping to lift her spirits. "Chicken!"

"I have no problem admitting to it, either, but go ahead and knock yourself out."

"Have you decided when you're going back home?"

"I don't know. I feel like such a fool."

"You shouldn't. It happens, Nedra."

She walked over to the railing of the balcony and closed her eyes.

"I can't believe he played me like this."

Donovon yawned. "You still love him, don't you?"

"That's what pisses me off! Maybe he can turn his feelings on and off like water, but I can't."

Her eyes filled with tears. She gulped down the rest of her wine quietly.

"Donovon?"

"Yeah?"

"He got a woman pregnant," she whispered.

Donovon didn't respond, even though he was shocked. Instead, he just listened to her.

"He told me it was an accident!" she yelled. "What happened? His sperm jumped into her womb? Now they're having a baby! Can you believe it?"

"I'm shocked."

Nedra's news was the worse case scenario.

"I didn't have the heart to tell Momma and Daddy about the baby. They're upset enough as it is. Maybe this wouldn't have happened if I had listened to those NFL women and moved on out there in the beginning. Tyree wanted me there too, but no, I had to stay and be a career woman."

Donovon could see Nedra's depression and guilt sinking deeper into her soul.

"You only did what you felt was best for your career. Everybody's situation is different, and you can't always listen to people who don't know you."

She opened their third bottle of wine and filled up her glass. "I bet he's been having an affair with this woman for God knows how long and he decides to wait until a month before our wedding to tell me about her!"

Donovon observed Nedra as she stumbled back over to the railing. "Take it easy on that wine, Nedra. You don't want to make yourself sick."

She gulped the wine down and wiped her mouth. "I can't feel any worse than I already do."

"I don't know, Nedra. Maybe it was an accident. I'm sure he still loves you just like you still love him. Maybe you guys need to sit down and talk about this before making a hasty decision."

Nedra started laughing hysterically. "You must be psychic like Aunt Tina! He did have the nerve to tell me he was still in love me."

"I believe him," Donovon replied.

"Then you're just as crazy as he is!"

Donovon chuckled. Nedra was passing her limit on alcohol and it was time to cut her off. He picked up the wine bottle and took it back inside the house. When he returned, Nedra was lying down on the chaise lounge with her eyes closed and wine glass in hand.

"What I want to know is what you would do if Tyree showed up right now, told you he was sorry, and begged you to come back to him?"

Nedra opened her eyes. "I'd tell him to kiss my ass!!"

Donovon smiled. "Sure you would," he said sarcastically.

"I'm serious! You only get one chance to hurt me. Tyree is history as far as I'm concerned."

"You do realize this could've happened to you while you were messing around with that lawyer, don't you?"

She shivered and closed her eyes once again. "You didn't have to go there, Donovon."

"It's true and you know it. You cheated on Tyree first and you could've gotten pregnant. Wouldn't you expect him to forgive you?"

"That was before we were engaged, Donovon, plus Simeon and I were always careful. There was no way I wanted something like that to happen to me. I loved Tyree too much to jeopardize our relationship. That's why I was so careful. Tyree has shown me he didn't care enough about us to protect what we had."

"You're drunk," he said and laughed.

"Maybe I am, but I mean it, Donovon."

They stared at each other and turned toward the ocean when they heard thunder rumbling in the distance.

"Oh, Lawd," Donovon mumbled.

Nedra jumped up out of the chaise lounge and played in her hair nervously. "You know I don't do storms."

"How can I forget?"

"Don't make fun of me, Donovon McNeil."

He grabbed their plates off the table and motioned for her to get the glasses. "I can't believe you're still afraid of storms. They're so soothing to me."

She picked up their glasses and looked back out over the water. "Well they terrify me, and I'm really not up to this tonight."

"You'll be fine. Bring your drunk butt on in here so we can get the kitchen cleaned up before the storm gets here. And call your parents!"

She gathered the remaining items on the table, blew out the candles, and followed Donovon into the house in silence.

After the kitchen was cleaned, Nedra called her parents as she promised. She paced the floor and prayed that the storm would pass quickly. The conversation with her parents was comforting and sad. She knew they had spent a lot of money helping her prepare for her wedding, but they assured her they weren't concerned about anything but her happiness.

Donovon went into another room so he could call Vivica. She was very upset that he didn't call her the night before he left town. Donovon apologized as best as he could under the circumstances. Vivica was jealous of his relationship with Nedra, just like all his other girlfriends. She'd seen Nedra several times on her visits to Dallas, and it had caused her a lot of stress, mainly because Donovon always insisted that Nedra stay at his house.

"So you just jet off across the country any time she calls with one of her crises?"

Donovon stared out the window at the impending storm. "I told you, Nedra needed me, and I am not going to desert her because you're paranoid."

"I have a right to be paranoid, Donovon. How would you like it if I was running around the country with a male friend of mine?"

The thunder rumbled even louder, and the wind was starting to howl.

"I have to go, Vivica. A bad storm is rolling in and I need to get off the telephone."

"Are you sleeping with her?"

"No!"

"When are you coming home?"

"I don't know."

"What about your job?"

He walked over to the dresser and lit some candles.

"I've taken care of that. Look, I have to go. I'll talk to you tomorrow."

"Are you sure you haven't slept with her?"

"How many times do I have to tell you? No!"

"OK, well be careful and hurry home."

"Good night, Vivica."

"Good night, Donovon."

Donovon hung up the telephone and shook his head. He was reliving all his relationships once again, maybe because all the women knew in their hearts that his feelings for Nedra were much deeper than a regular friendship.

He turned out the light and stripped out of his clothes. The soft light of the candles mixed with the wine in his system calmed him. He was somewhat lightheaded but relaxed. He took one last sip of wine, crawled under the soft, cool sheets, and closed his eyes. His head was buzzing, but it made the lightning and thunder show even more appealing. He was exhausted and welcomed a good night's sleep after his long plane ride and conversation with Nedra.

Across the hallway he heard what sounded like sobbing. It was difficult to tell for sure, so he climbed out of bed and slid into his shorts. He walked over to Nedra's room and tapped on the door.

"Nedra? Are you OK?"

She didn't answer, so he opened the door and walked in. Nedra was lying across the bed, clearly in tears.

"Nedra, don't do this to yourself. You're going to make yourself sick and it's not worth it."

He sat down on the bed and put his head in his hands. He didn't know what to do to comfort her. On one hand he was glad she had broken up with Tyree. On the other hand he was sorry because of the pain he had to witness her go through. He pulled her up next to him and put his arms around her shoulders. The silky material of her lingerie awakened his body, and the powdery fragrance she wore clouded his senses as she continued to unleash a fury of tears.

"Sh-h-h-h. It'll be OK, so stop crying," he pleaded.

"It won't be OK! How can you say that?"

He turned her face toward his. "Because you're bigger than this. You might feel down right now, but you're not out, Nedra. I know it hurts, but it will get better with time. You can always forgive him and go ahead and get married."

"I can't do that," she yelled. "That baby will be a constant reminder of his betrayal. I can't live like that."

She leaned over, pulled some tissue out of the box, and blew her nose. He took some tissue and wiped away her tears. The thunder rumbled around them and she flinched.

Before leaving the room, he kissed her on the forehead. "Get some rest. We'll talk more in the morning."

"I can't sleep while it's storming. You know that."

"Just relax. It's not as bad as it sounds," he said as he stood.

"I'll see you in the morning. No more crying. OK?"

She blew her nose again. "I'll try."

"Do you want me to get you some more wine to help you sleep?"

"That would be nice, Donovon. Thanks."

"Don't mention it. I'll be right back."

Nedra lay across the bed and waited for his return.

The thunder and lightning continued outside as the storm seemed to get worse. Donovon poured Nedra a large glass of wine and hurried back upstairs. When he walked into the room he found her pacing the floor. She was gnawing on her nails when she turned to him.

"Here you are, Nedra. Drink up."

She took the glass out of his hand and swallowed the red liquid down without taking a breath.

"Thanks, Donovon."

She crawled into bed and put a pillow over her head. He slowly walked out of her room, closing the door behind him and praying she would somehow get a good night's sleep.

The storm had gotten worse and Donovon found himself trying to cool off from the subtle contact with Nedra. The wind howled even louder and then a loud clap of thunder shook the house. Nedra burst through his door and jumped into his bed, startling him.

"Nedra! What are you doing? You can't be in here!!"

She had pulled the sheet over her head and scooted close to him. He tried his best to push her away, but she wouldn't budge.

"Please don't make me get out, Donovon. You know I hate storms!"

His body immediately responded to the contact, and he felt trapped.

"Nedra, I'm sorry, but you have to get out!"

Another loud clap of thunder shook the house. Nedra's heart pounded in her chest and the high from the wine did anything but calm her. She hugged him even tighter and finally realized why Donovon was freaking out. She looked up at him curiously.

"Donovon, are you naked?"

"Yeah . . . I . . . I . . . just get out!"

She stared at him oddly. "Why?" she asked softly.

"Because I said so," he yelled as he tossed a pillow her way.

"Why are you acting so hostile?"

"Because this is not good."

She didn't respond.

"Nedra! Are you listening to me? You have to go! I mean it! It's just a little storm!"

She snuggled up to him without responding. A loud clap of thunder shook the house again, and Nedra screamed as she closed her eyes tightly. Donovon sighed and decided to leave her alone. It was obvious that she was terrified of this storm, and being on the coast made matters even worse. He lay there and did his best to comfort her.

There was a fierce wind blowing outside the window, and the lightning was putting on a spectacular light show. They lay there, side by side, holding hands. Their eye contact seemed to make them telepathic, and Nedra only blinked when the thunder boomed outside. Donovon noticed that Nedra didn't seem to care about the intimate position their bodies were in as he stroked her hand lovingly. He did his best to keep his body under control, but he was failing. He also noticed that she was beginning to calm down, but the room seemed to heat up to a thousand degrees.

The past few minutes had been sheer torture

for him, and he was unsure how much longer he could take it. Each time he swallowed, his mouth became even drier as he prayed for the storm to end so Nedra could go back to her room. He couldn't take much more of this intimate contact without being able to touch her like he'd always dreamed of. They'd both had a lot to drink tonight, and naked in bed wasn't where he envisioned them ending up. He understood that Nedra was still in a lot of emotional pain, and being together like this could be catastrophic. She lightly brushed her lips against his and caressed his cheek. The warm kiss she placed on his neck broke his one remaining thread of strength.

"Nedra, what are you doing?" he whispered.

Looking deeper into his eyes, she nuzzled his neck in silence. He moaned and closed his eyes as he felt her hands caressing him. He trembled from her touch and thought, *to hell with it.* A man would have to be a fool to dismiss her affection. The reality was he really wanted to make love to her, but not necessarily under these circumstances. However, he was a man, and feeling her lips and hands on his body felt heavenly.

The storm outside was still raging, and was spilling over into the bedroom. Donovon was surprised at the amount of passion Nedra had in her. Her kisses were heated as their tongues intertwined. He pulled her nightgown over her head, leaving them skin to skin, soul to soul. Kissing down her soft body and back again caused Nedra to wiggle in agony. He'd waited for this moment for years and there was no way he was going to rush now.

Breathlessly, she moaned. "Donovon, please . . . now."

He made eye contact with her. "Not yet. Hold on. I want to taste you."

"Oh God," she whined as he ran his tongue in a circular motion around each nipple and down to her navel. Her breathing was shallow and her body began to tremble when he went even lower as the thunder exploded around them.

The contact of his lips between her thighs caused her to arch upward. Donovon savored and tortured her with a pleasure he had saved especially for her. Nedra's screams were in rhythm with the flashes of lightning, which lit up the room. Donovon couldn't stand it any longer. He towered over her and kissed her hard on the lips. Nedra wrapped her legs around his body and begged him to love her. He pushed against her moist flesh, causing her to whimper even louder. When he entered her body, he felt like crying. It was even better than he had imagined. He made love to her with a fervor that had been bottled up inside him for years. Nedra worked his body just as vigorously. She moaned even louder, causing him to push harder and deeper. He was out of control and there was no turning back now. Unable to contain his emotions, he yelled and screamed her name. Her own screams of ecstasy gave Donovon notice that her peak was near. His thrusts went deeper until he felt her body shudder hard beneath him, and his release was just as intense.

"I love you, Nedra," he whispered in her ear.

Out of breath and drenched in perspiration, he found the strength to move off her body. Nedra immediately snuggled up to him in total exhaustion. She had finally experienced the love he'd carried for her all these years. She had been avoiding the inevitable with Donovon for years. Now that it had happened, she didn't know what to do. Maybe the person she had been looking for had been right in front of her all this time. Maybe her Aunt Tina was right all along, but timing meant everything, and it was off for both of them.

The fury of the storm continued around them as they lay there in silence. He caressed her body in a soothing manner.

"What are we doing?" he asked.

She kissed his neck. "We're showing each other just how much we care about each other."

"Care?" he asked.

"You know what I mean, Donovon. This . . . us . . . what we have is so special that it doesn't have a name."

He didn't know what all of this meant, but what he did know was that he was exhausted. "Get some sleep, Nedra."

She nodded as their eyes met for a second before they embraced and fell into a deep sleep.

The next morning Donovon woke up alone and with a headache. He knew it was from the consumption of wine the night before, and the sunlight beaming through the window wasn't helping. He slid into his denim shorts and walked out of the bedroom in search of Nedra. He was a little apprehensive about seeing her the morning after making love to her. Descending the stairs he found breakfast on the table, but Nedra was nowhere to be found. He figured the only place she could be was on the beach. Walking out on the deck, he spotted her sitting in the sand. He walked out on the beach and joined her on the blanket. She looked over at him and smiled. He brushed her damp hair out of her eyes.

"Good Morning, Roadrunner.

"Hey, Donovon."

"You look like you're feeling regrets already."

She sighed. "I'm sorry, Donovon, but I was an idiot last night. I shouldn't have drank so much. I hope you're not mad at me," she answered as she sat hugging her knees.

They stared at each other for a long time. She was stunning in her swimwear, and it was difficult for Donovon not to become aroused at the sight of her. He broke the silence.

"Why would I be mad?"

"Because I forced myself on you."

He laughed out loud and lay back on the blanket. "I would have to be a fool to be mad at you about that; besides, you didn't force yourself on me."

She looked into his eyes.

"I'm serious, Donovon. I don't want to mess up our friendship. It's the one thing in my life that's been good. Last night I was emotional, feeling unloved, and you were there. It was beautiful and much more than I could've ever dreamed of, but our friendship is so important to me to chance ruining it."

He played silently in the sand. She was right about one thing—it was much more than he could've ever dreamed.

"Nedra, our friendship is important to me too, but you have to admit there's something else going on between us."

She saw that dreamy look in his eyes. She held his hand tightly in hers.

"Donovon, what we did last night wasn't in our character and I want you to know that I love you—maybe more than I'm willing to admit, but I'm still in love with Tyree. This is so confusing, and it's pissing me off."

"That's understandable, and I don't expect you to forget about Tyree overnight, but I don't want you to ignore us either."

She laid her head on his shoulder.

"Donovon, I don't doubt one moment that we made love last night, but my main concern is making sure we didn't hurt our friendship. I need to know that you're still here for me," she pleaded."

Donovon tossed a seashell toward the surf. "You shouldn't have to ask me that, Nedra. I'm here, aren't I? I've always been here for you, you know that."

She giggled. "I just needed to hear it, Donovon."

"OK, now where do we go from here?"

"I don't know," she admitted while lying back on the blanket. "Being with you was unbelievably hot and I'm still tingling, but correct me if I'm wrong, you're in a relationship with Vivica and I'm an emotional wreck in the middle of nowhere."

He knocked sand off his shorts. "My relationship with Vivica is not as serious as you might think. You and I have been tight for a long time, and last night we took it to another level. It was all that, and I'm tripping because I don't know what to expect next."

Nedra was speechless. "I don't want you to do to Vivica what Tyree did to me. It hurts too much, and she doesn't deserve that. Last night was what it was, OK? We both had a lot to drink, Donovon, and honestly it shouldn't have happened."

He lay back on the blanket. "So that's it?"

"For now, yes, Donovon," she explained. "The alcohol clouded my judgement and I need to get my head together. It was selfish of me to sleep with you."

"My concern is with you, and what you're going through right now," he said softly. "I believe we acted out exactly what we've been feeling for each other."

"Your concern should be with Vivica, and how she would feel if she found out what we did. We didn't use protection, and you know what position this could put us in."

"She won't find out, and if you're pregnant, so be it. I will take care of my responsibilities. You know that."

"That doesn't make it go away. Look, don't worry about me. I have no choice but to dust myself off and move on with my life, but if I'm pregnant, that will make me just like Tyree. We were careless, and I don't want any more drama in my life. Understand?"

He looked over at her in silence. She leaned over and kissed him tenderly.

"What was that for?"

"For being my best friend who has and would do whatever it takes to make me happy," she answered, smiling. "I love you, Donovon, but I need to get my life together. My head is so screwed up right now, and I don't want to pull you into this."

"I hear you. Look, I'm here for you any time. OK?"

"That I've always been able to depend on," she happily responded.

Nedra had summed up their relationship after the most passionate night of his life. The way things appeared, they would remain friends, which caused his heart to ache.

The rest of the evening it was hard for Donovon to be in the same room with her and not want to touch her. He had to stay in control until he left for the airport the following day. Their relationship was back to normal, and for now, he would do his best to respect her wishes.

They played cards together out on the deck and when she looked up at him, he looked away.

"Are you going to be able to handle this?"

He stared at his cards and nodded his head. "I'm cool," he responded without making eye contact.

She leaned forward. "You're not acting like you're cool. Look at me. Talk to me."

He sat his cards down and looked up at her.

"This is not easy for me, Nedra."

"I know, but I told you no one else needs to get hurt."

He stood up and walked over to the railings in silence. She joined him, wrapping her arms around his waist.

"I never expected us to end up in bed, Donovon."

"Are you saying you've never thought about it?"

She ran her hands through her hair. "I'd be lying if I said no. It's only natural for us to be curious about each other."

They continued to watch the waves roll onto the beach. She reached up and gently turned his face toward her.

"Donovon, in case you're wondering, I'm not dismissing us. What I felt with you was a first for me. No man has ever touched me like you did, not Tyree or Simeon. To tell you the truth, what happened between us scared me."

"Why?"

"Because I do want more, but that would be so selfish of me. You're in a relationship and I was drunk. That's not the way I would envision us starting a romantic relationship. Besides, I will not be the cause of a breakup between you and Vivica."

"Don't you realize last night wasn't just sex for me? If you want more, all you have to do is say the word."

She put her finger of his lips to silence him. Tears welled up in her eyes.

"I know, Donovon, but this is how it has to be for now. OK?"

"It's not OK. We should be able work around any obstacles."

"You're right, but not at the expense of someone's feelings," she explained. "I just pray we get through this situation safely."

He kissed the back of her hand. "A baby with you wouldn't be the end of the world, Nedra."

"That's not the way I want to start a family. You know me better than that, Donovon."

He shook his head in frustration and then regrouped. "Look, I'd hate to even bring this up under the circumstances, but did you remember Toni's wedding is coming up?"

"Damn! I almost forgot about that," she scolded herself.

"All you have to do is say the word and I'm sure Toni can get someone to replace you if you're not up to it."

"No, I won't let her down. I'll be there."

"OK, I'm going upstairs to pack. My plane leaves tomorrow afternoon."

She swallowed hard. "Thanks for everything, Donovon."

He winked at her. "Good night, Nedra."

Before she could respond, he disappeared inside the house. She knew she had hurt Donovon, and he was the last person she wanted to hurt. It would be a few weeks before she knew whether or not she was pregnant, and she realized the ride to the airport was going to be a sad and difficult one. Nedra slowly gathered the cards, blew out the candles, and walked into the beach house.

The next day as Donovon flew home, he knew his life would never be the same. As he looked out the window of the airplane, he remembered the hug and kiss he gave Nedra in the airport. It wasn't the kind he wanted to give her, and he had let her make the decision for both of them. They would remain only friends.

* * *

Nedra's plane ride had her deep in thought as well. One look in Donovon's eyes and she knew he was in love with her. If they hooked up it would be because it was their destiny, and not anything else. Tyree had sent her to the beach house a broken woman. Donovon was sending her back to Tennessee feeling that she could and would be able to move on with her life.

The day after arriving back in Texas, Donovon fell into a dark mood. Vivica sensed he was sick, so she came over unannounced with some home-made chicken soup. She rung the bell and waited for Donovon to open the door.

"What are you doing here?" he asked sarcastically.

"Nice to see you, too," she replied as she walked past him.

He wasn't up for any company, especially Vivica. She sat the dish on the table and smiled.

"I brought you some soup since you seem to be under the weather."

Donovon closed the door. "Thanks for the soup, but I'm just fine. I'm just a little tired."

He sat down on the sofa and picked up the remote. She stared at him curiously.

"Why didn't you call me when you got in yesterday?"

He didn't answer her. He just scanned the channels instead.

"Donovon! Don't you hear me talking to you?"

He looked at her and frowned. "Who are you yelling at?."

"I'm sorry," she whined as she sat next to him.

"I'm just worried about you. Did everything go OK in Florida?"

"What do you mean?"

"Nothing! Damn! Why are you getting all defensive! Did something happen between you and Nedra that I need to know about?"

He jumped up off the sofa and threw the remote on the table. "Look, Vivica, I'm not up for any of your drama today!"

"You don't have to yell at me, Donovon, and I asked you a question."

"Why is everybody so worried about me and Nedra? Can't a man have a female friend without everybody thinking something's going on between them?"

She paced the floor. "Hell no!"

"Then why are you here? I've told you once, and I'll tell you again, Nedra is not going anywhere, so if you can't handle it . . . step!"

He was unconsciously doing everything he could to get her to break up with him.

Vivica's voice cracked when she spoke. "Is that what you want?"

Donovon looked at her and ran his hand over his head in frustration.

"Look, this is not working, Vivica. I just want to be alone."

"Fine! Good-bye!"

She grabbed her purse and walked out the door, slamming it behind her. Donovon sat back down and continued to channel surf. At the moment he was unsure if he had run Vivica off for good. They'd had arguments about Nedra before, but this time it seemed more intense. He looked at the telephone and thought about calling Nedra, but he changed his mind. Instead he turned off the TV and went to bed. Tomorrow he would try to suppress his feelings for the woman with whom he was in love.

Chapter Sixteen

I Do

A couple of weeks later, Nedra arrived for the wedding rehearsal for Donovon's cousin, Toni. This was going to be a high profile wedding since Toni was member of the city council and her fiancé, Anthony, was a college football coach. Nedra could see the love in their eyes when they looked at each other. She used to see the same thing when Tyree looked at her.

Nedra found out that her parents had arrived earlier that morning, but she had just arrived. The McNeils invited Nedra's parents to stay at their home for the weekend, but Nedra chose to stay at the hotel where the reception was being held. Donovon was still MIA, but he was expected any minute. Toni walked over to Nedra and hugged her lovingly.

"Nedra, I'm so glad you decided to come. I'm sorry to hear about what happened between you and Tyree."

"I know. I'm still trying to make sense of it all."

"Well, for what it's worth, he didn't deserve you," she said. "No one should be treated that way. Donovon was so angry when he found out what Tyree did to you. You know he really cares about you."

"That, I know. Where is he anyway?"

"The missing groomsman called and said his plane just landed and he would be here shortly," Toni said as she glanced at her watch.

"I can't wait to see him. We haven't been able to talk much since everything went down"

"I'm sure he's just as anxious. We'll be starting as soon as he gets here, so just relax."

"Thanks, Toni."

Twenty minutes later, Donovon rushed through the door and the rehearsal began. Nedra found it difficult to go through the ceremony with the romantic music playing. This was too much of a reminder of her failed engagement with Tyree. Several times tears welled up in her eyes and her head throbbed. Donovon watched from across the room and saw that she was struggling with her emotions and her hands were trembling.

Finally, after several practices of the ceremony, the wedding coordinator was pleased with the outcome. Rehearsal was dismissed and the guests were instructed to meet at a local restaurant for a private dinner. Nedra walked over to Donovon and gave him a big hug.

"Hey, Roadrunner. I'm so glad to see you."

"It's good to see you too," Nedra said.

"Do you want to ride with me to dinner?"

"I'm not going. I feel a migraine coming."

He leaned against the wall and folded his arms. "I noticed you were a little emotional and your hands were trembling. Are you going to be able to get through this?"

"Yeah, just tell Toni and Anthony I'm sorry about missing dinner."

He took her hand in his and led her toward the exit. "I'll bring you something to eat, OK?"

"I'm not really hungry."

"I'll bring it just in case you get hungry later."

"Thanks," she said.

He opened the door and allowed her to exit ahead of him.

In her hotel room a couple of hours later, Nedra lay across the bed feeling her migraine getting worse. Donovon called to let her know he was pulling into the parking lot of the hotel. She cracked her door and lay back down on the bed. Her cell phone rang and she answered without looking at the ID.

"Hello?"

"Nedra?"

She sat straight up in bed.

"I can't believe you have the nerve to call me. What do you want?"

"I've been worried about you," Tyree said.

"Oh, really?"

He sighed. "I still love you very much."

"You have a funny way of showing it. I don't even know why I'm talking to you."

"Nedra, wait! I didn't mean to hurt you. This thing that happened wasn't planned, but I can't walk out on my child. I feel terrible about the whole thing, but I didn't think it would be right to bring you into this situation."

"You should've kept it in your pants! Better yet, what happened to using protection?"

"I did use protection, but . . . I don't know what happened. I know I messed up and if I can turn back the hands of time, I would've never . . ."

"Do you love her?"

"No! I care about what happens to her, and I can't walk out on her. I don't believe in having illegitimate children. That's why I had to marry her instead of you. I love you and I needed to hear your voice, Nedra, and to apologize for hurting you."

"The damage is done! Go on with your new family and leave me alone!"

"I can't, Nedra!"

"Did it ever occur to you that I might've been able to deal with the situation and still be your wife? You didn't give me that option, so that tells me you didn't have any trust in my love for you."

"I messed up. I'm sorry, Nedra."

"Look, Tyree, I have to go! Don't call me again!"

Unexpectedly, Donovon took the phone out of her hands, startling her. The unexpected call from Tyree and the migraine had sent her over the edge. She ran to the bathroom and slammed the door. Donovon could hear her throwing up in the toilet.

"Tyree, why are you calling Nedra and getting her all upset? She's trying to move on with her life, but you're not helping her."

"Look, Donovon, I feel real bad about all of this, and I didn't mean to hurt Nedra."

"Well, you did, and you're making her life a living hell. She's in the bathroom right now throwing up."

Donovon could tell that Tyree was in tears.

"Just let me talk to her, please?"

Donovon turned to Nedra just as she re-entered the room.

"I'm not sure if she wants to talk to you anymore, Tyree."

She dabbed her eyes and looked up at Donovon. She shook her head that she didn't want to talk to Tyree anymore, but he needed to ask her so Tyree could hear her answer.

"Do you want to talk to him?"

"No!" she yelled. "He's done enough to me."

"You heard her. Now good-bye," Donovon said.

He hung up the telephone and turned to Nedra. "Are you OK?"

She wiped her eyes. "Not really, but thanks."

He sat the plate of food down on the table. "Do you want me to leave?"

"Of course not, but I'm sure your family's looking for you."

"Unless you've forgotten, you're family too."

"I appreciate you saying that, but you have immediate family members who expect you to spend time with them this weekend."

He just stared at her. "You're coming too, now get yourself together and come on."

"I'm really not in the celebrating mood, Donovon, and this migraine isn't helping."

He picked up her jacket. "You'll feel better once we get there."

"Where?" she asked.

He helped her into her jacket. "We're just hanging out, playing cards, stuff like that."

"I guess I can go for a little while."

"Good!"

She smiled back at him before walking out the door ahead of him.

Nedra did have fun playing cards and hanging out with Donovon's family members. Before long, they all knew they had to get some rest because the wedding was only twelve hours away.

Chapter Seventeen

Rejuvenation

The wedding ceremony was beautiful, and in some way, it was healing to Nedra. Her tears were frequent, but joyous. She was happy for the couple, but she couldn't wait to get out of her three-inch heels. Her parents were obviously enjoying themselves because they couldn't seem to stay off the dance floor. She couldn't help but laugh, and she hoped that her own marriage would be just as loving.

A couple of hours into the reception she walked over to refill her glass. She sipped her champagne and noticed Donovon heading in her direction. He looked unbelievably handsome in his tuxedo.

"Hey, beautiful. Are you ready to dance with me?"

"Sure, handsome. Lead the way."

They walked out on the dance floor and embraced each other. The sound of Stevie Wonder's "Ribbon in the Sky" radiated throughout the room. Nedra's parents had taken a break and joined the

McNeils at the table. Olivia McNeil picked up her glass and stopped halfway to her mouth. Cameron looked at her.

"What's wrong, honey?"

All she could do was point toward the dance floor. This caught the attention of Austin and Virginia Harris as well.

"What are you two looking at?"

"Look at the way Nedra and Donovon are dancing together," Olivia said.

All four heads turned and noticed the possessive manner in which Donovon held Nedra. Cameron laughed out loud.

"I've never seen them dance like that before. Has something happened that we don't know about?" Cameron asked.

"Not that I know of," Virginia whispered.

Nedra's grandmother walked over and sat down at the table. She took a sip of champagne.

"What is everyone looking at?" Leona asked.

Virginia pointed out onto the dance floor. "We're looking at the way Donovon and Nedra are dancing."

Leona looked over at the pair and waved them off. "Is that all? Anybody with eyes can see those two are in love with each other. I don't know why they're wasting all this precious time apart."

"Well if it's true," Olivia said, "I would love to have Nedra as a daughter-in-law."

"Wait, wait, wait, ya'll are getting ahead of yourselves. All they're doing is dancing," Austin added.

Leona sipped her champagne and thought to herself that something very special was brewing between her granddaughter and Donovon, and it was only a matter time before it came to light. All the rest of them could do was stare until the pair joined them at the table and sat down.

Donovon noticed them staring. "Why is everyone staring at us?"

No one would speak up, except for Leona. "Your parents want to know if you two are sleeping together because you were holding onto each other pretty tightly out on that floor. You looked like a married couple."

"Nana!" Nedra screamed.

"Don't yell at me young lady! I just asked what everyone's wondering."

Donovon was taken aback by their parents' curiosity. He chuckled. "I don't believe ya'll."

Donovon's mother tried to calm everyone down.

"Donovon, anyone with eyes can see that you were holding Nedra more intimately than you have before."

He sat back in his chair and laughed because he didn't know what to say. He was about to answer when Nedra touched his hand.

"Donovon, wait a second." She looked at their parents. "Our relationship has never been a secret with you guys. I've been through a lot of drama the past few weeks and luckily Donovon has been there for me. I would have to be a robot not to cling to him for comfort. If you want to know if we've been intimate, keep wondering because that would be between us. I love him and I always will. Now if you will excuse me, I'm going to call it a night."

She stood and Virginia elevated her voice.

"Sit down, Nedra, and stop being so dramatic. We're not trying to get into your business. A matter of fact, nothing would make us happier than you two getting together. All we did was make an observation."

Her father supported her mother. "Nedra, don't forget that we're your parents and we went through that hell with you. We love you, and if you and Donovon decide you want to be more than friends, fine. Leona was out of line for speaking her mind so forthrightly as usual, and we apologize. Don't we, Leona?"

Leona squinted her eyes at Austin without responding to him. "Nedra, Donovon, don't stress out over what I said. It's not like we all haven't wondered it before now. In any case, stay and enjoy the reception, and I apologize if I offended or embarrassed you two."

Nedra took a deep breath. "Apology accepted, Nana, and from all of you. Now, I really am tired so I'm going to my room. I'll see you guys tomorrow."

Donovon stood and shook his head at their parents.

"I'll walk you to your room. Good night."

In unison, they all said, "Good night."

After Donovon and Nedra walked away, Leona said, "They're sleeping together."

All eyes were on her as she swallowed her champagne.

"What?"

The ride up the elevator was quiet. Nedra and Donovon couldn't believe what had just happened. When the doors opened on their floor, he laughed.

"Now that was interesting."

"Nana can be a trip sometimes. That champagne has given her loose lips," Nedra said as she was reaching into her purse for her key card.

"I guess I was holding you a little closer than normal. It's hard not to, considering."

They arrived at her door and she looked up into his eyes. "It felt good. It always feels good in your arms, Donovon."

He leaned down and kissed her softly on the lips.

"You need to go away because I'm a little vulnerable right now. All this talk about love everlasting tonight has taken its toll on me," she explained

He leaned against the doorframe and lowered his head. "I understand this weekend has been rough on you, but you know how I feel about you, and you know what room I'm in if you need anything. Good night, Nedra."

"Thank you, Donovon. Good night."

Before walking off, he pulled her into his arms and gave her a deeper kiss. Nedra swayed slightly as he released her. Bracing herself against the door, she watched as he walked down the hallway until he was out of sight. No matter how bad she wanted to feel him, their timing was still off and she wouldn't break her own rules.

After breakfast the following morning everyone said good-bye to the newlyweds and each other. Both Nedra and Donovon knew it would be a while before they would get a chance to see each other again, because they now both had a lot of work to catch up on.

Chapter Eighteen

Oops!

A month later, Donovon received a call from Nedra as he was driving home from work. He was happy to hear from her because they hadn't had much time to talk since the wedding. His relationship with Vivica had improved, but he knew it wasn't what he wanted.

"Hey, stranger. Are you on your way home from work?"

"Yeah, and I can't wait to get in a bubble bath to relax these tired muscles. I wanted to call you the other night, but it was late, so I thought I would wait until tonight."

"Donovon, you know you can call me anytime," she said softly.

"Yeah, but it was late. So, what's up?"

Nedra cleared her throat. "I don't know any other way to say this, but to say it.

"Say what?"

"I'm late, Donovon. I've missed my period two months in a row, and I'm a little scared."

Donovon swerved out of control and into another lane. He dropped the cell phone on the passenger seat and fought to regain control of his car. Other cars blew their horns in anger at him. He immediately felt lightheaded. He finally made his way into the parking lot of a shopping plaza and threw the car in park. He picked up the cell phone, closed his eyes, and leaned against the steering wheel to catch his breath. He could hear Nedra calling his name as he picked up the phone.

"Donovon? Are you still there?"

His heart was about to beat out of his chest. He took a deep breath. "I'm here."

"Did you hear what I said?"

"Yeah, I heard you. When are you going to find out for sure?"

"I have an appointment next week. I'm sorry, Donovon."

"Sorry for what?"

"Possibly messing up your life with Vivica."

He raised his voice at her. "You think having my child is going to mess up my life? Damn, Nedra, I thought you knew me!"

"So you're not mad? I mean, what if I am pregnant? What about Vivica?"

"I'm not mad, and if you're pregnant, we'll deal with it. And just for the record, I'm the one who should've been more responsible."

"I'll let you go so you can get home. I just wanted you to know what was going on."

He put his car in drive and pulled back out into traffic. "I'm coming for the appointment."

"You don't have to."

"I know I don't have to, but I want to."

She bit her lip. "It's next Thursday at one o'clock."

"I'll be there Wednesday evening."

"Let me know what time your flight comes in, and I'll pick you up from the airport."

"No problem. You just take care of yourself and I'll call you back later."

"I will. See you."

"Bye."

Donovon hung up the phone and drove home in a daze. Nedra, on the other hand, knew if she was pregnant, it was going to change everything between them.

At home, Donovon immediately logged onto the computer and purchased his plane ticket.

A week later they nervously sat in the doctor's office waiting their turn. It didn't take long for the nurse to call her name. The two walked side by side to the examination room. Donovon sat quietly as Nedra was weighed and had blood drawn. Next, she was instructed to disrobe for the physical part of the exam. Donovon stood by anxiously as she prepared to take off her clothes.

"Do you want me to leave?"

She looked at him and shook her head. "No, you can stay."

"Are you sure?"

"I don't have anything you haven't seen, and considering why we're here, it's only right for you to stay."

Donovon still pulled the curtain to give Nedra some privacy as she undressed. Within minutes, her doctor entered to begin the exam. Donovon never knew what women went through for their physicals, but today he gained a newfound appreciation for them. Watching the doctor touch Nedra the way he did angered him because she looked like she was being violated. She saw the stress on his face and winked to reassure him that she was OK.

The doctor stood and removed his gloves. He handed some items to the nurse and helped Nedra into a sitting position.

"OK, Nedra, you can get dressed now. I'll be back in just a second."

"Thank you."

He patted Donovon on the shoulder before he walked out.

"You can breathe now, son."

Donovon had no idea his body language revealed how he was feeling inside. He closed the door behind the doctor and helped Nedra down off the table.

"I never knew you guys had to go through something like this. I was getting ready to kick his ass for touching you like that."

She laughed as she slid into her undergarments. Donovon swallowed as he handed her bra to her. She was beautiful. Once she was fully dressed, they sat down and waited on the doctor. She held Donovon's hand tightly as her leg trembled. Dr. LaSalle walked through the door minutes later with Nedra's chart in hand. He sat on the stool and delivered the news.

"Well, Nedra and Donovon, you're not pregnant, but you do have some fibroids I want to keep an eye on, otherwise you're healthy."

She closed her eyes briefly. Donovon let out the

breath he'd been holding. He was a little disappointed with the news, but he saw the relief in Nedra's eyes.

"I will, Dr. LaSalle."

"As far as your cycle, have you been under any stress lately?"

"As a matter of fact, I have, but things are getting better."

"Good, because that's the only reason I can find that could be throwing your cycle off. Make sure you get plenty of rest, too."

He stood and shook Donovon's hand.

"It was nice meeting you, Donovon. Nedra, I'll see you back next year for your annual."

"Thank you, Dr. LaSalle."

They quietly left the office and walked out in the hallway.

"Donovon, how are you feeling about this?"

"I'd be lying if I said I wasn't disappointed, but God knows best."

Donovon pushed the button on the elevator and turned to her. "Can I ask you something?"

"Sure."

They entered the elevator together and Nedra pushed the appropriate button.

"Why won't you give us a chance? The love is there and we came real close to becoming parents today."

"Donovon, have you forgotten about Vivica? I haven't. Don't you have any feelings at all for her?"

"I care about Vivica, but love? No way."

The elevator doors opened and they walked out into the parking lot. Inside the car, Donovon turned to Nedra. "If you're wondering, my feelings are never going to change."

He started the car and pulled out into traffic.

"Just so we understand each other, I want you to know that I will not come between you and Vivica under any circumstance."

He sighed. "I hear you. Now, let's get you home."

Once again, Donovon had been shot down by Nedra, and he figured he would just have to live with it as long as he was in a relationship.

Chapter Nineteen

After The Storm

Six months passed, and Nedra was rewarded with a promotion from office manager to regional manager. It was God sent, and the promotion gave her the financial security she had always dreamed of. Her internship with the company while in college had helped her get the promotion, and she was excited to be progressing as a permanent employee. She had dated guys off and on, mostly men from work or church. None of these relationships progressed into anything serious. In fact, Nedra was a little reluctant to open up to anyone since her break up with Tyree. Donovon had backed off also, but they still remained good friends even though they didn't get a chance to see each other very much.

At lunch on this day, Nedra joined her friends and was complaining about how hard it was to meet a nice guy. She had thought about calling Simeon on more than one occasion, but decided against it since she ended their relationship after her internship. She had to admit he was a good companion and was magnificent in bed, but she didn't see anything more serious happening between them. She'd been under a dry spell for long enough and was ready for a serious relationship. Donovon was still dating Vivica, and they seemed to be getting along much better.

She took a bite of her lunch. "The only men I've been meeting lately are policemen who've been stopping me for speeding," Nedra said.

Her coworker, Lawrence, laughed. "Nobody told you to buy that race car. It's not going to be your last ticket either."

"If you must know, it was a gift," she explained.

Lawrence took a bite of his sandwich and teased her.

"I wish someone would give me a Mercedes as a gift."

Ednita raised her glass in agreement. "You and me both."

Nedra lifted the fork to her mouth and rolled her eyes. "All right, you guys, I can't help it that I have a very generous grandmother. I'm an only child. You should see what she gave my friend, Donovon, for graduation."

Lawrence leaned back in his chair. "What was it?" he asked.

She wiped her mouth. "I'll let him tell you when you guys finally get a chance to meet him."

"I can't wait to meet this Donovon you talk about all the time. He sounds wonderful."

"He is, Ednita."

Ednita looked at her watch and screamed. "Oh my gosh! We'd better finish up so we can get back to the office."

Lawrence picked up the check and reached into his pocket for his wallet. "It's my turn to buy lunch today," he said. "By the way, what are you going to do about that ticket, Nedra?"

"I guess I'll have to go downtown and take care of it."

They all stood up. As they walked off Ednita said, "Good luck."

Weeks later, Nedra took off work early so she could go to court for her ticket. As she sat in the lobby, waiting to be called, she decided to look over some work. An hour had passed and she was still she waiting. Crossing her legs, her navy skirt rode high on her thighs. Within minutes, she was approached.

"Excuse me, but haven't we met before?"

The voice shot chills all over her body. In front of her stood Simeon Mathews, and as expected, he looked fabulous.

She looked up, smiled, and played along with him.

"You do look familiar . . . wait! I remember you. You have a biblical name. Samuel, is it?"

"No, it's Simeon. We met at that United Negro College fundraiser a little over a year ago."

She snapped her fingers.

"Yes! That's it. How are you?"

He smiled warmly and shook her hand. "Just fine. Your name is Nedra, right?"

"I can't believe you remembered my name."

He walked closer with a gleam in his eye. "I have a pretty good memory when it comes to beautiful women."

Nedra laughed. "OK, enough of this game already. How are you, Simeon?"

He sat his briefcase down and pulled her tightly into his arms. "Damn! You still feel good! I've missed you something bad."

"Sure you have."

Sitting down next to her he couldn't take his eyes off her. "I'm being dead serious, Nedra. You weren't kidding when you said no strings. I didn't expect to fall for you like I did, then you left me all alone."

"Now you're really pulling my leg," she playfully teased.

"No, I'm not, and by the way, do you still have that infamous boyfriend you always made a point to remind me of?"

Clearing her throat, she looked away solemnly. He leaned closer.

"Did I say something wrong?"

He stared at her with those piercing eyes. She was once again shaken by his presence. Running into Simeon wasn't something she planned on, but she figured her luck would run out sooner or later.

"Nedra?"

"We broke up. Well, actually we were engaged, but it didn't work out."

"I'm sorry, Nedra. I met him at your graduation and he seemed to be a nice guy."

She turned to him and frowned. "Yeah, why did you do that?"

He held his hands up in defense and smiled.

"Hold on, Nedra. I only came because I wanted to see you and personally give you my gift, but after I got there I realized it wasn't a good idea and

I didn't want to upset you. I didn't know who the young man was when I first started talking to him. It was only after he introduced himself to me that I knew. That's why I used a fake name because I didn't want to leave a trail. I told him we were old friends and asked him to give you the gift. I was trying to protect you, Nedra. I didn't want him to suspect anything."

"Well he did, and he was pissed."

"I guess using the fake name wasn't a good idea, but after you saw the gift, I figured you would know it was me and just play along innocently."

"I'm not good at lying, Simeon, but if you had given me a heads up I could've handled it. It took me a minute to catch on, but by the time I did it was too late. I had to do a lot of convincing to calm Tyree down."

"I'm sorry, Nedra. I didn't know it would go down like that."

She pulled out a breath mint, popped it in her mouth, and sighed. "Well it did, and he didn't like it. He knew you were more than a friend, especially since you gave me a lingerie gift certificate. I just told him I didn't know anyone named Byron."

Simeon unbuttoned his expensive jacket and crossed his legs, very happy that Nedra was single.

"So you're finally single and free?"

"Unfortunately, I am."

He took her hand and caressed it with his thumb like he always did. It sent a shock wave over her body.

"Nedra, seriously, I'm sorry your engagement didn't work out. It was obvious you cared about him and he cared about you."

She pulled her hand back. "Thank you," she said softly.

"I guess I did stir up too many questions. You didn't tell him about the tickets to Hawaii, did you?"

She shook her head and laughed. "No way! It was nice, Simeon, but I couldn't accept a gift like that from you."

He kissed her hand and laughed. "I can't help it that I like pampering you. In all honesty, I was hoping you would call me so you and I could sneak off to a little R&R, but you held your own. I did my best to stay away from you, but it wasn't easy. I'm interested in you, Nedra, and I care about the things going on in your life. I knew you had been rehired with your company, but I didn't know you and your friend had broken up. I decided to stay away because I knew you had all my numbers, and if you wanted to hang out, I wanted it to be your call."

"I appreciate you doing that, Simeon."

"Good! Now what are we going to do to make up for all this lost time?"

Nedra smiled at him. Time had been good to Simeon and he was even more handsome than he was the last time she'd seen him. She was still a little upset with him for showing up at her graduation, but it was water under the bridge at this point. He'd apologized.

Nedra tugged on her short skirt and squirmed in her seat. "I don't know. What do you have in mind?"

"How about we start with dinner?"

"It sounds nice, but I don't know how long I'm going to be down here."

"What are you in for?" he asked while looking at his watch.

She pulled the tickets from her purse and he burst out laughing. He took them from her hand and looked at each one closely.

"I see you still have a heavy foot, Miss Harris."

"It's not my fault. This city is full of speed traps. Are you going to or coming from court?"

"Coming from," he replied. "Why don't you let me help you so we can get out of here together?"

"You don't have to hang around if you have somewhere to be. I'll be fine."

He stood and picked up his briefcase.

"What would you say if I told you I could make these tickets go away?"

She looked at him suspiciously. "How?" she asked.

"I have my ways," he admitted proudly as he winked at her. "Have dinner with me and I'll tell you all about it."

"I don't know. I don't want you to get into any trouble for helping me out."

"Oh no! I happen to have some good friends on the bench and some of them owe me a favor. Seriously, I want to spend some time with you so we can catch up with what's been going on with you."

Nedra stood there weighing her options. She had no idea how much longer she would have to wait for court, and she didn't want these tickets to affect her insurance. Simeon Mathews was definitely charming, and maybe he could help her out of her dry spell once and for all.

"I don't know. It's kind of short notice."

He held her hand.

"Why don't you stay here and think about it while I go take care of your tickets? I'll be right back."

She smiled. "OK, thank you."

"I'll be right back."

Nedra sat down and pulled out her cell phone to call Donovon.

"Hello?"

"Hey, Donovon. Are you still at the office?"

"Yeah, what's up? Are you still in court?"

"Yeah, but I think I'm going to get out of paying for those tickets I told you about."

"How?" he asked.

"You're not going to believe who I ran into."

Donovon was still at work finishing up some paperwork. "Simeon?"

"How did you know?"

"Well, who else could it be? I knew it couldn't be Tyree."

Donovon could hear the excitement in Nedra's voice. "Be nice. He's going to take care of my speeding tickets for me."

"What does he want from you in return?"

Donovon's heart thumped in his chest as he worried about Nedra hooking back up with this lawyer. She played with her hair nervously.

"We're going out to dinner."

Donovon tapped his pen on the desk. "Where are you going?"

"I don't know. Oh! I see him coming. I'll call you later."

Before he could respond, Nedra slid her cell

phone back into her purse. She stood as Simeon approached. He smiled and handed her a slip of paper. Nedra looked over the piece of paper, which exonerated her of all the tickets. She looked up at him in amazement.

"How did you do this?"

"I told you, I know people."

She tucked the paper inside her purse. "Thank you very much. You didn't have to go out of your way to do that, but I appreciate it anyway."

"You know there's nothing I wouldn't do for you. Now, where do you want to go for dinner?"

Nedra blushed. "What about Sal's?"

"Sal's sounds good to me."

Simeon pulled her into his arms and kissed her passionately. As expected, she melted in his arms. He released her.

"Are you ready to go?" he calmly asked.

She looked at him in amazement because he didn't skip a beat.

Breathlessly she asked, "What was that?"

"You like?"

Her body shivered.

"It was very nice. You definitely haven't lost your touch."

"You haven't seen anything yet. Come on, my car is parked outside this door."

"No! Wait! I can't leave my car here."

He took a step back. "Yes, you can. You can use my parking pass and leave it in the garage until we get back."

"OK, thanks."

*   *   *

Nedra arrived to work the next day full of sunshine. She hurried to her office and dialed Donovon's number.

"Good morning, Donovon."

"I see you're in a great mood this morning. I guess dinner with your boy went well last night."

Nedra danced around her office before falling down in her chair and placing her feet up on her desk.

"Yes, it did. Conversation was great, he still looks handsome, yadda, yadda, yadda."

"Please tell me you didn't sleep with him?"

She sat down and took offense to his comment. "Come on, Donovon. Don't be like that."

Jealously sank deeper into Donovon's heart. "Are you getting ready to open up those doors again? I thought you wanted to let sleeping dogs lie?"

Nedra didn't like Donovon's comment. She wanted his support, not to fight with him. "What's the problem? He was good to me when I was here before."

Donovon felt a headache coming on. He was feeling like he was going to be left out in the cold again, especially if Nedra was going to start dating this lawyer.

"You weren't praising him when he was trying to break up your relationship with Tyree."

Nedra sat down and twirled around in her chair. "Simeon just had a hard time letting go when I moved away. We got real close when I was seeing him. He's really nice and he explained all that to me."

Donovon flipped through some paperwork on his desk and Nedra was silent on the phone.

"I have to go, but I want you to know you're still my only love."

"Sure I am. Get to work. I'll call or e-mail you later."

She smiled. "Have a good day."

"You too, Nedra."

She hung up the telephone and started going over her paperwork.

Chapter Twenty

Starting Over

Nedra decided she would give her relationship with Simeon a serious try. She didn't know how well it would work out since there was a huge age difference between then, but nevertheless, it was worth a try. Simeon had always been charming, loving and attentive to her, and since they were official, he had raised the bar.

Donovon wasn't happy about the reunion, but he had to respect Nedra's wishes and rules regarding their relationship. He knew Nedra would never come between them, so he ended his relationship with Vivica once and for all. His heart and mind was never too far from Nedra. The night they shared at the beach house made him love her even more. He could never see himself with anyone else seriously, because Nedra knew him better than any other woman, except for his mother. She was also the only woman who had ever made him feel the things he felt, both emotionally and physically.

Nedra was happy with her relationship with

Simeon. They basically picked up where they had left off. He couldn't be happier to have her back in his life, and especially in his bed. Nedra was a woman who needed healing, and he wanted to make sure it was him and only him giving her loving. Since she could date him openly, she decided to let Simeon have his way, because after what she'd been through, she needed to be catered to. One of the first things he did to start off their relationship was to take that trip to Hawaii. It was one of the most romantic places on earth, and if Nedra was going to bounce back from her heartache, Hawaii was a great place to start.

Simeon was careful with Nedra's heart because he knew she was delicate. All he wanted was for her to trust that he would love her like no other man could, and he would provide her with the finer things in life.

In Hawaii, he made it a point not to make her think he only wanted her for her body. They enjoyed all the amenities the island had to offer, whether it was scuba diving, private boat rides, shopping, whatever. He just wanted to make her happy. Nedra especially enjoyed the breathtaking views from the window of their helicopter tour.

When she told her parents she was going to Hawaii with Simeon, they were apprehensive about her jumping into a new relationship so soon. They had hoped that Nedra would wake up and see Donovon for who he was, but for reasons unknown to them, she decided to go in an opposite direction. Her father wanted to meet Simeon as soon as possible, especially since he was so much older than his daughter. Nedra assured them that as soon as time permitted, she would make arrangements for them to meet.

The couple came back from Hawaii rested and with stars in their eyes. Simeon didn't want to be separated from Nedra, but he realized her body needed to rest. On the island, she seduced him as much as he seduced her, making it hard for either of them to keep their hands to themselves. The pair was spontaneous and adventurous, so whenever they had enough privacy to make love, they did. Nedra had never let herself be as uninhibited as she was with him. He was always relaxed, confident, and thorough, and he always made sure she was satisfied first. Because of Simeon's unselfishness, Nedra proudly started wearing the platinum diamond ring he'd given her years earlier as a going-away present. She was finally happy that her life seemed to be back on track. Simeon introduced her to his sister and a few other family members, making it a point to let them know how special she was to him.

Donovon's heart was bruised, but he decided to keep his comments to himself after seeing how starry-eyed she was over him. He couldn't wait to meet this man so he could judge for himself if Simeon was all Nedra portrayed him to be, because if he wasn't, there was going to be hell to pay.

Chapter Twenty-One

Back Together Again

The economy hadn't been the best in the world lately, and Donovon had unfortunately become a casualty of downsizing. He was now looking for a new job. As fate would have it, Nedra's company was looking for someone to run their sales department, and she strongly urged Donovon to apply since it would bring them together again. Nedra thought of how great it would be to have her old friend close to her if he got the job. Their demanding careers and the fact that Nedra was with Simeon hadn't allowed them a lot of time to get together much over the past year. Donovon felt like they were slowly drifting apart. Nedra assured Donovon that he was still number one on her list, and that Simeon understood that.

Donovon was reluctant to apply for the job at Nedra's company, but he decided to take Nedra up on her suggestion and interview for the position. Thankfully, he was hired and he was pleased to find out that his salary was going to be even more than it was at his previous job. Donovon was still dating Vivica, but their relationship had cooled off tremendously. Since she wasn't interested in moving to Tennessee, it left them no choice but to end the relationship for good.

Donovon was excited about his new position and the fact that he would be working with Nedra. When he flew in for his interview weeks earlier, she had the opportunity to introduce him to his new coworkers, Ednita and Lawrence, as well as other personnel. Everyone welcomed Donovon on board. Learning that he and Nedra had been friends for years seemed to fascinate them.

Donovon stayed with her when he came in for his interview. Simeon didn't care much for the setup, but because of their history, Nedra told Simeon it wasn't up for discussion. She told him he was welcomed to stay as well, but if he didn't trust her, they didn't have much else between them. Simeon didn't want to rock the boat, so he unwillingly went along with Nedra's plans.

She owned a small house out in the suburbs because she loved the tranquility of the surroundings. While Donovon was there, he found an upscale apartment downtown, which was located conveniently near their office.

A few weeks later, Donovon returned and started settling in to his new apartment and new job. Donovon and Nedra had begun catching up on each other's lives, which made things feel like old times once again. He still loved her dearly, but he had decided if things heated up again between them, it would have to be initiated by her. He also decided he was going to do everything in his power to keep his jealously under control. Nedra and Simeon were closer than he first thought, and he couldn't wait to look into the eyes of the man who was getting all of her time.

The following Saturday night, Nedra had dinner at her house so Donovon could finally meet Simeon. He couldn't help but stare at Simeon, the man who Nedra couldn't stop talking about. There was something about him that didn't quite add up. For one, he was wealthy, handsome, and intelligent, but yet he wanted a woman nearly ten years younger than he was. Simeon turned to Donovon and smiled.

"Nedra tells me you two have been friends for a long time."

"Yes, we have, and she means the world to me."

Simeon frowned momentarily as Donovon kissed her hand.

"She is a remarkable woman."

Nedra blushed. "That's so sweet of both of you. Now who wants dessert?"

Both men acknowledged their desire for the sweet peach cobbler Nedra had prepared. Dessert was a hit with both men, and afterward they retired to the living room for coffee. The three continued to talk amongst each other until late into the night. Donovon was still picking up bad vibes from the man Nedra was so fascinated with. He was determined to keep a close eye on him—a very close eye.

Before lunch the following Monday, Nedra had received two-dozen pink roses. She was overwhelmed, and all the ladies in the office made their way to her desk to admire them. Ednita was at her desk smelling the flowers when Donovon came to get them for lunch.

"Well, well, well. What have we here?"

Ednita was still admiring the flowers. "Aren't they beautiful? Her lawyer friend sent them," Ednita said.

Donovon walked over and sniffed the scented flower. He looked over at Nedra, who seemed to be glowing. "What did the card say?"

"Donovon!"

Ednita chimed in and said, "Yeah, what did it say?"

Nedra grabbed her purse and walked toward the door. "I'm not telling. Now are you guys coming to lunch or not?"

Ednita looked at Donovon. "I guess we'll just have to wonder about this one."

"I guess so," Donovon answered. "Let's grab some lunch."

That afternoon in Donovon's office, Nedra showed him the card, which read:

> *A beautiful woman like you should always have beautiful things around her. I'm glad you're back in my life.*
>
> *With Love,*
> *Simeon*

Donovon handed the card back to her. "He's smooth. I have to give him that."

"I could've called him as soon as I moved back here, but I didn't. I was trying to start out fresh. Is it a sin that I like his company?"

"It's not a sin, but he seems like a con man to me."

Nedra shook her head in defeat. "I don't know what else to say, Donovon. It's obvious you don't like Simeon, and you probably never will, but can't you at least be happy for me? I've been so down since Tyree and I broke up, but I'm better now. You need to stop concentrating on my love life and work on your own. When was the last time you had a real date?"

"We're talking about you, not me."

"No, for real, Donovon, you need to loosen up and find someone to spend time with. There's no reason for you not to be dating someone."

"If it happens, fine. If it doesn't, I'll survive. I just moved here, remember?"

She grabbed his hand and gave it a squeeze. "I know, but I want you to be happy like I am."

"Just remember, you don't always have to look for someone new. Now are you ready for lunch?"

"Yeah, I'm starving."

She knew exactly what he meant by his statement, but she was not about to risk messing up their friendship. If it was meant for them to be together as a couple, it would happen. In the meantime, she was with Simeon and he was doing and saying all the right things. Boyfriends come and go, but a good friend will be with you no matter what.

Chapter Twenty-Two

Looking For Love

A couple of months later, Donovon found himself searching the mall for a Mother's Day gift for his mom. Over the years, it had become even more difficult to find just the right present. She loved jewelry, but she also loved simple, inexpensive items. She worked hard every day and hardly ever took a day off. This year, he thought of the perfect gift, which was a day of pampering complete with a massage, facial, and the works. This shopping trip reminded him of all the gifts Nedra had acquired since she'd started dating Simeon again. Not a week went by that she didn't have some new jewelry, clothes, etc. Dismissing his thoughts of Nedra, he walked into a boutique and purchased his mother's gift with a smile. He made his way through the parking lot to his car. As he deactivated the car alarm, he noticed a beautiful, statuesque woman struggling with her shopping bags.

He didn't want to startle her as he walked toward her so he yelled, "Do you need some help?"

The young woman looked his way and then dropped several bags on the ground. Disgusted, she went ahead and dropped all of them. Donovon decided to go over and lend a hand.

"Let me help you with those."

"Thank you," she answered in appreciation.

Donovon helped her put the bags in the car and dropped the keys in her hands.

"There. You're all packed and ready to go."

She extended her hand to thank him. "Thank you so much for helping me. My name is Brea."

Donovon shook her hand. "My name is Donovon. Donovon McNeil."

"Well, Donovon McNeil, thank you for being the perfect gentleman, and I hope you will allow me to treat you to lunch to show my appreciation."

"That sounds nice, but I insist on treating you to lunch. It seems you've had a rough afternoon. I think you could use the nourishment," he said while looking at her car full of shopping bags.

She giggled. "In that case, you're on."

"Let's get your bags out of the car and put them in the trunk for safety purposes."

Brea was impressed. This handsome gentleman seemed to know all the right things to do. They walked together back into the mall and into Ruby Tuesday for lunch, and what Donovon hoped was a chance to get to know this gorgeous woman a little better.

The seasons had changed once again, and time had been good to both Nedra and Donovon. Brea had turned out to be a very nice and sensual woman. She was a breath of fresh air in Donovon's life and allowed him to loosen up a lot. He wasn't working the long hours he used to work, and spending time with Brea took his mind off of Nedra and Simeon just a little bit. He still kept a watchful eye over Nedra, not only because he was in love with her, but because Simeon seemed a little too good to be true.

Chapter Twenty-Three

The Nightmare Begins

The seasons changed, and for unknown reasons, so had Simeon, and the paradise Nedra had been enjoying was starting to crumble. They had been getting along great up until now, but Simeon's cases were becoming more demanding on his time, and because of it, he didn't have a lot of extra time to spend with Nedra. He had become increasingly frustrated and easily irritated when he worked on high profile cases, and even more despondent when he lost. Nedra understood the ups and downs of being a lawyer, and she always gave him the space she felt like he needed. The problem was, when she pulled back to give him space, he would accuse her of sneaking around. His mood swings were hard for her to deal with, so her best relief was going to the gym. So far she'd always been able to keep herself toned up, and now that she was nearing her mid-twenties, she didn't want to start slacking off.

Simeon was definitely keeping her busy in the bedroom, sometimes more than she wanted. Their relationship had hit a plateau, but Simeon had become somewhat irrational when it came to their sex life. His sexual appetite was enormous, and while he was very capable of pleasing her, he started requesting things that she felt uncomfortable with, like wanting to videotape them in bed having sex. What caused Simeon's behavioral changes, she didn't know, but she prayed it wasn't drugs. She knew he drank, but whatever it was had to change or she was going to have to move on.

On one evening, it was two a.m. when Simeon decided to arrive at Nedra's house. She had been waiting up for him since midnight. He'd called hours earlier to let her know he was on his way over, and since she hadn't heard from him, she thought he had been in an accident. Simeon walked in whistling as if nothing was wrong. Nedra stood and folded her arms in anger. She was dressed in pink pajamas, but she still managed to look sexy.

"What took you so long to get here? I was worried," she said. "I called your cell, but it went directly to voicemail."

Simeon walked toward her with a blank look on his face. When he passed by, Nedra could smell the alcohol and something else on his breath. He walked into the kitchen and hung his jacket on the back of a chair. Nedra followed him, still seeking answers. She was upset and he didn't seem to care.

"I'm not going to let you disrespect me,

Simeon! I can't believe you would walk up in my house smelling like some cheap whore! Who is she?"

He walked past her and then stopped dead in his tracks. He slowly turned. Out of nowhere he slapped Nedra so hard, it knocked her over the sofa, into the coffee table, and onto the floor.

He stalked around the sofa to where she lay. "Now look what you made me do! Damn it!"

Her lip was split and her cheek was starting to swell. She was sobbing uncontrollably and was dazed. She never dreamed in a million years that Simeon would hit her. Yes, they'd had their arguments, but they had never escalated to this magnitude. She was hurt and in shock.

Simeon looked remorseful seeing the blood on her pink pajamas and the tears streaming down her face. He pulled her up into his arms and cupped her face. He frowned as he looked closely at her injured lip. Before releasing her, he leaned down and kissed her sore lips tenderly.

"Go clean up, baby," he whispered in a calm and soothing voice. "I'm so sorry I hurt you. I don't know what came over me."

After he walked out of the room and into the kitchen, Nedra tried to gather her thoughts. She touched her lip and flinched at the pain. She made her way upstairs to the bathroom so she could inspect her injuries in the mirror. Tears still streaked down her face as she took a terry cloth towel and wiped away the blood. As she stood in the bathroom mirror, Simeon walked up behind her. Without saying a word, she turned and looked at him.

"I'm so sorry, Nedra. I love you."

He pulled Nedra into his arms and rocked her, but Nedra pulled away.

"I'm OK, Simeon. Just leave me alone."

He stared at her.

"I didn't mean to hurt you, Nedra. I love you too much to hurt you."

She didn't respond as she did her best to clean up her wound. He left the room and then came back with an ice pack in his hand.

"Here's some ice for your lip. I'm getting ready to hit the shower. Hurry up and come to bed so I can make it up to you."

Son of a bitch!

Nedra slowly exited the bathroom and made her way back into her bedroom. She thought to herself that he should be tired after doing God knows what, with God knows who, and to say she was pissed off was an understatement. Also, he was crazy if he thought she was going to have sex with him after he had used her as his personal punching bag.

When she heard the shower turn on she took her cell phone and made her way back downstairs. She needed to talk to Donovon. She was so confused. How could Simeon claim he loved her and treat her like she was trash?

In the kitchen she dialed Donovon's number, not remembering the time. As she listened to it ring, the tears started streaming down her face again when she felt her cheek and lip throbbing.

A groggy voice finally answered on the second ring.

"Hello?"

"Hey, Donovon. Did I wake you?"

"What time is it?" he asked while yawning.

"I'm sorry It's a little after two a.m. Are you alone?"

He laughed. "If I wasn't it would be a little late to ask now, wouldn't it? What's going on? Why are you calling me so late?"

"I just wanted to talk to you, that's all," she whispered.

"Nedra, I've known you for years and you're not fooling me. I know something's wrong. Now tell me."

She could still hear the shower running, so she knew Simeon was still occupied. Struggling for words, she answered, "It's Simeon."

Nedra had his full attention now.

"What has he done?"

"We got into an argument and things kind of got out of hand."

Donovon sat up in bed. "What do you mean got out of hand?"

"Well, you know . . . he sort of—"

Cutting her off, Donovon pulled back the comforter and sat up on the side of his bed.

"Did he touch you?"

She started crying and Donovon knew he had his answer. He was out of his bed and getting dressed. Brea stirred, but did not wake up. He looked over at her and walked downstairs so he could talk.

"I'm on my way over there," he stated angrily.

"No! Don't! I'll be OK. I just needed to hear your voice."

He pulled a glass out of the cabinet and poured some milk. While sitting at the table he got even angrier.

"This is pissing me off, Nedra. I'm not going to sit here and let him put his hands on you."

"Donovon, please. I can handle it," she tried to convince him.

He took a sip of the milk in silence.

"Nedra, I'm going to ask you something, and you'd better tell me the truth."

"What?"

"Has he ever touched you before?"

"No. We've argued, but this is the first time he ever hit me."

"If you're not dressed, get dressed. I'm on my way over there to pick you up."

"No, Donovon! I'm sure Brea is there, and you need to stay there with her."

"I don't give a damn if Brea is here. I'm on my way!"

Sipping her tea, she stifled her tears. "Please don't, Donovon. I'm fine, seriously. If you come over here it'll only make things worse."

He was silent. "Donovon, are you still there?"

"Yeah, I'm here."

"Don't be shocked when you see me," she announced.

He wanted to throw his glass against the wall.

"Did he mess your face up or something?"

"I have a split lip and my cheek is swollen."

Donovon made fists with his hands. "Nedra!"

"I'm sure it's the stress of the trial he's working on," she defended.

"What the hell does that have to do with anything? I know he'd better not put his hands on you again."

Hearing the shower turn off, she went into a slight panic.

"I'd better go. He's getting ready to get out of the shower."

"Damn it, Nedra!"

"I'm OK."

"This is not good, Nedra."

"I have to go. Good night, Donovon."

She hung up the telephone and turned to see Simeon standing in the doorway with a towel around his neck. He had a disgruntled look on his face.

"Who were you talking to?"

Walking past him, she said, "It was only Donovon."

Simeon looked at her and gave her a warning. "What goes on in our relationship is between us, and it doesn't concern him. Stop telling him our business."

This is no relationship. Who is he fooling?

"He's my best friend, Simeon," she reminded him.

He ran his finger over her cheek and kissed her. "I trust no man around you, especially Donovon McNeil."

Nedra wanted to pull away from him because she didn't want him to touch her. She despised him now, but the last thing she wanted to do was make him angry again.

"It's late, Simeon. I'm going to bed."

He released her arm and caressed her body as she brushed past him.

"I'll be right up, sweetheart."

Out of his view, she rolled her eyes and proceeded upstairs.

*   *   *

Donovon, on the other hand, was having a hard time getting back to sleep. He was still worried about Nedra. He knew Simeon Mathews was bad news from day one. Why Nedra didn't see through him before now, he didn't understand. The flowers, jewelry, and clothes were all just a cover. Men only did that to gain control over women, and Nedra didn't even see the setup.

He turned and looked at Brea sleeping peacefully. She was nice and fit well with him for the moment, but she was starting to show signs of falling in love with him, and he needed to head it off before it was too late. His heart could only belong to one woman, and it wasn't Brea.

She stirred in her slept and cuddled closer to him.

"Who was that on the phone, baby?"

"It was only Nedra."

"Is she OK?"

"She will be."

Nibbling on his earlobe, she purred, "I hope whatever's going on with her works out."

"So do I."

She hugged his neck and started kissing and caressing his body. Donovon couldn't help but continue to worry about Nedra as Brea was trying to get his mind and body on her.

"I'm sorry, Brea. I have to make a run," he said suddenly, breaking the kiss.

"Where?"

Climbing out of bed, he hurriedly dressed. "Don't worry. I'll be back shortly. I just have to do a favor for Nedra."

Before she could respond, he was out the door.

* * *

Nedra was finally settling down for the night. She was glad Simeon was still downstairs; however, about thirty minutes later he walked into the bedroom and apologized to her once more. Before he could climb into bed beside her, the doorbell chimed.

"Now who could that be at this hour?"

Simeon walked downstairs to answer the door. He looked through the peephole and cursed.

"What the hell is he doing here?"

Opening the door, he was shocked to see the barrel of Donovon's nine millimeter pointed between his eyes. Simeon laughed and shook his head in disbelief.

"Donovon! What's up, man? Why are you rolling up on a brotha like this?"

Without moving an inch, he asked, "Where's Nedra?"

"She's asleep. Why? Did she tell you to come over here?"

"No, and don't play with me, Simeon. I'm going to ask you once again. Where is she?"

"Look, put the gun down so we can talk about this rationally," he suggested

Becoming angrier, Donovon gave him a look Simeon had seen in the eyes of murderers he had defended.

"Simeon, if you don't get Nedra down here right now, I'm not going to be responsible for my actions. Now get her down here. Now!"

Simeon finally understood that Donovon might just pull the trigger.

"Nedra! Get down here! You have company!" Simeon yelled without moving an inch.

Nedra slowly descended the stairs and peeped around the corner. She was shocked to see Donovon standing there holding a gun on Simeon. She also saw the rage in his eyes—a look she'd never seen before.

"Donovon, what are you doing here?"

"Get your coat," he said without taking his eyes off Simeon.

"What?"

"I said, get your coat. I'm not leaving you with him."

"I'm OK, Donovon, really."

"You heard her. My baby's fine," Simeon said with a grin on his face.

He took his eyes off Simeon for one minute and looked at Nedra. She trembled because she knew Donovon was beyond angry.

"For the last time, Nedra, get your coat!"

Nedra reached into her closet and reluctantly slid into her coat.

Simeon reached out to her and slowly pleaded with her. "Babe, what are you doing?"

"She's coming with me."

Simeon walked over to her and pleaded with her to stay. "Come on, Nedra. You're not really leaving, are you? You know I didn't mean . . ."

"Didn't mean what?. To smack the shit out of her?"

"Whatever, Donovon!"

Nedra looked at Simeon with tears in her eyes. "Simeon, I need to get out of here so I can think straight. You really hurt me tonight."

He threw up his hands. "Ain't this a bitch! Nedra, baby, I told you I was sorry."

"That's not good enough, Simeon. I never expected you to hit me. I thought you loved me."

"I do love you!"

Still holding the gun on him, Donovon instructed Nedra to go to the car. She quietly did as she was told. Once she was out of earshot, Donovon gave Simeon a few words of warning.

"If you ever put your hands on her again, I'll kill you. Do you understand?"

"You'd better be ready to back up what you say, Donovon," Simeon replied arrogantly.

"Oh, don't you worry about that. I'm more than capable of proving myself to you. This is Nedra's house, and you will not disrespect her or her home, so you need to be out by dawn."

Simeon looked at Donovon with a smirk on his face and then closed the door. Donovon walked slowly back to his car. He climbed in and Nedra started sobbing.

He tilted her chin. "Damn! He did a number on you. We need to go to the police station and report him."

"No. I just want to go to bed."

"You need to get yourself together because I could've killed that fool tonight."

"I'm sorry, Donovon," she whispered.

He didn't respond. Instead they rode quietly back to his house.

Chapter Twenty-Four

Reality Sets In

Donovon was happy that Nedra called out sick from work. He knew she would be the subject of office gossip if she came in displaying her swollen lip. Several coworkers stopped by and asked about her because they knew he was her friend. After they left, he decided to give Nedra a call.

"Hello?"

"How are you feeling?"

"I look awful, Donovon," she moaned.

"Have you been keeping the ice on your lip?"

"Yeah, but people will know once they see me."

He stood, walked over to the window, and sighed. "Do you have any sick time you could use?"

Touching her swollen lip, she grimaced. "Yes, but . . ."

He cut her off mid-sentence. "Use it, Nedra, and get things settled with Mathews or I'll settle them for you."

"I hear you, Donovon."

"Good!"

She held the phone in silence because she knew everything Donovon was saying was true. Simeon had come into her life showering her with love, gifts, and attention. He whisked her away on weekend getaways and he made it a point to go out of his way to make sure she was satisfied in every way. It was only recently that Simeon started showing signs of being angry and out of control. This was the first time he had actually hit her, and she felt confident that he would never do it again—especially after Donovon had paid him a visit.

"Look, Donovon, I know you care about me, but there's no reason for you to get involved with this. OK?"

"First of all, I love you. Secondly, I'm already involved. Don't you realize that men who hit women never stop?"

"I don't know what to think right now. Look, get back to work. I'm fine."

"OK, I'll see you later."

"OK."

Nedra took three days off work so she could recuperate. Even though she was back at work, Donovon couldn't get the image of Nedra's face out of his mind. He also couldn't believe that Nedra was giving Simeon another chance. Since the incident happened, Simeon had not only apologized to her, but he had also apologized to Donovon. Nedra accepted it, but he didn't have to. Simeon was also back to his old tricks, sending Nedra flowers, taking her on shopping sprees, etc. Donovon was concerned, and he had a right to be.

Nedra popped into his office on her first day back and called out to him.

"Are you ready for lunch?"

"You guys go ahead. I'm meeting Brea for lunch."

Walking further into his office, she smiled. "Well, well, well. Are things getting serious with you two?"

Donovon leaned back in his chair and blushed.

"You sure are nosey today."

Coming around his desk, she leaned over in front of him, grinning.

"What are you grinning about?"

Folding her arms, she laughed. "I can't believe you're not going to tell me."

"There's nothing to tell," he answered as he picked up his keys.

"I disagree, Donovon McNeil, and you bet not run off and elope without telling me."

"You have got to be kidding. I'm dating Brea, but that's all. If it looks like I'm getting ready to do something stupid, please stop me."

He opened the door so she could exit ahead of him. They walked down the hallway together toward the elevator.

"Enjoy your lunch."

"You too. I'll see you later."

"OK, and be careful," she answered as the elevator doors closed.

Turning on her heels, she walked back to her office to get her purse so she could also get lunch.

Simeon often worked late. It was also often that he took detours before coming over to Nedra's house. This night he sat in a bar with a shapely redhead beside him. He'd had several drinks and couldn't seem to keep his hands off the woman. She giggled as he whispered in her ear. The sound of his cell phone ringing interrupted their exchange.

Looking at the ID he said, "Damn! Hold on a sec, babe."

"Hello?"

"Simeon, I'm at the gym and my car won't start. I need you to come pick me up."

"I'm kind of busy right now, Nedra. Can you call roadside assistance?"

"Yes, I could call roadside assistance, but I called you."

She shook her head in disbelief. Here she was, giving him another chance, and he was treating her like dirt once again. Nedra was furious that he was acting like her situation wasn't serious, plus she heard a female giggling in the background, so he couldn't be too busy. She didn't know what had happened to the kind and gentle Simeon she'd met a long time ago. She was beginning to think more and more that drugs were involved, and she decided she would have to watch him a lot closer.

"Nedra, I said I was busy, babe!"

"Fine! Good-bye!"

She threw the phone down on the floor of her car and burst into tears. Simeon was taking advantage of her, and she knew it. Why she stayed with him, she didn't know. It's not like she didn't have a strong will. Her mom and dad made sure she understood not to let people walk all over her. So why was she letting Simeon do it? She shouldn't have to sacrifice her dignity for love.

Pulling her bag up on her shoulder, she dialed Donovon's number.

"Hello?"

"Donovon, I'm sorry to bother you, but I'm at the gym and my car won't start. Roadside assistance is going to take forever to get here. Can you come help me?"

Donovon could hear her voice quivering as she spoke.

"I can't get in touch with Simeon," she lied as she tried to stifle her tears.

Donovon shook his head in disgust because he knew Simeon didn't give a damn about Nedra now that he'd used her up. Luckily, Donovon was on his way home from work so he assured her he was on his way.

"Sit tight, Nedra. I'm on my way."

"Thanks, Donovon."

"Don't mention it."

It took Donovon about thirty minutes to get to her with rush hour traffic. When he arrived, she was sitting in her car with her head resting against the steering wheel. She didn't even see him approach, so when he knocked on the window, it startled her.

She opened the door and climbed out.

"I didn't mean to scare you."

"It's OK. I was sort of in a daze.

She had on a lime green warm-up suit with matching Nike tennis shoes. Donovon was very upset that Simeon wasn't available for her. Anything could happen to a woman stranded and alone. It was a blessing that her car had stopped at a familiar place.

"Pop the hood," he requested.

She popped the hood and joined him under it.

"When was the last time you had this thing serviced?"

"It's overdue," she answered while leaning under the hood next to him.

Donovon inspected a few items under the hood.

"You can't play with these foreign cars, especially a Mercedes."

Nedra leaned against the car as Donovon rumbled through his trunk.

When he returned to the hood of her car he started working quietly.

"I don't know why you stay with him."

"Stay out of this, Donovon"

Back under the hood, he looked around at the wires.

"Look, I don't want to mess around with your car. Get it towed so somebody can look at it. I can pick you up for work until it's ready."

"You don't have to do that, but you can take me to pick up a rental car."

"I have no problem picking you up, but if you want a rental, I'll take you to get one."

"Thank you."

"Come on and sit in the car with me until the wrecker service gets here," he said while wiping his hand on a towel. "Then I'll take you to get a rental."

She walked over and hugged him lovingly.

"Thanks, Donovon. I don't know what I would ever do without you."

He hugged her back. "You're welcome."

She watched him as he put his tools back into his trunk and closed it.

"Thanks for coming to help me."

"You're welcome."

After the wrecker service came and picked up her car, Donovon took her to pick up her rental. Hopefully she would seriously think about everything he'd been trying to tell her about Simeon.

Chapter Twenty-Five

Round Two

Nedra didn't see Simeon for a few days, which gave her a little more time to think about their relationship. He'd called to check on her, but he hadn't come by until three days later. When he walked in, Nedra could smell the cheap perfume and liquor. Nedra was working on her computer, ignoring him. He leisurely walked in and kissed her on the cheek.

"Whose car is that outside?"

"It's a rental."

"So where's your car?" he asked sarcastically.

"Like you really care," she said without looking up from her computer.

"I do. You're my woman."

"You have a funny way of showing it, Simeon."

He was clearly drunk.

"Who took you to pick up the rental?"

"I had a real man come and help me," she lashed out at him.

His hands were quicker than lightning. He

grabbed her by her collar, pulling her up from the chair. He shoved her so hard against the wall that she made an imprint. Nedra screamed as he slammed her a couple more times against the wall. Before releasing her, he kissed her hard on the lips.

"If I ever find out that you're messing around on me, I will kill you!"

He angrily walked out of the room as Nedra slid to the floor in the fetal position. She had difficulty catching her breath, and she sobbed hysterically. She couldn't believe he had put his hands on her again. She wanted to call the police, but she was afraid he would make good on his threat.

She lay there for what seemed like hours. Nedra could hear him talking to himself and walking around the house, which made her even more afraid. She wished he would just leave. He walked back into the room with a beer in his hand and sat down.

"How much longer are you going to lay on the floor?"

Afraid he might kick her, she pulled herself up into a chair. Rubbing the back of her head, she looked over at him in disbelief.

"What's going on with you, Simeon? Is it drugs? If it is, I can make sure you get some help."

He walked toward her, pulled her into his arms, and kissed her tears.

"Baby, I'm not on drugs. It's just that I'm under a lot of stress and it doesn't take much to irritate me. I love you, Nedra. That's why I freak out like I do, and I get sick to my stomach when I think about another man looking at you or touching you. I can't handle that, and I won't."

"This doesn't feel like love!" she said, pulling away from his embrace. "I've been in love before, and you can't love me if you treat me like this. I want you out of my house!"

He reached up to touch her hair lovingly. She flinched and turned away from him. He grabbed her by the throat. He wasn't choking her, but he had a firm grip on her. He kissed her over and over as he started crying.

"Don't say that, Nedra. I do love you! I would do anything for you, baby!"

She was able to push him away from her body so she could get out of the house. She ran downstairs, out the door, and jumped in her car. She could hear him yelling her name as she fled the house. Her heart was beating rapidly in fear that he was chasing her. The only place she felt safe was with Donovon.

It had started to rain, and by the time she made it to his apartment, she was soaking wet. She knew he was going to be angry with her, but she decided to ring the doorbell anyway.

Donovon wasn't expecting anyone, and when he opened the door, his heart sank. She was standing there with water dripping from her clothes and hair.

He shook his head and motioned for her to come inside. She walked past him in shame, because the last thing she wanted to hear was I told you so. As she walked in, she was met by Brea, who stood there in shock.

"Nedra, are you OK?"

Donovon stood behind Nedra and he motioned for Brea not to say anything else.

"I'm fine, Brea, and I'm sorry for intruding on your evening."

Ignoring Donovon, Brea looked her up and down. "Nedra, are you hurt? Is there anything I can do?"

"Thanks, but I'll be fine," she replied while walking upstairs. "Again, I'm sorry for interrupting on your evening."

Nedra disappeared upstairs. Donovon walked over to Brea.

"I'm sorry about this," he said.

"What's going on with her?"

Taking her by the hand, he led her into the family room.

"She's having some relationship issues, and that's all I can say."

"Do you still want to catch a movie?"

He stood and looked at his watch. "Let me go check on Nedra first, and we'll see."

"OK," she answered as she sat down and grabbed a magazine.

Upstairs, Donovon knocked on the bedroom door.

"Come in."

He opened the door and found her staring out the window at the rain. He walked over and stood next to her.

"What did he do this time?"

Leaning her head on his shoulder, she hesitated.

"He got pissed off because you helped me with my car."

"If he has a problem with it, he needs to see me. Did he hurt you?"

Nedra didn't want to tell Donovon the truth because she knew this time he would put Simeon in his grave for real, so she lied. She pulled a Kleenex out of the tissue box and wiped her eyes.

"He didn't hurt me, but he was talking crazy. It was partly my fault because I provoked him by telling him I had a real man help me with my car. He's insanely jealous of every man."

"It doesn't matter, Nedra. He's not supposed to put his hands on you!"

"He doesn't know it was you who helped me, but I'm sure he knows you're first person I would call."

Walking closer to inspect her, he asked, "Are you sure he didn't touch you?"

"I'm sure," she lied with a smile.

"You can't keep letting him intimidate you."

"I know. Can I crash here tonight?'

He stood with a smirk on his face.

"You know you don't have to ask."

She put her hands over her face. "I know, but you have company and I don't want to be in the way."

"Speaking of which, will you be OK by yourself for a few hours? Brea and I were just heading out to the movies."

Pulling back the linens on the bed, she smiled.

"You know I don't mind. Go! Just give me something to sleep in and you won't even know I'm here."

"Look in my dresser and get a shirt," he said on

his way out of the bedroom. "There's food in the fridge and whatever else you want. If you need me, call my cell. I'll be back a little later."

"OK. Thanks again, Donovon."

"You're always welcome."

"Thanks."

"Sweet dreams, Nedra."

Laughing, she said, "Good night, Donovon, and tell Brea I'm sorry."

"She's cool. See you later."

On the drive home the next morning Nedra tried to figure out how she got to where she was with Simeon. When she returned home, Simeon was nowhere to be found. He didn't live with her, but he had a key to the house so he could come and go as he pleased. Who he was with or where he was when he wasn't at her house, she didn't know. She hadn't spent much time at his house lately, and according to him, his house was where he worked. Her house was where he unwound.

She made sure she left Donovon's house without disturbing him and Brea. As she dressed and headed to work, she felt the back of her head. It was still sore from being slammed against the wall by Simeon. At work she couldn't concentrate. She occasionally rubbed her head as she sat at her desk. Donovon stopped in to say hello.

"Hey! What time did you leave this morning?"

Smiling, she said, "Early."

"You didn't run into Simeon, did you?"

"No, thank God."

He played with the trinkets on her desk. "Why did you leave so early?"

"I didn't want to disturb you and Brea."

He laughed. "Brea didn't stay over."

"Why not? Is it because I was there?"

He sat down in the chair across from her and fumbled with his tie.

"Donovon? Is it because I was there?"

He made eye contact with her. He had beautiful eyes.

"Brea's cool, but sometimes she has a hard time understanding how tight you and I are. It's nothing new."

"Will people ever trust us?"

"No, so I guess we're going to have to live with it."

Nedra felt bad, so she offered her assistance.

"Do you want me to talk to her?"

"Nah! She's just going to have to get over it because we have a history, or have you forgotten?"

They sat there staring at each other. Nedra fumbled with her ink pen and Donovon continued to play with her trinket. Neither of them had spoken about their passionate past since it had happened. She knew she was in love with Donovon, but their lives had gone through so much, and they never seemed to be in sync to get together.

"We have a history, indeed—an unforgettable history."

Nedra could sense he had some things on his mind.

"Can I ask you something, Nedra?"

"Sure," she said, giving him her full attention.

He walked over to her window and looked out. "Do you ever think about what happened between us in Florida?"

Chills ran over her body and she closed her eyes briefly.

"As a matter of fact, I do." She stood and hugged him. "I think about it a lot."

Donovon held her close.

"I could never forget that weekend, Donovon."

He smiled, kissed her forehead, and walked toward the door.

"I was just checking. I guess I'll see you at lunch."

She sat down in her chair and pointed at him. "Yes, and it's your turn to pay too!"

Chapter Twenty-Six

If At First You Don't Succeed . . .

Nedra didn't take Donovon's advice like she should have. Instead, she let Simeon convince her that his irrational behavior was due to exhaustion, caused by his job. Once again, she decided to give her relationship with Simeon another try. He came to her crying and apologizing for the things he'd done to her. She was a little reluctant, but when he checked himself into the hospital for a few days, she believed he was being sincere.

After two months had passed, things between Nedra and Simeon were back like they were when they first met. Against Donovon's advice, she allowed Simeon to take her on a romantic weekend trip to the mountains to make up for everything he'd done. He'd attended anger management classes and had started going back to church. Because of Simeon's behavior, it had been weeks since they'd made love, but she was so impressed with his efforts she was ready to bring intimacy back into their lives.

Back from their trip, Nedra had all but buried the unpleasant incidents with Simeon. He was going out of his way to impress her. She was happy that he was attending anger management classes to get control of his temper. Donovon, on the other hand, wasn't fooled by Simeon's game. He let Nedra know that he totally disagreed with giving the relationship a third try, and he wasn't quiet about it either. While discussing it one day, Donovon lost it.

"Nedra! You must have lost the good sense God gave you!"

On the other end of the telephone, Nedra yelled back.

"Things are better now, Donovon! He's a changed man!"

"Men like Simeon don't change! You're just being stupid now!"

She was silent on the telephone as she listened to Donovon yell at her in anger. Closing her eyes, she spoke softly to him. "I just want to be happy, Donovon. You can understand that, can't you?"

He tried to calm himself down.

"Nedra, I offered you happiness with me, but you didn't want that, remember?"

Her voice was cracking now. "I know, Donovon, but there were extenuating circumstances back then."

"So instead you're deciding to settle? I'll be damned if I let you commit suicide like this with the likes of Simeon Mathews! I'm getting sick of this back and forth shit!"

She had heard enough. "Look, I have to go, Donovon. I'll talk to you later.

"Nedra," he pleaded.

"I have to go!"

She hung up the telephone without saying good-bye, something she'd never done before. Donovon was still holding the phone. He felt like he might've been too harsh with her. But he couldn't believe that such a strong, educated, black woman was allowing someone to control her life. She was bigger than that, and he wouldn't rest until he made her see otherwise.

Nedra's conversation with Donovon had upset her, but she wasn't about to let it mess up the evening she had planned with Simeon. She knew he probably had a grueling day in court, so she wanted everything in their surroundings to be soft. When he walked into the house and saw all the candles, he was surprised.

"What is all this for?"

"Come on in," she said while removing his coat. "I just want you to come in and relax. I know you probably had a rough day in court."

Kissing her, he smiled. "I did. Thank you, baby. Mmmmm, something smells wonderful."

Taking him by the hand, she led him over to the table and motioned for him to sit down.

"I cooked your favorite."

Loosening his tie, he smiled. "You didn't."

"Oh yes I did. Shrimp alfredo, coming right up," she proudly admitted.

Taking her hand into his, he looked her in the

eyes. "Nedra, baby, I'm so sorry about everything—"

Cutting him off, she nuzzled his neck. "It's OK,
Simeon. I don't want to look back. Let the bad
things that happened between us stay in the past."

He stood and kissed her again and again. Nedra
was feeling well-loved as he whispered his love for
her into her ear. He stepped back for a moment,
pulled a small box out of his pocket, and handed it
to her.

"What's this?"

He sat down in the chair and pulled her into his
lap. "Go ahead . . . open it."

Nedra opened it with anticipation. She was
stunned when she laid eyes upon the diamond
ring before her. She was speechless. "Wow!"

"Is that all you can say?"

"Oh no, baby. Thank you. It's beautiful."

"Wait. Let me put it on you."

Nedra held her right hand out, but Simeon
reached for her left hand instead.

Nedra tilted her head with confusion. "Simeon,
what are you doing?"

"Nedra, I do love you, whether you believe me
or not. I know I haven't been the easiest man to
deal with over the past few months, and to show
you just how much I love you, I want you to wear
this ring. I want to marry you. Will you please be
my wife?"

"Are you serious?"

"I couldn't be more serious," he said while kissing her hand. "So what do you say?"

Nedra was in awe. On one hand, she believed he
really did love her because of the lengths he went

to lately to make sure she was happy and satisfied. She knew there was nothing he wouldn't do for her. On the other hand, she'd seen his dark side. You don't hit someone you claim to love, and she wasn't completely convinced his irrational behavior was stress related. However, two months had passed and Simeon hadn't even raised his voice to her.

"Well? Are you going to marry me or what, Miss Harris?"

"Let's enjoy tonight, Simeon. I'm a little shocked and need a chance to let this absorb."

"I can do that. Now, let's eat so I can get to dessert," he said while stroking her thigh."

Nedra's dinner pleased Simeon, and her acceptance of his ring all but told him she wanted to be his wife. He did love her, more than life itself.

After dinner, Simeon hurried Nedra upstairs to her bedroom. The short red dress she had on was no match for his hands as he quickly removed it. She lay back on the bed and smiled as he removed his tie and shirt. Nedra sat up and helped him unbuckle his pants and push them to the floor. She sighed as she lay back on the bed in red satin undergarments. Simeon's eyes glazed over as he kissed her neck, lips, and stomach. She squirmed as he removed her bra and then her panties. Her breath was very shallow and she lay there with anticipation. Simeon wanted to give Nedra the pleasure and joy she deserved, and he wasn't about to rush. He began by kissing her breathless while stroking her center. He nibbled on her breasts and lips until her skin was sizzling. He kissed his way down her body and back up again. Nedra closed her eyes because everything he was doing to her was sheer torture.

"I love you, Nedra," he whispered.

She felt the rhythm of her heart speed up when he started sucking her toes. This was a first for her, and the sensuality of it caused her to pant loudly. He took pleasure in watching her body go through the different changes as he pleasured her in different ways.

"Simeon."

He knew what she wanted, and he was ready to give it to her. Before disappearing between her thighs, he whispered, "Don't take your eyes off me."

The moment she felt his lips on her, she screamed. He had a special way of flicking his tongue against her sensitive area, and he wouldn't stop until he'd had his fill of her. Simeon was turned on by her moans and whimpers as he savored her for several long minutes until her toes curled uncontrollably. He was very receptive to how her body responded to him, and when she was near tears he finally joined his body with hers and made love to her until her body shook violently against his.

Later, as Nedra lay totally exhausted, her body was still tingling, and she felt like an electrical charge was running through her. When she closed her eyes, she could still feel his lips all over her body. Simeon was sleeping soundly as she admired the huge diamond on her finger. As she studied it, she realized it had to be at least four carats. She loved the diamonds on the band, and it glistened in the candlelight. She still hadn't given him an answer, and she was unsure if she could. Simeon wasn't a patient man, and she knew he wouldn't wait long for an answer. Since Tyree, she had been afraid to commit to any relationship—until now.

* * *

Donovon was furious with Nedra. She showed him the ring in his office the next morning and told him she was considering marrying Simeon. Donovon was so angry, he couldn't even speak.

"Come on, Donovon. I believe he's changed. It's been months and we haven't even had an argument. He even took an anger management class."

He jumped up out of his chair and made a fist with his hands. "Just because he hasn't hit you in a while and he went to anger management classes doesn't mean he won't hit you again. Where's your brain, Nedra?"

She felt her head throbbing. She wanted Donovon to be happy for her, but in the back of her mind, she knew he was going to be furious.

"I have a brain, Donovon. Can't you just be happy for me?"

"No! He's dangerous! That man doesn't love you. He only wants to control you."

"I appreciate your concern for me, but Simeon has changed, whether you want to believe it or not, and I would appreciate it if you would try to get along with him."

He released her and shook his head in disbelief. "I know if your Dad knew about this, he would feel the same way I do."

"Donovon! You wouldn't dare tell my parents!"

"I will if I have to. Somebody needs to talk some sense into you. It's obvious that I can't."

"I'm sorry I told you," she yelled as she walked out of his office.

"So am I!"

She slammed his door, which let everyone in the office know they were feuding. After she was gone, he picked up a glass and threw it against the wall. There was no way he was going to let this wedding take place.

Donovon and Nedra didn't see or speak to each other for the rest of the day. It was hard for both of them to concentrate on work when they were so upset with each other. On the way home, Nedra called Donovon, but got his voicemail instead. As she waited for his answering machine to pick up, she couldn't help but feel sad. After listening to his message, she spoke.

"Look, Donovon, I'm sorry about this morning. I didn't tell you about the ring to upset you. I want you to be happy for me. I value your advice, but I've made my decision. Please try to understand, because I'm going to need you just like I have over the past years. I will never forget us. Call me later, and I do love you, Donovon."

She hung up and continued her drive home, hoping for a quiet evening of rest and relaxation.

Donovon walked into the house and threw his keys on the table. He had skipped lunch, so he picked up some beer and ribs with all the fixings on the way home. A ballgame was coming on later, so he wanted to make sure he had everything set. Earlier he had talked to Brea, who noticed he wasn't in a talking mood. She tried to get to the bottom of his solemn mood, but he didn't let his guard down. He usually didn't let Brea know when he was upset with Nedra because she wasn't completely comfortable with the relationship anyway.

"Baby, are you sure you're OK?"

"I'm sure," he said as he pulled a beer out of the refrigerator. "Look, it's just some stuff at work that's getting on my nerves."

"Are you sure? I mean, I can come over to help take your mind off of it."

Popping the top on the beer, he sighed. "I know, but I won't be good company. I'm just going to watch the game and then crash. I'll talk to you tomorrow."

"If you change your mind, give me a call."

"I will. Thanks for checking on me."

"No problem," she answered, smiling. "Enjoy the game."

"Good night, Brea."

Brea hung up the phone, but she was sure the cause of his solemn mood had more to do with Nedra than work and she needed to know what was going on. Grabbing her purse, she decided to pay Nedra a visit. She remembered where she lived because she had gone to dinner with Donovon there, and double dated with Nedra and Simeon on several occasions. In fact, Brea found out that she and Simeon had a lot in common. He was a lawyer and she was a paralegal.

As Nedra poured dressing on her salad at home, she thought about Donovon. She was sad that he hadn't returned her call yet. It was at that moment that the doorbell chimed. She wasn't expecting anyone, and Simeon wasn't due to come by for another couple of hours. When she looked out the window and saw Brea's Infiniti, her heart jumped into her throat.

She swung the door open in a panic.

"Brea! What's wrong? Has something happened to Donovon?"

Brea saw it with her own eyes. She saw the deep love Nedra had for *her* man.

"Calm down, Nedra. Donovon's fine. He's at home watching a game."

Nedra put her hand over her heart and leaned against the door. "Thank God. What brings you over here?"

Pointing to a chair, she asked, "Do you mind if I sit down?" Nedra closed the front door.

"No, go right ahead."

Brea sat down and crossed her legs.

"Can I get you anything to drink?"

"No, I'll make this quick. I don't know what's going on between you and Donovon, but I don't like it. He is *my* man and you need to stay away from him. You're screwing up his head, and I don't appreciate it."

Nedra sat back in her seat. She was taken totally by surprise. "Excuse me? What are you talking about, Brea?"

"Don't play dumb with me. I know you two are more than friends. I'm not a fool!"

"Look, Brea, you have the wrong idea here. I mean, yes, I love Donovon. He's my best friend and I would go to hell and back for him, and he would do the same for me, but whatever you think is going on, isn't."

"So you admit it?"

Nedra stood and put her hands on her hips.

"What exactly are you trying to get me to admit, Brea? That I love Donovon? If so, that's never been a secret."

Brea rose slowly out of her chair and pulled her purse up on her shoulder. "That crap about you being friends ain't fooling anybody, Nedra."

Pointing her finger at Brea, Nedra had heard just about enough. "Now you wait just a damn minute!"

"No! You wait! I have eyes, and I'm warning you: stay away from him!"

Without responding to her, Nedra walked over to the door and opened it. "You can't tell me what to do, and you definitely can't keep me away from Donovon."

"We'll see about that," Brea promised.

"Whatever!"

Brea looked her up and down and slowly walked out the door. Nedra slammed it, furious that Brea would confront her like this. She grabbed her cordless phone and dialed Donovon's number. He picked up on the second ring.

"Yeah?"

"I just thought you should know that your little girlfriend just left my house confronting me about you!"

"What are you talking about, Nedra?" he asked, holding the phone away from his ear.

"Hello!! Donovon!! Are you listening to me? Brea just left my house!! She was in here warning me to stay away from you. You need to get your girl in check because she's lucky I didn't clock her ass!!"

Before he could respond, Nedra slammed the phone down. Donovon's blood pressure started to elevate, first, because Brea had approached Nedra. Second, their cat fight had interrupted him from watching the game. He cursed and dialed Brea's cell phone.

"Hello?" she casually answered.

"What the hell is wrong with you?"

"I knew your little girlfriend wouldn't waste any time calling you. Is something going on with you guys? Tell me the truth, baby, because if you are, I can handle it. But I won't allow you to make a fool of me."

"Brea, you were out of line. If you want to know about Nedra, ask me! You got that?"

She was silent on the line.

"Brea!"

"I'm here."

"What did you say to her?"

"I told her she's using the friendship as a cover. I know you love her, Donovon, so don't lie."

"What?"

"It's true, Donovon. There's no hiding it. I'm a woman and women can pick up on these things."

"I don't believe this," he calmly mumbled.

"Does she know you're in love with her?"

He was silent for a moment.

"Stay out of this, Brea. You're messing with things you don't understand."

Through tears, she nodded and said, "I understand completely, Donovon."

"Good-bye."

The phone line went dead. Donovon slowly hung up the telephone, opened another beer, and tried his best to get back into the football game.

Chapter Twenty-Seven

Make Love, Not War

The next morning, Nedra and Donovon stared at each other from across the conference room table for their Tuesday morning meeting. Neither had the opportunity to greet the other when they arrived earlier that morning. Their eyes revealed a lot that needed to be said, but it would have to wait until later. She almost didn't hear her boss ask her about the upcoming business trip. She broke eye contact with Donovon and responded to him.

"Yes, I have everything set up and ready to go."

Her boss thumbed through a stack of papers and looked up at her. "Do you have a copy of the itinerary?"

"Yes. I got it a few minutes ago."

Her boss scanned some reports and shook his head.

"I don't like these numbers." He turned to Donovon and Lawrence. "I want you guys to go also. This will give you a chance to go over the client's files and revise whatever needs to be revamped. Lawrence, make sure the SUV has been serviced before you leave today."

Lawrence nodded and entered information on his Palm Pilot. "Got it."

"If nobody has anything else, I guess we can all get back to work," their boss said as he adjourned the meeting.

Nedra stood and put all of her paperwork into a folder. Donovon couldn't help but admire how nice she looked in her beige suit. The skirt was short and displayed her beautiful legs, but it was also professional. As she turned to leave, Donovon stopped her.

"Nedra, wait up a second."

She waited for him to catch up to her. They walked out the door together and toward their offices.

"We need to talk. Do you have a second?"

"Sure," she answered as she walked stride for stride with him.

He opened the door so she could enter his office. She sat down as Donovon hung up his jacket. He came around in front of her and sat on the edge of his desk.

"Look, I'm sorry I didn't call you back last night. Brea was out of line. I don't know what she said to you, but I want you to know that I'm sorry."

Nedra leaned back and crossed her legs. "Why are you apologizing for her?"

"I don't know, Nedra. I just don't like it when we argue. I'm sorry for going off on you about Simeon, but I meant every word I said. He's dangerous and you don't need to marry him."

She stood up and hugged him, lingering in his arms. Her perfume caressed his nostrils and his heart started to thump against his ribs.

"Thank you, and I appreciate you taking care of me. I just want to move forward and get past all of this."

"So do I, Nedra."

Before releasing him, she kissed him softly on the lips. "No more arguing, OK?"

"Agreed."

His lips were tingling from the sensual contact. Picking up her folder, she turned to him and smiled.

"Get back to work, McNeil, and get plenty of rest tonight. We're pulling out no later than six thirty sharp."

"Yes, ma'am," he answered as he walked her to his door.

"Does Brea know we're going out of town?"

He shoved his hands in his pockets and leaned again the wall.

"Yeah she knows. She tried to apologize to me for showing up on your doorstep but I wasn't hearing it. She had the nerve to ask me if she could go to Atlanta with me, but I told her it wasn't a good idea. She wanted to know where we were staying and even offered to get a separate room so we could start over."

Nedra folded her arms and watched Donovon's body language.

"Did you tell her where we were staying?"

"Yeah I told her, but she knows I'm stilled pissed off at her for fronting you like that. My relationship with Brea is over."

"If you say so, Donovon, but if you're serious, you need to make sure *she* knows it's over."

"I guess."

Before walking out of his office, she wiped the remnants of her lipstick from his lips. "I'll talk to you later," she whispered.

"Bye, Nedra."

Chapter Twenty-Eight

Breaking Point

Simeon left court and headed to his usual spot. After several glasses of liquor, one of his lady friends approached.

"Well, well, well. Where have you been hiding?"

Motioning for her to join him, he smiled up at her.

"I haven't been hiding. I'm engaged, so I'm trying to be a good boy."

The lady laughed out loud. "Really? That would be a first."

He swallowed the strong, brown liquid. "Yeah. Why? Have you missed me?"

She stroked his leg and licked his ear. "You bet. Now, why don't we get out of here and go somewhere quiet so I can congratulate you properly?"

Simeon swallowed another glass of liquor and removed her hand. "I thought I told you I was engaged."

"And the problem is? Honey, I know you and

you have an appetite that one woman can't quench. So, what are you going to do?"

Simeon was about to get up and leave until the woman put the cherry from her drink seductively into her mouth.

"Ah, what the hell!"

She clapped her hands in excitement.

"Baby, I'm going to make you feel so good that you'll reconsider getting married."

He laughed and tossed a tip on the table. They both stood at the same time and walked out of the bar into the parking lot. Simeon opened his car door for the woman and pushed his seat back.

"Are you ready for this, baby?" she asked.

He laughed, leaned back in his seat, and closed his eyes. He immediately heard the sound of his zipper, which alerted him that she wasn't going to waste any time. She looked into his eyes and winked before lowering her head. The moment he felt her warm, wet lips engulf him, he hissed and grabbed a fistful of her hair. She was an expert in her field, and Simeon was in ecstasy as he watched her take in all of him. He loved the sensations she was giving him, and as she quickened her pace, he felt the explosive wave of heat build up in his body. She tightened her grip on him and worked him over even harder. As his body shivered beneath her, he pulled her hair even tighter and he watched her work her magic on him. Simeon's restraint had been broken down, and he couldn't hold his tongue any longer. He cursed loudly as he exploded into her. Simeon was well aware that what he was doing was wrong, but a man would have to be a fool to pass up pleasure of this magnitude.

* * *

Nedra woke up at four a.m. to get ready for her trip. She thought maybe Simeon would've spent the night with her, knowing she was going out of town for a few days, but he didn't. As she climbed into the shower, she thought that he could've at least called to wish her a safe trip. She toweled off and hurriedly dressed. She didn't want to get behind schedule, so she made sure she packed all her essentials the night before. They would be in Atlanta until Friday, and in a way she was looking forward to a change of scenery. She sat her bag beside the door and decided to check the house once more. Returning to the living room, she decided to leave Simeon a note just in case he came by.

> Simeon,
> 　I was hoping to see you before I left for Atlanta. I guess you had to work late and didn't feel like driving over. Anyway, I'll see you Friday. You know how to reach me.
>
> 　　　　　　　　　　Love,
> 　　　　　　　　　　Nedra

As she taped the note to the mirror in the hallway, she heard a horn blowing outside. She peeked out and saw both Lawrence and Donovon pulling into the driveway. Before Donovon could get out of his car, she locked her door and approached them with her luggage. Donovon met her on the sidewalk and carried her luggage the rest of the way for her. Lawrence popped the hatch so Donovon could put her luggage in the back of the truck.

"Good morning," she said energetically.

"Good morning," the two men grumbled in unison.

"I guess it's a little early for you two, huh?"

"Something like that," Lawrence answered.

Donovon stood quietly beside the truck as he held the passenger front door open for her.

"You don't mind if I leave my car over here, do you? I didn't want Lawrence to drive all the way downtown to pick me up, and then have to double back over here to get you. "

"No, that's fine. And you go ahead and take the front. Your legs are longer than mine, and I'll be comfortable sitting in the back."

"If you say so."

Donovon opened the back door for her and helped her climb in. Before buckling her seatbelt she decided to offer her assistance.

"Lawrence, do you want me to drive so you can catch a nap?"

"Funny, Nedra. I'm just fine and will be even better once I stop by Mickey D's to get some coffee."

"I second that," Donovon grumbled.

The ride to Atlanta was mostly quiet between the trio. Nedra was anxious to get there and get to work. As she looked down at the diamond ring resting on finger, she realized that Simeon still hadn't returned her call.

Hours later, they checked into their hotel rooms before heading to their corporate office. Each one went about their jobs with their fellow coworkers. The day was short, but the next day they would start bright and early. Nedra was tired and could tell that Lawrence and Donovon were too. As they drove back to their hotel, Lawrence asked them about dinner plans.

"Do you guys want to grab some dinner on the way in or eat at the hotel?"

"It doesn't matter to me, Lawrence," Nedra responded.

Lawrence looked over to Donovon. "What about you, my man?"

"I don't care either. I just want to get back to the hotel as soon as possible. I'm wiped out."

"The hotel it is."

He pulled up in front of the valet station and shut off the engine. Lawrence exited the vehicle, handing the keys to the valet. Donovon opened the door for Nedra just as his cell phone rang.

"Hello?"

"Hey, Donovon. I was just checking to see how your day went," Brea greeted.

"Oh, you're talking to me now?"

"I'm sorry, Donovon. This thing between you and Nedra is hard to deal with, and I'm not sure I can handle it. If I didn't care for you so much, I wouldn't have reacted like I did."

Donovon frowned. "It's been a long day, Brea. I'm going to crash just as soon as we have dinner."

"I'm sorry your day was long, and I'm sorry I upset you."

Walking behind Nedra and Lawrence, he cut their conversation short.

"Forget it. Look, I'll talk to you later. Good-bye, Brea."

"Good-bye."

He caught up with Nedra and Lawrence as the hostess led them to a table.

"Is everything OK?"

Pulling out her chair for her, he took off his jacket and laid it across the back of his chair.

"Yeah. It was Brea."

"Oh," she sarcastically responded.

Lawrence was already giving the waitress his drink order. She asked both Nedra and Donovon for their order and disappeared. She was back in a flash with their drinks and appetizers.

Lawrence took a sip of bourbon and closed his eyes. "Ahhhh! Now that hits the spot."

Nedra shook her head and laughed. Donovon looked around the room and admired its décor.

"This is a nice hotel."

"It's cool," Lawrence admitted. "I'm glad we're close to the office so we don't have to fight that traffic."

"I'll drink to that." Donovon held up his glass of wine and laughed.

"Why are you so quiet, Nedra?" Donovon asked.

She massaged her neck. "I'm just tired."

He nodded in agreement. It wasn't long before their entrees arrived and the threesome dug into their meals. There wasn't much conversation during dinner, but each complimented the chef on their meals. Nedra had consumed approximately four glasses of wine when Donovon glared at her.

"Don't you think you need to slow down a little?"

Taking another sip, she sat her glass down and wiped her mouth. "I'm OK. This is really good."

"Don't let it sneak up on you, because you know

what can happen. We have to get up early in the morning."

Lawrence laughed at Nedra. "Damn, girl, you drink like a fish. I didn't know you could drink like that."

"Forget you! You guys are acting like I'm an alcoholic or something."

The two men laughed together.

"I don't want you losing control up in here. I don't think a table dance would look good on your resume," Lawrence joked.

Donovon couldn't help but laugh at Lawrence's comment. He was sort of known as the office comedian, and he was well liked by everyone. His green eyes and handsome smile definitely attracted the ladies, and at twenty-seven years old he had a lot more wisdom than most people his age. He was a little mysterious about his past and always avoided it when any of them would bring it up. All Nedra and Donovon cared about was that he was good at his job and he was a good friend to them.

"You're so ignorant. And for your information, I'm not drunk, Lawrence."

"If you say so. Are you guys finished? If so, I'll tell the waitress to bring the check. Nedra, do you want one more refill?" Donovon laughed again. "I think she's had enough."

Nedra's head swung around. "You're not my daddy, Donovon. Yes, Lawrence, I do need one for the road."

Donovon stood with a smirk on his face. "Excuse me a minute. I'll be right back."

He made his way to the restroom, which gave Nedra time for one more drink and for Lawrence to take care of the check. When he returned, Nedra and Lawrence were waiting for him at the door. Lawrence grabbed a few pieces of peppermint out of the bowl and they walked to the elevator. They got on, Donovon pushed the button, and they rode up in silence.

Lawrence looked over and nudged Nedra. "Do you need a designated escort to your room?"

She slapped him on the arm playfully. "Leave me alone, Lawrence. I told you I'm not drunk."

"But you're buzzing real good, aren't you?"

Nedra laughed as they exited the elevator and headed to their respective rooms. "Good night! I'll see you guys in the morning."

"Good night," the men answered in unison.

Within minutes, they were all inside their rooms preparing for bed.

Nedra still had not heard from Simeon. She dialed his number again and got his voicemail. When she heard the tone, she spoke softly into the phone.

"Simeon, I was trying to catch you before I went to bed. Please call me so I'll know you're OK. You're starting to make me worry about you."

She hung up, looked down at her engagement ring, then grabbed her toiletries and headed to the shower.

Chapter Twenty-Nine

Reminiscing

An hour or so had passed and Nedra lay in bed watching TV, bored. She thought about calling Donovon to see what he was doing, but she didn't want to disturb him. He had mentioned on several occasions that he was exhausted and wanted to get some sleep. Little did she know, he was down the hall, just as bored as she was. Lawrence, on the other hand, had gotten a second wind and was busy playing an NFL game on the hotel's PlayStation.

Scanning the channels, Donovon gave up and walked over to the window. Looking out over the Atlanta skyline he turned to look at the telephone. Taking a chance, he called Nedra's room to see if she was up.

"Hello?"

"Did I wake you?"

Flipping over on her back she sighed. "Nah, I was just lying here bored to death."

"Me too." He sighed.

They were silent for a moment as if waiting on the other to come up with a suggestion.

"Do you want to come over and hang out with me?"

"Are you sure?"

"Get your butt down here, Donovon."

He laughed. "I'll be over in a sec."

"I'll be waiting."

They hung up the phone and Nedra continued to try to find something decent to watch on TV. Within minutes, there was a knock at her door. Dressed in her flannel pajamas, she opened the door.

"Come on in."

Donovon stepped through the door and closed it behind him.

"Have you found anything to watch yet?"

Tossing him the remote, she crawled up on the bed. "No, you try."

Donovon sat down on the edge of the bed and scanned the channels.

"Here we go!" he yelled. "*Kiss the Girls* with Morgan Freeman and Ashley Judd! This is a good movie. Have you seen it?"

Nedra had already curled up on the pillows. "I don't think so."

Donovon scooted back on the bed next to her. "I think you'll like it."

She nodded, laid her head on his chest, and began to watch the movie.

"Donovon?"

"Huh?"

"This is just like old times, huh? I miss hanging out with you like this."

He caressed her back. "My door is always open for you, Nedra."

She looked up into his eyes. "I'm going to do better," she whispered.

"You'd better. Now be quiet. The movie's starting."

It was way into the night when Nedra got up to go to the bathroom. Donovon was snoring, so she did her best not to wake him. They used to hang out like this all the time when they were in college. When she crawled back onto the bed, Donovon stirred out of his sleep.

"What time is it?"

Laying her head against his chest again, she said, "It's about two. Go back to sleep."

He sat up. "I need a bathroom break myself."

She watched him slide out of bed and into the bathroom. His T-shirt and sweats showed off a very fit physique. All the women he dated were very protective of him, and they had a reason to be. Seconds later he returned to the room and stood over her.

"I'd better get to my room so I can get some sleep."

"You don't have to leave," Nedra said through a yawn.

Teasing, he decided to challenge her. "Are you sure you want to share you bed with me again? You know what happened the last time you drank a lot of wine."

"Don't be silly. I'm sure I'll be able to contain myself this time."

He picked up a pillow and fluffed it. "It's not you I'm worried about. It's hard for me to be close to you like this."

They stared at each other in silence. They were both remembering their night in Miami. To break up the awkwardness, he hit her with the pillow playfully.

"Donovon! Stop playing. It's late."

He hit her again. "I thought you wanted to have some fun in Atlanta."

Nedra sat up on her knees and grabbed another pillow, swinging at him. "See what you've started?"

She giggled as she chased him around the room, hitting him with the pillow. He fought back playfully. This went on for a minutes until Nedra dived on his back, causing them to fall onto the bed.

"OK, Nedra, you win! Dang! I forgot how strong you were. Lifting weights at the gym has paid off for you."

Breathing hard, she giggled. "I can't believe you picked a pillow fight with me."

"I wanted to see if you still had it in you."

She straddled him and held his arms above his head. Staring down at him, she chastised him.

"Donovon McNeil, you are too old to be so silly. Now go to sleep. Good night."

He lay there, staring up at her. She saw the strange look in his eyes. It was the same look she'd seen at the beach house. She released his arms and shifted to move off of him, but he grabbed her hips, holding her there.

"Donovon," she begged as chills ran over her body.

He rolled her over, changing positions with her. Her heart was beating loudly in her chest. Without saying a word, he leaned down and kissed her tenderly on the lips. Nedra gasped as he magically toyed with her mouth. The softness of her body caused his lower body to harden and throb. She squirmed under him as he kissed her neck tenderly.

"Donovon," she called out breathlessly.

Making eye contact with her again, he ignored her pleas. She moaned as he kissed her harder on the lips. The sensations felt incredible, but she wasn't supposed to be enjoying them.

Gasping for air, she yelled again. "Donovon!"

He pulled himself away and hurried out of her room, slamming the door behind him. Nedra lay there in total shock. Donovon hadn't made a move on her in a long time. Lying there, she tried to compose herself, but it was difficult because she could still feel his lips on her body. Sitting up, she picked up the telephone and dialed his room.

"Yeah."

"What was that?" she questioned.

He sighed. "I'm sorry. I don't know what got into me. It won't happen again. OK?"

"It felt good."

He was silent.

"Look, Donovon, I know it hasn't been fair to you that I haven't given us a chance, and the reason is that I'm scared. I'm afraid of failing at loving you just like I've failed at all my other relationships. Your friendship has been the one relationship that I've had with a man that has been secure. I can't risk ruining that."

He was still silent.

She sighed. "Are you hearing me?"

"Yeah, I hear you, but I disagree with your reasoning. Kevin was an idiot and he took you for granted. You were too trusting of him, Nedra. The signs were right in front of you, but you just didn't see them. Now Tyree, I don't know. Maybe it was the stardom and the money that made it hard for him to resist temptation. I do believe he really loved you, but because he was a preacher's kid, he felt like he had no choice but to do what he did."

"I really can pick them, can't I?"

"Sometimes you have to pick through some bad apples before you find a ripe one. Don't be so hard on yourself, Nedra. The day will eventually come when you'll open your heart to the right man for you. You'll see."

Now it was her time to be quiet.

He broke the silence. "It's late and we both need to get some rest."

"You're right. Good night."

"Good night, Nedra."

Chapter Thirty

The Morning After

The next morning at breakfast Donovon sat across the table and watched as Nedra tried to call Simeon for the millionth time. Lawrence hadn't joined them yet, but he was on his way. Nedra hung up her cell phone, disgusted. She picked up her glass of orange juice and took a sip. Donovon poured cream in his coffee and pulled a biscuit out of the basket centered on the table.

"Are you still having trouble getting in touch with your future husband?"

She slid her phone back into her purse. "I don't understand why he won't return my calls. I guess it's as clear as the writing on the wall if I would just read it."

"I told you. You've wasted too much time with him already."

"I should've never accepted this ring," she said while staring down at her hand. "I don't know what I was thinking."

"You accepted it because you believed in him and the fairy tale. You are a trusting and loving woman. You shouldn't have to change a person in order for them to be what you need in your life."

They could see Lawrence approaching the table.

"When we get back home, I'm giving him back the ring."

"Are you sure?"

"Yes, I'm sure," she said with confidence.

"Hey guys! Sorry I'm late," Lawrence explained as he sat down at the table.

Nedra picked up her menu, and for the first time in a long time she felt relieved.

"You're fine, Lawrence. We were just getting ready to order."

Donovon's mind was traveling a thousand miles an hour. Could he really trust that Nedra was ready to completely walk away from Simeon? Time would tell, but he hoped she was serious before Simeon seriously hurt or killed her. Then he could finally love her like she deserved.

Later that evening, they returned to the hotel after another long day at work.

"One more night," Nedra mumbled as the threesome walked through the hotel lobby.

Lawrence pushed the elevator button and started dancing.

"So are you two up for some clubbing tonight? We leave tomorrow, so it wouldn't hurt to party on our last night."

The elevator doors opened up on their floor and Nedra threw up her hands in defense.

"Count me out. You two can go right ahead. I'm going to get out of these shoes, order room service, and pray a decent movie's on tonight."

Lawrence turned to Donovon and rubbed his hands together. "That leaves you and me, playa. Are you game?"

He glanced over at Nedra, who was opening the door to her room.

"Why not? Count me in."

"Good!"

They continued down the hallway to their rooms. Before opening his door, Donovon looked at his watch.

"So what time is this night out on the town going to start?"

"How about in an hour?" Lawrence replied as he looked at his watch. "We can catch the train downtown to grab some dinner, then hit the clubs."

"OK, I'll see you in an hour," Donovon said.

Nedra moved about her room, undressing. What she needed tonight was a hot, soapy bubble bath. Before starting her ritual, she placed a call to room service and ordered a chicken dinner with all the fixings and a bottle of wine. She knew she probably wouldn't see the guys until the morning, so tonight was her night for a little private pampering.

The tub in her room was massive, and luckily the hotel accommodated it with aromatherapy candles, which set the room aglow. She turned out the lights, closed her eyes, and lay back in the bubbles. It was so peaceful and beautiful, but she couldn't help but feel sad. She opened her eyes, looked at the sparkling diamond on her finger, and cried. Her cell phone rang, startling her. She thought it was Simeon finally calling back, but it was her mother.

"Hello, Momma."

"Hey, baby! How are you?"

"I'm fine," she solemnly answered.

"It doesn't sound like you're fine," her mother said with concern. "What's wrong?"

Playing with the bubbles, she assured her mother that everything was fine. "It's nothing, Momma. Where's Daddy?"

"He's cooking dinner. Now tell me what's wrong."

Splashing the water, she lied. "It's nothing, really. I guess I'm just ready to get back home."

"How are things going in Atlanta?"

"It's been fine. Tomorrow is our last day."

"You've been so sad lately, and I'm worried about you."

"I know, Momma," she answered, smiling. "But you don't have to worry."

"I can't help it, Nedra.

Seconds later there was a knock at her door, and it was loud enough for her mother to hear it.

"Was that someone knocking?"

"Yes. It's my dinner arriving. I love you, Momma, and tell Daddy I love him as well. Thanks for checking on me. I'll call you when I get home."

"Drive safely tomorrow."

"Will do. Good night."

She pulled the drain in the tub, slid into her robe, and answered the door. The waiter brought in her platter and placed it on the table.

"Will there be anything else?"

"No, I think I have everything I need," she answered as she signed the ticket.

She handed the ticket back to him and thanked him.

"Have a good night and enjoy your dinner."

"Good night."

After closing the door, she walked over to inspect her dinner. Everything was hot and she couldn't wait to dig in. Just as she was about to begin eating, there was another knock on her door. Frowning, she answered the door to find Donovon and Lawrence standing there grinning.

She cracked the door and looked them up and down.

"Well, don't you two look nice? What can I do for you guys?"

Lawrence laughed. "We smell food. What you got up in there?"

"None of your business! I thought you two were going out to dinner."

Donovon teased her as well. "Let us in, Nedra, so we can sample your dinner."

"No way! Besides, I'm not decent!"

"That's an even better reason to let us in."

"You're dreaming! I hope you have a great time tonight. Now if you don't mind, my dinner is waiting on me."

"Come on, Nedra."

"No, Donovon! Good night!"

She closed the door and could hear them laughing as they walked down the hall to the elevator.

Chapter Thirty-One

Party Time

The club was full as expected. There were so many women out it had Lawrence's head spinning. Donovon wasn't doing as much hunting as Lawrence was. The night was almost over and he already had a pocket full of phone numbers

"Donovon, did you see the body on that one? She'd make a brotha turn in his playa's card for real!"

Sipping on his vodka, Donovon laughed. "She was fine, but you better pay closer attention to the Adam's apple."

"No shit! It is kind of scary doing this, because you just never know."

They laughed as they sat watching people coming and going throughout the club. They had danced with several ladies and knew they should be heading back to the hotel. An hour later, they decided to call it a night.

On the cab ride back, Lawrence turned to Donovon. "Can I ask you something?"

"Sure."

"Why haven't you and Nedra hooked up?"

"Because she's my friend."

Lawrence elbowed him and continued to quiz him. "I know that, but you have eyes, don't you? The woman is gorgeous! Don't tell me you haven't thought about getting with her."

"I've been looking at Nedra for years, and yes, I have eyes, so I know she's gorgeous."

"So, have you thought about it?"

"I'd have to be a robot not to think about it a time or two," Donovon admitted.

"So answer my question. Why haven't you two hooked up?"

Donovon didn't know he was frowning, but he was. "Nedra's engaged, Lawrence, and I'm dating Brea."

He sat back in the seat and mumbled.

"You don't love that woman. I've seen you two together. There's something about her that doesn't fit you. Now, Nedra, she turns every man's head and it's not all because of her physical attributes. I don't see how you can just be friends with her. Whew!"

Donovon looked at him again and shook his head. He then felt his cell phone vibrate. He looked at it and noticed that he had missed a call. He decided to check the message and found out that it was Brea.

"Hey, baby, I hope you're out enjoying yourself. I just wanted to call you back and tell you I'm going to apologize to Nedra when I see her, and I have a nice surprise for you when you get back. See you soon."

Lawrence watched Donovon's facial expression as he hung up the cell phone.

"Who was that?"

"Brea."

Lawrence shook his head with disgust. "See what I mean? You're not even enthusiastic about her calling, and she's supposed to be your woman."

The rest of the ride to the hotel was in silence. It was late, both of them were tired, and Donovon had a lot on his mind. Lawrence was right about one thing—he didn't love Brea.

When they exited the cab, Donovon paid the driver. "Are you coming up?" Lawrence asked.

Donovon walked toward the bar in the hotel garden area. "A little later. I want to chill out here for a while."

"OK. I'll see you in the morning."

"Good night, Lawrence."

As soon as Donovon took a seat at the bar, the bartender approached to get his drink order. He normally didn't drink strong liquor, but for some reason, tonight he needed his conscience to be quiet. Four vodkas and an hour later, he made his way toward the elevator. On the ride up, all the alcohol he had consumed had kicked in with a vengeance. He started sweating and couldn't help but think about what Lawrence had said on the cab ride back to the hotel.

Exiting the elevator, he slowly made his way toward his room. When he got to Nedra's room, he stopped and braced himself against the wall. His heart was pounding and his head was spinning. Leaning against her door, he found the strength to knock. Nedra was startled out of her sleep by the sound of knocking at her door. She tiptoed over to it and peeped out. It was Donovon, and he didn't look well. She opened the door and he practically fell into her room. She was able to keep him from hitting the floor by helping him over to her bed.

"What's wrong with you, Donovon?"

His eyes were closed, but he was able to mumble. "I think I had a little too much to drink."

Standing there in her pajamas, she looked down at him. "Why did you do something so foolish? We have to go to work in a couple of hours!"

"Stop yelling at me, Nedra. I'm sick."

Pushing him over in her bed, she frowned. "What you need to do is sleep it off. Move over!"

She helped him out of his jacket and shoes. He fell back onto her bed, so she covered him with an extra blanket. Within seconds he was snoring. She turned out the lights, crawled under her comforter, and went back to sleep.

A couple of hours later, Nedra woke up to the sound of Donovon throwing up in her bathroom. She jumped up out of bed went to his aid.

"Are you going to be OK?"

He couldn't answer her as he leaned over the toilet. She grabbed a cold cloth and placed it on his head. They had been through a similar scene before when they were in college together, and when she thought about it, she started laughing.

Donovon found the strength to ask, "What's so funny?"

"You. Don't you remember homecoming senior year?"

"Don't remind me," he moaned.

She continued to laugh as she walked over to her table and turned on the coffee maker. He pulled himself up off the floor and sat on the side of the bathtub with his head in his hands.

"You never could handle liquor well, Donovon. What did you drink?"

"Vodka."

She grimaced at him. "Not good, babe."

"I know. I'm going to pay for it the rest of the day."

"You got that right."

He sighed and asked for a toothbrush. She handed one to him, as well as some mouthwash.

"What brought this on? Talk to me."

He shook his head and took a deep breath. In silence, he walked over to the sink and brushed his teeth.

"There's nothing to talk about," he said after rinsing out his mouth out with the mouthwash.

"Come in here so I can pour you some coffee."

He sat at her table and looked out over the skyline as he waited for the coffee. Nedra made herself a cup as well.

"You really look pitiful. What am I going to do with you, Donovon?"

He took the cup from her hand. "I don't know." he said softly.

They sipped their coffee in silence for a moment.

"Are you feeling any better since you coughed up your dinner?"

"If you can make the room stop spinning, I'll be fine."

"How much did you drink?"

He laid his head down on the table. "I don't know. I lost count," he mumbled.

"That's dangerous, Donovon," she scolded him. "Don't do that again."

"I won't."

She stared at him and admired his handsome features. Finishing off her coffee, she realized Donovon had dozed off to sleep. There was no way she could get him down the hall to his room by herself. She didn't want to wake Lawrence, so she helped him up and back to her bed. He immediately fell into an alcohol-induced slumber. Nedra caressed his face, then kissed him softly on the lips before going back to sleep herself.

Chapter Thirty-Two

Busted!

Nedra's alarm clock went off around the same time there was a knock at the door. She slowly opened the door and unexpectedly stood face to face with Brea. She bit down on her lower lip and looked over to see Donovon still in a deep sleep. She tightened the belt on her robe nervously because she knew this looked bad with Donovon in her bed.

"Nedra, have you seen Donovon? He didn't come back to his room last night."

Over Nedra's shoulder, Brea noticed movement in the bed. She recognized the physique immediately. Angry, she stormed into the room and started yelling.

"No wonder you didn't make it back to your room last night, because you were up in here, getting your freak on with your girl, you son of a bitch!"

Nedra tried to get Brea's attention. She stood between her and the bed and called out to her.

"Brea, it's not what it looks like! Donovon is hung over from going out last night."

"Oh really? I bet you took real good care of him, too!"

Donovon got up out of the bed, fully clothed, and hung his head. "Brea, nothing happened between me and Nedra. All I did was sleep in her room last night."

"It doesn't matter what you have on now. You were here with her all night, Donovon! I can't believe you would do this to me! Didn't you get my message?"

He was holding his head in pain. All the yelling was causing the throbbing to get worse. He tried to talk as quietly as possible, but Brea was still yelling.

"Brea, when you told me you had a surprise for me when I got back, I didn't know you meant surprising me here at the hotel. I thought you meant at home."

Tears were streaming down her cheeks.

"I've never been as humiliated as you two have made me feel right now. If you want to be together that bad, go right ahead! I've had about enough!"

Donovon stood and tried to hurry her out of the room.

She pushed him away.

"Don't touch me! Just stay the hell away from me!"

Nedra didn't know what to say. As a woman in Brea's position, she actually could see why she was so angry. The situation didn't look good, and she probably would react the same way if she caught Simeon in bed with a friend of his. She felt it was her duty to do what she could to help Donovon.

"Brea! Please listen. Nothing happened . . ."

From that point, all Nedra saw were stars. She couldn't believe Brea had slapped her. Donovon sobered up quickly when he saw the look in Nedra's eyes. He quickly pushed Brea out of the way before a full fight ensued.

"What the hell is wrong with you? Don't you ever put your hands on her again, do you understand?"

Brea stood there breathing hard, not caring what Donovon was saying. Nedra took a deep breath and turned to Brea.

"I'm sorry you don't understand what Donovon and I have between us. Nothing happened, Brea, but if you ever touch me again, I won't be responsible for my actions."

As Nedra walked toward the bathroom, Donovon grabbed her arm. "Are you OK?"

Nedra nodded that she was and closed the door behind her. When he turned, Brea had her arms folded and she was mumbling to herself.

"Is she OK? What about me?"

Brea was livid that his concern was with Nedra and not with her. Donovon grabbed his jacket and Brea by the arm and pushed her out the door. He angrily escorted her down the hallway to his room as she continued to voice her disgust. Once inside, he got in her face because it was his time to yell.

"First of all, how in the hell did you get into my room? Secondly, from what I got out of our last conversation, you were fed up with me, so don't come down here trying to lay claims on me! Thirdly, you've lost your mind if you think putting your hands on Nedra is going to solve anything! Your issue is with me, not her!"

Brea laughed. "You'd be surprised how easy it is

to get what you want just by being a good tipper. I gave the maid a hundred dollars to let me in your room and to find out what Nedra's room number was, and it was worth every penny. You're a piece of work, Donovon. You don't care about me. Like I said before, you're in love with her. Well, you don't have to worry about me anymore. I came down here to see if I was making a mistake, but I guess not. I hope you two have a wonderful life together."

He opened his suitcase and pulled out a bottle of Tylenol. "You are going to apologize to her."

Walking toward the door, Brea laughed again. "You must be crazy. There's no way in hell I'm going to apologize to her. If you want her, you got her!"

He looked up at her, clearly angry as he popped the pills into his mouth. After taking a sip of water, he shook his head.

"You're a piece of work, Brea."

"So are you!"

He went into the bathroom and threw some water on his face.

"I think you need to go home. You've caused enough trouble here."

She stood in the doorway with her arms folded. "Just so there won't be any kind of misunderstanding this time, I'm leaving, and I mean it this time."

She slammed the door as she exited his room. Donovon didn't even acknowledge Brea's exit. He sat on the side of his bed and dialed Nedra's number.

"Hello?"

"Nedra, I'm so sorry about all of this. Brea had no right to put her hands on you."

"She had a right to be upset, Donovon. You shouldn't have been in my bed."

"It's not like we haven't shared a bed before."

"We're not in college anymore, Donovon. Look, Donovon, maybe we need to chill from hanging around each other so you and Brea can work this out."

"You're talking crazy now."

"No, I'm serious. I'm a woman, and it would be hard to accept your man having a female best friend that seemed to always be hanging around."

"Brea can step for all I care. Look, we'll have to talk about this later. It's almost time to get ready for work."

"OK. I'll see you in a few."

Donovon and Nedra hung up their telephones and dressed for work.

They checked out of their rooms because they only needed to work a half day to complete their assigned projects. They were ahead of schedule and would get home several hours earlier than originally predicted. It wasn't long before they were ready to head back home. Nedra drove while Lawrence slept in the backseat. Donovon slept the first hour of the return trip and welcomed the serenity after their horrendous night. The rest of the way home, they talked about work, music, and anything else except their relationship.

Nedra pulled up in the driveway and parked. Donovon climbed out to get their luggage out of the truck.

"Do you want me to walk you in before I pull off?" he asked.

"No, I'll be fine. I'm going to grab a bite to eat and go to bed. Be safe driving home."

"I will."

"Good-bye, Lawrence! Donovon, I'll holler at you in the morning."

Donovon opened his trunk. "Sounds good. Later."

Donovon climbed behind the wheel of his car and waited for Lawrence to back out of Nedra's driveway. They both backed out and pulled off.

Chapter Thirty-Three

The Truth Hurts

Nedra entered her house and turned on the lights. When she turned around, Simeon smacked her hard across the cheek. Her legs gave way and she hit the floor hard. He stalked over to her and yelled obscenities.

"I told you if I ever caught you messing around on me, I would kill you."

Nedra was stunned as she looked up into Simeon's enraged eyes.

"What are you talking about, Simeon?"

He pulled her up by her hair and pushed her over to the sofa. "I should be asking you that! Thanks to a telephone tip, I found out that you were in Atlanta messing around on me."

Nedra was rubbing her face, which was swelling. No one could've contacted Simeon but Brea.

"I wasn't messing around, Simeon. I was working, and whoever called you gave out bad information. I'm calling the police."

Nedra walked over to pick up the telephone,

but he grabbed it out of her hand and ripped the telephone from the wall. She was really afraid now, because he just might kill her. Just as he started toward her, the doorbell rang. Relieved, she hurried to open it. When she swung the door open she was startled to see Lawrence standing there with a concerned look on his face.

"Lawrence! What brings you back?"

He frowned when he noticed she was out of breath, her hair was tousled, and her clothes were out of place. He could see Simeon standing behind her and tears in her eyes.

"Are you OK?"

She closed her eyes briefly and swallowed. "I'm fine, just tired. What's up?"

"You left your laptop in back of the truck," he said as he extended the black case out to her.

He noticed her hands trembling as she reached out for it.

"Thanks. I was going to need that."

"Are you sure you're OK, Nedra?"

She nodded in silence.

"Oh, let me introduce you to my fiancé, Simeon Mathews. Simeon, this is my coworker, Lawrence."

Simeon ran his hand over his head with frustration.

"What's up, man?"

He didn't even shake Lawrence's hand. Instead he disappeared out of view. Lawrence didn't like the vibe he was getting from Nedra.

"You need to come with me," he whispered. "I can see something's not right here."

"I can't," she whispered back.

"You can and you will," he demanded.

Simeon walked back over to the door. "Aren't you two done yet?"

"It was nice meeting you, Simeon. Nedra, I'll wait for you outside."

She turned to Simeon. "I have to go to the office and download the information off my laptop. I would appreciate it if you would be gone when I get back or you will find your ass in jail. Do you understand?"

"You belong to me, Nedra! You're not walking out on me!"

Angry, she threw the ring at him and screamed, "I don't belong to you, and I want you out, Simeon, or I'm coming back with the police!"

She closed the door and hurried out to Lawrence's truck.

Nedra got an earful from Lawrence as soon as she got in the truck. He lectured her on domestic violence even though she didn't reveal anything specific to him. He told her he could see the signs because his mother had been a victim. She listened attentively and told him she appreciated his concern, but that she had everything under control.

Lawrence pointed to her face. "Nedra, I can see where he hit you. Damn! Do you want me to call Donovon?"

"No! Please! I don't want him to know about this. He would kill Simeon for sure."

"So would I," Lawrence replied softly.

She rubbed the area and repeated again to him that she had everything under control.

* * *

Hours later, Nedra cautiously returned to her house. Lawrence walked in with her and made sure Simeon wasn't once again waiting to ambush her. He purchased her a can of mace, but she refused to take the gun he offered her. She assured him that mentioning the police was enough to make Simeon go away, because he wouldn't want his image tarnished.

After Lawrence left, she locked the doors and tried to calm her nerves. Her stomach growled as she searched for food in her refrigerator. Closing it, she picked up the telephone and ordered some Chinese food. It was going to take about thirty minutes for them to arrive, so she carried her luggage upstairs to unpack. She was glad Simeon took her advice and left, but unfortunately he didn't take all his belongings with him. Her jaw was still very sore from the punch he'd so happily welcomed her home with, so she made her way back downstairs to gather some ice and placed it against her face.

A half hour later, Nedra paid the deliveryman for her dinner. By the time he'd arrived, she'd changed into some knit jogging pants and thick socks. She curled up on her bed, turned on the TV, and got ready for some good eating. Sitting there, she decided to check her caller ID box. On it were two unknown numbers, and her cell phone number from when she called home during her trip. She tried not to think about the fact that Brea was the only person who could've called Simeon, and that Simeon took her call when he didn't return any of Nedra's phone calls. She opened her nightstand to get out a pencil so she could jot down the unknown number, but she accidentally dropped it.

"Dang!"

Moving her dinner tray out of the way, she hopped out of bed to look for the pencil. She found it under the bed and placed it on her nightstand. As she sat there in a daze, thinking about Simeon and recent events, something out of the corner of her eye caught her attention.

"It can't be," she mumbled to herself.

She picked up the pencil and leaned down closer to the small garbage can beside her bed. Inside it was a condom and foil wrapper. Using the pencil, she lifted the condom out of the garbage can and placed it on a sheet of newspaper.

"Oh no he didn't!!" she yelled angrily.

Nedra couldn't believe Simeon had slept with someone in her bed while she was out of town. Even more sickening was that he was careless enough to leave the evidence behind for her to find. She was so furious, she couldn't think straight. As she sat staring at the condom she wondered who it could've been, even though at this point it really didn't matter. She still felt like she needed to give him a piece of her mind once and for all. First thing in the morning, she would box up the rest of his belongings and have them sent to his house for good.

Nedra had a hard time going to sleep after her traumatic day surrounding Simeon. Eventually she drifted off to sleep. Hours later, she was awakened by a presence in the room. When her vision cleared, she found Simeon standing over her. As soon as she gasped, he dragged her out of bed by her neck and threw her to the floor.

"Simeon! No!"

"Shut your damn mouth," he yelled.

She tried to scoot away from him.

"Where do you think you're going?" He grabbed her leg and dragged her back toward him.

"Simeon, please!"

Simeon knocked a table out of the way and pulled her up off the floor. "I'm just protecting what's mine, and you belong to me!"

"I don't belong to you! Just get out of here, Simeon," she begged.

He leaned down close to her. "You've pushed me for the last time! How dare you threaten to call the police on me? If I'm going to jail, I'm going to make it worth it."

Afraid of what he might do next, she tried to reach her purse so she could get to the mace, but he was holding her too tightly. He kissed her hard on the lips and slipped his hand into the waistband of her pants.

"I love you, Nedra!"

"No, you don't, Simeon!"

He was groping her and she couldn't stop him.

"I just want you to leave, and just so you know, I found your condom in the trash. I can't believe you brought another woman into my house. That's not love, Simeon."

When he opened his mouth for more lies to fly out, she put the palm of her hand up to his face and yelled.

"Talk to the hand, Simeon, because I'm not going for any of your lame excuses anymore. You're not the same man I met when I first moved here, and I want you to get out of my house!"

Simeon laughed and stopped groping her. He unexpectedly released her and Nedra inched her way over to her purse.

"That condom is not mine. You must've had somebody in here, and now you're trying to blame it on me."

She threw a drinking glass at him and yelled. "You bastard, Simeon! I have been nothing but faithful to you, and this is how you show your love? By hitting me any time you feel like it?"

He ducked, causing the glass to miss his head by inches. Quicker than lightning, he stalked over to her and grabbed her just as she reached her purse. He knocked her to the floor and straddled her body. Nedra was frantically trying to get the can of mace, but Simeon grabbed her hand.

"Mace! You were going to mace me! You bitch!!"

Crushing her body, he threw the can of mace across the room and screamed at her, "Who the hell have you been sleeping with, Nedra?"

Trying to knee him in the groin, she screamed for help, but he covered her mouth. She tried with all her strength to push him away, but she was unsuccessful. She could smell liquor on his breath as he leaned down and kissed her neck.

"You belong to me, Nedra, and you always will!"

The tears were stinging her eyes. She struggled to free herself, but she was tiring and he knew it. His hands were all over her as he ripped her clothes from her body. He pulled a gun from his pocket to add even more fear to the situation. While holding it to her head, he kissed her all over her body.

"You make me so hot, Nedra. Don't I make you feel good, baby?"

She was so afraid she was unable to answer him.

"Answer me!!"

"Yes," she whimpered.

Prying her thighs apart, he gritted his teeth and unzipped his pants. "You're my woman and no one else's. Don't you ever forget that!"

"Simeon! Please! Don't!"

He ran the muzzle of the gun across her cheek and kissed the tears running down her face.

"I'll never let you leave me."

Her cries were constant. She had no choice but to lie there as he forced himself on her. He moaned and groaned loudly with pleasure as he took what used to be beautiful between them and made it horrible. With the gun in his hand, he ordered her to moan. He wanted her to tell him how good he felt and how much she loved him. He thrust his body violently into hers for what seemed like hours. Finally, his body shuddered as his sperm flooded her body. He slowly loosened his grip on her neck as he lay on top of her, totally drained. The gun was still in his hand when he leaned down to kiss her breasts. She tried to push him away, but he grabbed her throat once more, causing her to scream out in pain.

"Tell me you love me."

She did as she was told and prayed he would leave without killing her. He kissed her greedily and she had to make herself kiss him back. She felt sick to her stomach, but she had to hold it in for her own sake. He rolled off her body and watched as she picked up her tattered clothing. He zipped up his pants and placed the gun back in his pocket. He walked over to her and pulled her into his arms.

"Nedra, if I ever catch you with another man, you're dead."

Nedra was numb and at the point of helplessness. He had violated her so horribly that she didn't care what happened next. She just wanted him gone.

"We're through, Simeon. And if what you just did doesn't prove it, nothing will."

Simeon became enraged. He began hitting her once again. She couldn't believe a man could hit a woman like Simeon was hitting her. When she hit the floor, her head hit hard. Before she could gather her senses, he was on top of her, squeezing the life out of her.

"This relationship is over when I say it's over!"

She tried again to loosen his grip, but he only tightened it more. She realized he was finally going to make good on his threats. She would never have the opportunity to get married, have children, or do anything else with her life. She was too young to die, especially like this. She was her parents' only child and they were going to be heartbroken to know that she had stayed in such an abusive relationship and kept it hidden from them.

As she started to black out, she wondered how she let herself get into this situation. Looking up into Simeon's enraged eyes, she heard a loud pop as she fought for one last breath just before the room went dark.

*   *   *

Nedra woke up, not knowing how long she had been unconscious. She slowly pulled her bruised body from the floor and entered the bathroom. She turned on the shower and began to wash the nauseating scent of Simeon from her body. Her cries rocked her body as she released all the anguish and hurt she had held in during the ordeal. After toweling off, she hurriedly dressed and pulled her suitcases from the closet. She had to hurry because if he returned before she could escape, she believed he would kill her for sure. She looked around the room and saw that he had shot several bullets into her ceiling. That must have been the loud noise she heard before blacking out. Tonight was the last time Simeon Mathews would lay a hand on her. Ever.

She packed as many of her belongings as she could and put them in her car. In the morning she would call her realtor and make arrangements to sell her house. Having the locks changed would allow her some time until she could get the rest of her possessions. It wouldn't hold Simeon back for long. She knew he wouldn't think twice about kicking the door in and doing what he seemed to do best—terrorize. He was no longer capable of love.

Chapter Thirty-four

The Last Straw

Donovon was in a deep slumber when he was jarred out of his sleep by the sound of his doorbell. He slid his six feet, four inch frame into his robe and hurried downstairs. He turned on the porch light and looked through the peephole and found Nedra standing there looking defeated. Seeing her bruised face on the other side of the door with suitcases in hand made his heart thump against his ribs.

He swung open the door in a panic. "Nedra, what the hell did Simeon do to you?"

All she could do was enter, lay her head against his broad chest, and sob. He pushed the door closed and wrapped his strong arms around her. Donovon already suspected what had gone down; however, tonight was the first time she had ever showed up with suitcases.

"Is it Simeon?"

She nodded in silence.

She was embarrassed and unable to look at him.

He tilted her chin so he could see her eyes, the bruised and swollen area on her cheek, and the bruises around her neck. Turning her face from side to side, he inspected her closely and could feel his blood pressure rising to the boiling point.

"Goddamn, Nedra! His ass is mine! Come into the kitchen so I can get you some ice."

Nedra led the way into the kitchen and sat down at the table. Donovon gathered some ice and sat down opposite her. She took the ice out of his hand and sighed.

"Thank you, Donovon."

"No problem," he answered with sadness in his eyes.

They sat there for a moment and then Donovon jumped up from the table, startling her. He hurried out of the room and ran up the stairs.

Nedra yelled up the stairs at him. "Where are you going?"

He dressed quickly and met Nedra downstairs in the foyer.

"Donovon! What are you doing?"

He stuck his wallet in his back pocket and kissed her forehead. "Don't worry about it. I'll be right back."

Nedra grabbed him by the arm and tried to stop him. He picked up his keys off the table and smiled.

"I'll be fine. Make yourself comfortable. I'll be right back."

Donovon jumped in his car and sped off into the night.

Nedra didn't know what to do. Her stomach was in knots with worry. She realized there was nothing she could do but wait for Donovon to return, so she climbed the stairs and entered the guest room to unpack her bags.

Over in the upscale section of town, Donovon cruised the area. He'd been there before with Nedra, but only once. Luckily he had a good memory. As soon as he saw the Escalade in the driveway with the personalized plates reading "Big Time," he knew he had found the right house. He drove around the block and parked his car on a side street. He exited the car and walked down the secluded street, cautiously looking over his shoulder. He didn't know what he would do once he saw Simeon, and at this point, he didn't care. Simeon's mistreatment of Nedra had been bottled up inside him for too long, and now he felt himself ready to explode.

As he approached the house, Donovon was all set to confront him until he saw Simeon exit the house. He was talking on his cell phone and was totally distracted from his surroundings. Donovon ducked behind some shrubbery and waited for Simeon to get closer to him. He could hear him tell the person on the other end of the telephone to put on something sexy because he was on his way over. When Simeon got to the door of his truck, he hung up the phone and reached for the door handle. Donovon was on him quicker than lightning. His fist connected with Simeon's face, knocking him into the side of the vehicle. He proceeded to punch him as hard as he could in the face, ribs, and abdomen. Simeon tried to scream out, but Donovon's punches were too fierce. He continued to punch Simeon as hard as he could.

When Simeon slid to the ground, Donovon kicked him brutally until the assault was unexpectedly interrupted. The garage door went up on the neighbor's house and a man stepped out into the driveway and lit a cigarette. With a small dog by his side, he walked down to the edge of the yard, constantly blowing smoke into the air while his dog emptied its bladder. Worried that the neighbors might call the police, Donovon gave Simeon one last kick and pulled his gun out of his back pocket. He held the gun to Simeon's head.

"If you even breathe, I will blow your ass away. Forget you ever heard the name 'Nedra.' If you come near her again, you'll be dead before your body hits the ground."

Simeon was nearly unconscious and bleeding from the brutal attack, but he heard every word Donovon said. He slowly pulled himself up off the ground and looked around, but Donovon was nowhere to be found. Pulling a handkerchief from his pocket, he wiped the blood from his face.

"Ain't this a bitch?" he mumbled.

His eyes were already starting to swell. His neighbor didn't see him struggling to get to his feet. Instead, he re-entered the garage with his dog and lowered the door. Simeon stumbled back into his house and turned on the bathroom faucet. He looked up into the mirror and saw the cuts and bruises. His ribs were throbbing and his gold shirt and navy pants were filthy. He pulled some gauze from under the sink and began to talk to himself.

"Damn! Simeon Mathews may be down right now, but he's not out. Ouch!!"

Walking across the room, he pulled his nine millimeter from the closet and laid it on the bed.

Glancing around the room, he stared at the picture of Nedra on the dresser.

"OK, Nedra. I see how you want to play. Let's just see how far your boyfriend is willing to go."

He moaned in pain as he removed his jacket. The rest of his clothes followed. He cursed as he climbed into the shower.

Donovon had been gone for nearly an hour. Nedra sat in the kitchen patiently waiting for him to return. She finally heard the garage door open and relief swept over her body. She met him at the door with tears in her eyes. He exited the vehicle and immediately Nedra noticed his swollen knuckles and the blood on his shirt. He walked toward her with satisfaction.

"Donovon, what happened?"

She took him by the hands and led him over to the sink so she could wash his hands.

He pulled away so he could inspect her bruises once more. "Are you keeping the ice on it?"

She frowned and put his hands under the stream of water. "Yes. I'll live. You didn't do anything crazy, did you?"

"I did what I should've done a long time ago. Come here so I can put the ice pack on your face."

They sat down at the kitchen table, facing each other. Nedra couldn't take her eyes off his swollen hands. Before giving him the ice pack, she held it over his knuckles and stared at him.

"Where did you go, Donovon?" she asked softly.

He looked her in the eyes. "You don't want to know. Now leave it alone," he answered as he held his hand out for the ice pack.

She gave it to him after realizing Donovon wasn't going to reveal any information. He turned her cheek and examined her swollen face once more. Clenching his fists, he closed his eyes and took a deep breath.

"I don't know why you won't have Simeon arrested."

"You know why. No one would believe he could do something like this."

"You never know until you try, plus you have the bruises to prove it," he yelled angrily.

"He'll kill me for sure, Donovon."

"So you're just going to live in fear?"

"I have no case. He'll just say it was rough sex or something."

"This is crazy, Nedra. What exactly did he do to you?"

"I don't want to talk about, Donovon. Not tonight."

They both sat there in deep thought. She knew Donovon would place a call in a heartbeat, but he didn't know what it would take to convince her to get help. Nedra sat at the table with her head lowered as Donovon continued to hold the cold compress to her face in silence. No words were spoken. They were always able to communicate with their eyes. Nedra found it amazing that she could connect so well with him. She didn't understand it, but Donovon knew very well why. She was his soul mate. She flinched at the contact of the cold pack as he repositioned it. He ran his hand down her back.

"It's OK, Nedra. I'll take care of you."

She looked at him, seeing his love, devotion,

and sincerity. The tears stung her eyes and she tried to fight them.

Why couldn't Simeon be as loving as Donovon? There had to be a reason for his temperament. He wasn't always like that. It had to be the stress of his job.

"Nedra, don't let Simeon intimidate you just because he's some hotshot attorney. No man has the right to put his hands on a woman like this."

She touched his hand softly.

"I know, Donovon, and I'm not going back this time."

He didn't believe her. She always went back. The suitcases were the only difference this time. Could he be so lucky? He would just have to wait and see. In the meantime, he would make sure she was safe and far away from Simeon.

The house Donovon was living in now was a two-story, Victorian home he was house-sitting for friends of his parents. The couple was retired and traveling around the world. He offered to give up his apartment to take care of it for four months until they returned. The rooms were massive and cozy, just like he eventually wanted for his own home one day. He just prayed that he would be able to convince Nedra that he wanted her in his life for more than a friend. He wanted her for his wife. First, he would have to settle this matter with Simeon.

"Are you hungry?"

"No, I just want to take a bath and go to bed. Thanks for taking me in again."

"No problem."

They rose from the table and Donovon followed her upstairs with the ice pack. Nedra was quite familiar with the room across from Donovon's. She'd spent a few nights there in the past, not always because of a bad night with Simeon, but sometimes because she wanted to be close to a real friend.

"Everything looks the same around here."

Donovon didn't respond. He entered the bathroom and turned on the faucets. After adding some fragrant bath salt to the hot water, he returned to find Nedra placing her clothes into the dresser.

"Holler if you need me. I'll be downstairs."

"Thanks, I will and I . . ."

He pressed his finger to her lips. "Don't mention it, Nedra."

With that comment he walked out, closing the door behind him. Nedra clutched her robe to her chest and let out a relaxing breath. At least for the rest of tonight she would get a good night's sleep. She made it a point never to allow Simeon to find out where Donovon lived once he moved into this house. It would be a disaster if he ever found out, because he just might kill Donovon along with her.

After about fifteen minutes of soaking in the hot, soothing waters, Nedra heard a knock on the door.

"Come in!"

Donovon entered the bedroom and stood outside the bathroom door.

"I know you're not decent, but I brought you some herbal tea to help you relax."

"OK! Hold on a minute."

Nedra grabbed a towel and covered her body.

"OK, you can come in now."

Donovon entered with the cup in his hand and froze. Even though she had covered her body, he knew what beautiful curves she had and he could still see her chocolate thighs through the bubbles. He had changed into some comfortable sweatpants and a T-shirt. He had to concentrate so his body would not give away his desire for her.

"Thanks, Donovon. This is just what I needed."

He handed the cup to her, sat on the toilet in silence, and watched her sip the tea.

"Donovon, have you heard from Brea?"

He frowned. "No, and I don't plan to. Why are you so worried about Brea, especially after she pimp slapped you?"

She giggled. "Come on, Donovon! Seriously, though, I think she called Simeon and told him about us being together in Atlanta."

"For real?"

"Yes," she answered. "He said he received a telephone call from someone telling him I was messing around on him in Atlanta."

Donovon fumbled with some potpourri on the countertop. "I'm not surprised."

Sadness filled her eyes as she continued to sip the tea. "I wish I'd never met Simeon."

"That makes two of us." He stood, taking the empty cup from her. "I don't want to talk about him anymore. Call me if you need me," he said.

Still clutching the towel, she looked up at him. "I just want to let you know that even though it seems I'm going through hell right now, I'm still here for you too."

"I know, and thanks for being concerned. I'll leave you so you can finish your bath."

She smiled as he stepped through the door, but he paused.

"Nedra?"

"Yes?"

"If he comes anywhere near you again, I'm not going to hesitate to pull the trigger."

Before she could respond, the door to the bedroom slammed closed. She hurried out of the tub so she could talk some sense into him. She couldn't allow Donovon to come into harm's way. He was too important to her, and Simeon had gone off the deep end.

What the hell was I thinking getting Donovon involved with my problems? I have to fix this before things get further out of hand.

Her heart felt like it was racing. She quickly toweled off and slipped on her gown and robe. When she got into the hallway, she knew Donovon was in his room because she could see the light under his door. Without even thinking, she burst through the door.

"Donovon!"

He stepped out of his closet with an empty look on his face. "Yeah?"

She walked over to him and put her hands on her hips. "Look, I know you care about me and you want to protect me, but this thing between me and Simeon can't escalate any further. I don't want you hurt."

He hung his jacket in the closet and laughed.

"I'm not worried about the likes of Simeon Mathews. I'm not afraid of him, and I meant what I said. You don't have to worry about me, because I can take care of myself. Look at your face and neck, Nedra! Damn! Somebody has to stand up to him!"

She looked down at the floor in defeat. When she spoke, her voice cracked. "I couldn't live with myself if Simeon hurt you."

"But you expect me to sit back and watch him continuously beat the shit out of you? You're crazy, Nedra!"

He was right and she knew it. He hung one last item up in his closet and then turned to her. He tilted her chin so he could see her eyes. "Simeon doesn't want to mess with me. You can stay here as long as you like. In fact, I'm going to enjoy the company. Stop worrying and let me worry about him. OK?"

Smiling, she nodded in agreement and stretched up to kiss his cheek. He kissed the top of her head and looked at his watch.

"With that settled, it's late and we both need to try and get some sleep. It's been a long night, and I'm exhausted."

"I can't sleep, Donovon. Will you stay up and watch a movie with me?"

He closed his closet door and sighed. "I'll try, Nedra, but I doubt I last long. You better be glad it's the weekend."

She wrapped her arms around Donovon's waist and looked up into his loving eyes.

"It's OK if you want to go to sleep, Donovon, because I know you're tired. I don't want to be alone if I decide to close my eyes because I'm afraid I'll see Simeon in my nightmares."

Donovon could see the fear in Nedra's eyes.

"OK, Nedra, I'll watch a movie with you and I'm here in case you have a bad dream."

She released him whispered, "Thank you."

He walked over to his movie collection and thumbed through the stack. "I have just about anything you want to watch."

She followed him over to his bookshelf and pointed her finger at him playfully.

"Bootlegger!"

"Pick out something." He laughed. "I'm going downstairs to turn off the lights and grab some sodas."

"OK," she said while scanning the tapes. "But don't complain about what I pick."

"As long as you're here, I have nothing to complain about," he said. And with that statement, he left the room.

Upon hearing his return, she pulled the movie, *The Long Kiss Good night*, from the shelf. He entered the bedroom, balancing a large bowl of popcorn and two cans of Pepsi.

"Let me help you with that."

"I got this, woman. Just pop in the movie. What did you pick out?"

Nedra climbed onto his bed and took the bowl of popcorn from his hands.

"I picked something with action!"

He joined her on the bed and opened his soda. "After tonight I would've picked a comedy myself, but it's your choice."

He passed her the Pepsi and pushed the play

button on the remote. Nedra stacked their pillows into a comfortable position.

"I'll never be able to repay you, D," she said.

"You already have," he said.

Thirty minutes into the movie both of them were sound asleep.

Chapter Thirty-Five

A New Day

The following Monday, Nedra and Donovon went to work as usual. Donovon had already called ahead to alert their security department about Simeon. Nedra provided them with a picture to help identify him in case he tried to gain entrance to their building.

The bruised area on her face was sore and noticeable. Lawrence walked into her office and froze.

"Nedra, what happened to your face? Did that guy put his hands on you again?"

She shuffled some papers on her desk and smiled. "I'm OK, Lawrence. Calm down."

Lawrence closed the door. "Does Donovon know?" he asked.

"Yes, he knows. Actually, I'm staying with him until this thing blows over."

Lawrence inspected her face and lectured her. "This kind of thing never blows over, Nedra. You need to take some pre cautions. Now if you had taken that gun like I tried to get you—"

"He would've shot me with it!" she said, interrupting him.

Lawrence sat quietly in the chair. He scratched his head and offered to help. "Look, Nedra, if you want me to, I can make this thing with Simeon go away."

"How?"

"I have my ways."

She stood, walked over to her filing cabinet, and opened a drawer. "Thanks, but no thanks. Too many people are already involved."

"If you say so. Anyway, here are those numbers you wanted."

She took the folder out of his hand and scanned the figures. "Thanks, Lawrence."

"You're welcome."

"No, thanks for everything."

He stood, shoved his hands in his pockets, and turned to walk out of her office. "Don't mention it."

A week had passed and Nedra was still living in fear every time she left Donovon's house. She was nervous because she didn't know when or if Simeon would show up to harm her. He'd been calling, intimidating her over the telephone, especially after she sent the engagement ring back to him by express mail. She was afraid to go back to her house, and she still didn't want to get the police involved. She decided to get a moving company to pack her things and put them in storage for now. Donovon offered to accompany her to retrieve her personal items, but she declined. She felt it would be safer to get them out of storage than for anyone to go back to the house.

A few days later, Simeon pulled up at Nedra's house just as the realtor put a "sold" sign in the yard. He questioned her about the previous owner of the house, but the realtor knew the situation and told Simeon the house had been bought and sold by a business, and she had no knowledge of the previous owner. He got back inside his car and slammed the door in anger.

"I guess I'll just have to pay you a visit at your office," he said to himself. He turned the key and sped off down the street.

Nedra wanted to show Donovon how much she appreciated his friendship, so she planned a delicious menu for dinner. She wanted to surprise him, so she left work early to cook. Inside the kitchen, she hurried around so she could have dinner ready for Donovon by the time he walked through the door. The radio on the countertop was playing some of the top jazz tunes, and Nedra danced as she chopped the vegetables and stirred the pot. Glancing at the clock, she tasted her dish and set the table.

Donovon walked through the kitchen door and was immediately met by the aroma of dinner. The succulent smell caressed his nostrils as he walked further into the dining area and saw the table set for two. Nedra met him in the dining area with a huge smile.

"What's the occasion?" he asked.

"No occasion. I just wanted to cook dinner for you. I need to do something around here to earn my keep."

She motioned for him to sit down.

"I'll be right back," she said.

Moments later, she returned with a platter containing two Cornish hens.

"Can I help?" he asked as he loosened his tie.

Walking toward the kitchen again, she yelled back at him. "You can do the dishes."

"I knew there was a catch to this," he said, laughing.

She returned with salad and the rest of the side items.

"Everything looks and smells delicious, Nedra. You didn't have to do all of this."

She sat down opposite him. "I wanted to. Now say the blessing so we can dig in."

Donovon proceeded to say grace and they started eating their dinner. As they enjoyed Nedra's peach cobbler for dessert, Donovon looked over at her.

"I hate to ruin the moment, but have you heard from Simeon?"

She sighed and sat her fork down. "He calls every day or so just to say something crazy over the phone. He's trying to scare me."

"What did he say?"

"He told me he was sorry for everything, and if I came back, he promised he wouldn't hurt me again. I told him it was over and I wasn't coming back, so he started threatening me again."

Donovon noticed her mood had become solemn. "The bruise on your face is almost gone."

She took a bite of the peach cobbler. "Finally. He's never going to leave me alone, Donovon. I

don't know why it's so important for him to have
me when all he does is hurt me."

"He's a control freak, Nedra. If he's not in control, he loses it. He needs to be locked up."

"I don't want to talk about him anymore."

"OK, but make sure you save any messages he
leaves on your phone."

"I will," she said, standing. "Are you up for a
movie tonight?"

"I'm always up for a movie."

"Good! When I finish the dishes, I'm all yours."

She took his empty plates and walked toward
the kitchen.

"Where are you going?"

She laughed. "I was just kidding about the
dishes. Go relax. I'll do them."

"We'll do them together."

"If you say so. Let's go."

An hour into the movie, Nedra and Donovon
were, once again, sound asleep. Her head was resting against his chest, and as usual his arms were
around her waist. When Donovon stirred from his
sleep, the TV screen was blank. He glanced at his
watch and saw that it was late. He couldn't remember at what point he had drifted off to sleep, but
Nedra's warm body lying against his had awakened
other parts of his body. He closed his eyes, trying
not to notice the sensual rhythm of her breathing,
as well as the perfume on her skin.

Damn!

He tried to push her body away from him, but it
caused her to shift her body slightly, and one of
her hands slid down to his thigh.

He tried again to move her body away from his, but she snuggled even closer. There was only one thing he could do, and that was to wake her up. Hopefully she wouldn't notice his obvious arousal.

"Nedra?" he called softly.

Her eyes were still closed and she stirred again.

"Nedra, the movie's over. It's time to go to bed."

Her eyes slowly opened. She had never felt as safe and secure as she did at this moment. She looked up into his compassionate eyes.

"What time is it?"

Fighting for strength, his voice was strained when he replied.

"I'm not sure, but you'd better get to bed."

"I'm already in bed, Donovon."

He tried to pull his T-shirt down to hide himself, but she had already felt the evidence of his arousal.

"I know, but you're in *my* bed."

"Can't I stay in here with you?"

"I don't think that would be a good idea," he said, staring into her glazy eyes.

"Why?" she asked, not moving an inch.

"I think you already know why."

Instinctively she ran her hand down his thigh and gently touched him. "Donovon, please don't push me away. Not tonight."

He realized it was just like Miami all over again. She leaned in and kissed his lips softly. He reluctantly pulled her closer and ran his tongue over her lips. Donovon *was* the best kisser she had ever experienced in her life. He kissed the corners of her mouth and sucked her tongue into the sweet depths of his mouth. He heard soft moans escape her as he explored her heavenly body. He pushed her away and searched her eyes. He was at the point of no return, but he had to see if there was any regret in her eyes. There was none. Brea was right, and so was everyone else, including their parents. He'd always been in love with Nedra.

"Don't stop, Donovon."

Linking her arms around his neck, she straddled him and planted kisses on his neck, chest, and lips.

"Nedra, are you sure about this? You've been through so much."

She put her finger to his lips before kissing her way down from his neck to his stomach. His heart was pounding in his chest and he felt like it was about to burst. Before he could utter another word, her warm, moist lips engulfed him. He cried out as she moved over him slowly and with determination. He closed his eyes and begged for mercy as she showed him just how much he meant to her. There was no way he could watch her because he felt like he was dying just from the sensations shooting through his body. Nedra took pleasure in hearing Donovon hiss and moan as she continued to feed off of him. His body began to shiver, but he wasn't ready for this heavenly feeling to end.

He stopped her, rolled her onto her back, and removed her clothing. Her beautiful brown skin was a shade lighter than his, and the contrast was exciting. Nedra pulled his shirt over his head and inspected his rippling abs. She couldn't help running her hands over the silky hair on his chest, causing him to flinch.

Donovon wanted her so badly that he could hardly wait. He lowered his sweats and immediately covered her body with his. He felt as if he had died and gone to heaven when he pushed his rigid body into her warm, wet center. She arched into him and received the sheer power of his desire. His body moved in and out of hers with precision and want. Nedra was loving how naturally they fit together. Never in her wildest dreams did she think their relationship would come to this again, but it had, and it was perfect.

Donovon kissed the curve of her neck and breasts as he filled her body with his. His groans were nothing short of wonderful, and Nedra was excited that she was able to please him. She kissed him with every ounce of passion she owned. Donovon meant everything to her. Everything.

Moments later, she began her own climax and trembled in his arms. He held her tightly as he also shuddered in an explosive release. His seed entered her and his name tore loudly from her throat. Their bodies lay intertwined and sated, glistening with perspiration. Their breathing was rapid and loud. He kissed her with fire as her body rippled with yet another release, causing her to scream his name once more.

Burying her face into his neck, she continued to hold on to his powerful body. He rolled over, pulling her atop his body. She looked into his eyes and kissed his heaving chest. He had a body like a black Adonis. He was absolutely beautiful. He pushed her hair away from her eyes and smiled.

"I didn't get a chance to please you like you pleased me."

She smiled as a lone tear slid out of her eye.

"We have time for that, Donovon. Today, I wanted you to feel my love for you."

"This is for keeps, Nedra."

"I'd like that."

She smiled and turned with her back to his front, scooting up against his body. She grabbed his arm and wrapped it around her waist.

"Good night, Donovon."

"Good night, Nedra."

Chapter Thirty-Six

Insatiable

The next morning Nedra stretched out of her sleep, forgetting where she was. The sun's rays illuminated the room. After remembering where she was, she turned over to find Donovon missing. A single yellow rose rested on his pillow. She sat up and noticed a scroll of paper with a ribbon neatly tied around it. She picked up the rose and sniffed the perfumed scent. Nedra placed the rose across her lap and slowly unrolled the small piece of paper. The beautiful words jumped from the page.

Good morning Nedra,
  I wanted you to have something beautiful to wake up to like I did. Even though this rose doesn't compare to your beauty, it's the closest thing I could find on such short notice. Anyway, I've gone to the gym. I hope to get back before you wake up. If you need me, don't hesitate to page me. We'll talk when I return. I hope you had a good night's sleep.

                                        Luv Ya!
                                        "D"

His words were intimate, yet friendly. Last night was a long time coming for the both of them. All these years she'd had a deep love for him, one that she couldn't and wouldn't deny any longer.

She gathered her rose and note and proceeded across the hallway to her room. Once there, she found an empty vase to put the rose in. She tucked the note away in her purse. Nedra pulled some khaki shorts and a T-shirt from her suitcase and placed them on the bed. She looked over and noticed her cell phone had a message on it. There was no doubt who'd left the message either. Right now she didn't have the strength to listen to it. She took a deep breath and ran her fingers through her hair. A chill ran over her body as she gathered her undergarments and shower gel and retreated into the bathroom for a shower.

Donovon had left the gym an hour ago. He was still in a daze from the previous night with Nedra, and now he was just driving in circles. He knew by now that she was awake and probably waiting to talk. After picking up some buttery croissants, he decided to head home.

When he pulled into the garage, she was standing on the steps. Seeing her radiant smile made his heart skip a beat. She seemed to be as cool as a cucumber. Her shapely legs and the roundness of her breasts immediately shattered his train of thought.

"Good morning!"

He stepped out of the car and gave her a kiss. "Good morning."

"What's in the bag?"

He handed the bag to her as he picked up his gym bag. "Croissants. I know you love them."

She looked up at him with those soft brown eyes. "I love you."

He blushed upon hearing her admission. She'd said it many times before, but today he knew she meant it with all her heart.

"Are you hungry?" she asked.

He put his hand over his stomach. "Starving," he said.

Nedra took him by the hand and led him into the kitchen.

"Come on in so I can make us some breakfast."

Donovon followed her into the kitchen and sat down his bag.

Across town, Simeon dialed Nedra's cell phone, only to have it go into her voicemail again.

"Damn it! Nedra, when I get my hands on you, you're going to be sorry!!!"

A sultry voice called out from an adjoining room.

"Simeon, baby, what's taking you so long?"

"Mind your damn business and go fix me a drink!"

The woman strolled into the room and started massaging Simeon's shoulders.

"OK, baby, and when I get back, I'm going to fix *you* up real good."

Simeon watched his last night's lay exit the room dressed in his designer shirt. He lay back on the pillows in deep thought about the plan he was going to set in motion. He would have Nedra, or no one would. His thoughts were interrupted when the woman reentered the room with his drink. She handed it to him and he sat it down on the nightstand. Just as she was about to join him, he pulled her down on the bed. He wrapped her long red hair around his wrist and yanked.

"Come on, baby, not so rough."

"Ah, sweetheart, you know you like it that way. Now come on over here and do what you do best."

He lay back on the bed and closed his eyes. Over the next few hours, the young woman was at his beck and call and did anything and everything he asked. Once he was finished with her, he tossed her a velvet box with diamond earrings in it.

"Thank you, Simeon!"

"It's nothing. Next time, don't stop until I tell you. Got it?"

"Anything for you, baby."

"Now go get dressed. I have a lot of work to do, so I'll call you later."

"I'll be waiting," the woman said as she kissed him on his cheek.

He motioned for her to leave, then put his hands over his eyes. No woman had ever denied him . . . not until Nedra.

You'll learn Nedra. If it kills me, I'll teach you.

Sunday morning Nedra attended church with Donovon and then enjoyed a ride to an apple orchard in the country. Donovon loved homemade apple pie and Nedra wanted the best apples.

"Have you called your mom and told her what happened?" Donovon asked as they walked around the farm.

"No way!"

"Are you ready for tomorrow?"

"Not really."

"Nedra, security won't let Simeon in the building. I'll see to that."

She sat down under a tree and sighed. "I can't live my life like this."

He sat down beside her and picked up a ripe apple. "I told you it might be a good idea to at least take out a restraining order. You also should've pressed charges when you had the chance."

"Simeon knows just about everyone in law enforcement. Who do you think they'll believe?"

"He's not above the law. He can't have everyone down there in his pocket."

Nedra just shrugged her shoulders in silence. About that time an elderly gentleman approached them with a nice basket of apples. They stood and inspected the apples.

Nedra picked up an apple and gave it a squeeze. "They're perfect!"

"Thank you!"

Donovon paid the gentleman and loaded them into the car for their return trip home.

That evening they shared a wonderful Southern dinner complete with fried chicken, macaroni and cheese, turnip greens, and the best apple pie ever made. After clearing the table, Nedra and Donovon retreated to his room. Before going to bed, Nedra needed to clear out her voicemail. She knew the majority of the messages were going to be from Simeon.

Donovon took the phone out of her hand. "Let me do it for you."

She nodded in agreement and handed him the phone. Donovon sat there listening to message after message. Nedra sat there and watched his facial expressions change with each call.

"Nedra! If you think you can just pack up and leave, you have another thing coming! It would be smart on your part if you came back. Don't make me have to look for you!"

The second message was no different.

"Look Nedra! I'm not playing with you! You're only making things worse for you!! If you think what I did to you the last time we were together was bad, just wait."

The last message was even worse.

"Look, bitch, that's it!!! You've gone too far this time. Now you're going to have to suffer the consequences! It's on now! Get ready! Do you hear me!"

The last message made it plain and clear for Donovon. Simeon needed to be dealt with, and quickly. After Donovon listened to the last message, she looked at him.

"Is it bad?"

He smiled. "Nothing we can't handle together."

One particular message bothered Donovon. Nedra never did tell him what happened to her that night, and every time he asked, she would avoid answering the question.

Nedra pulled back the covers of the bed and climbed in. Tonight her prayers would be specific in asking God to protect not only her, but Donovon as well.

Donovon couldn't sleep. He was being tormented by Simeon's messages, and it was obvious Simeon didn't take his warning seriously. He looked down at Nedra, who was clinging to him. Glancing over at the clock, he saw it was 11:45 p.m. and getting later. With no sign of sleep in sight, he threw back the covers and opened the French doors leading onto the balcony. Even though it was early autumn, the nights were still somewhat humid. He had to admit, he was a little unsure about how he would react when he saw Simeon again. Standing out on the balcony looking at the stars made him think about the woman he loved, who was sleeping in his bed. He closed his eyes and took in a variety of scents from the garden below. Freshly cut grass and the rose garden in the backyard were soon joined by another familiar scent.

"What are you doing out there in the dark, Donovon?" she asked softly.

He turned and saw Nedra standing there in her long, lavender nightgown. He swallowed hard and held out his hand for her to join him. She folded her arms across her breasts and stepped out into the night air. He pulled her into his arms and warmed her body.

"Did I wake you?"

"I missed you."

"I'm sorry. I was just out here thinking."

Hugging her closer he kissed the top of her shiny auburn hair. "It's going to be all right, Nedra. Stop worrying."

"I'm not worrying."

She turned and buried her face against his chest. He was so manly. He was perfect. Donovon wrapped his arms around her body as she shivered.

He tilted her chin upward. "Then what's wrong?"

He pulled her tighter against his body in silence. She wrapped her arms around his neck and sighed.

"I love you so much, Donovon. I hope you don't hate me for wasting so much time."

He laughed.

"I'm serious, Donovon . . ."

Whatever she was about to say was smothered as his mouth covered hers. Her legs became instant jelly. Donovon was full of raw desire and his body awakened her soul every time he entered her space. Her breasts swelled at his touch. He toyed with her lips as his tongue darted in and out of the warm depths of her mouth. He pulled her even closer as the evidence of his desire pressed against her body. Her whimpers and moans were driving him crazy. He picked her up and she naturally wrapped her legs around his waist as he made his way back into the bedroom. They never broke contact as they tumbled onto his bed. He peeled the nightgown away from her skin and planted kisses down to her navel. Just as fast, she pulled his T-shirt over his head and tossed it on the floor. Greedily, she tugged at the drawstring on his pants. His mouth found hers once again as he removed them.

She lay there and stared at his all-male body. "You're beautiful, Donovon."

He ran his hand up her inner thigh and stroked her into silence. His voice was soothing and barely above a whisper.

"Nedra, you're the one who's breathtaking."

He began kissing her feverishly, and she panted as he made his way lower and devoured her. Nedra sucked in her breath and held it, in fear of screaming. Donovon wanted her to feel the same pleasure she'd given him, and then some. He held her tightly in his grasp as he consumed her essence. She clenched the sheets and shuddered beneath him as his tongue and lips danced with her core. Donovon feasted on her greedily until he felt her body spasm against his lips. He quickly moved his body between her thighs. A gasp caught in her throat as his body joined with hers. He decided to take it slow and easy as he moved in and out of her heat. Each time he returned, he slowly dove deeper. Trying to get closer, she wrapped her legs around his waist securely. Donovon represented true love and power, and he was finally hers. He wanted Nedra to know what it felt like to be cherished beyond her wildest dreams. She had given him her body, and now there was no doubt he also had her heart. Now the only thing left for him to do was to make her his wife.

Chapter Thirty-Seven

Taking A Stand

Nedra had been nervous ever since she'd gotten up. For some reason she felt Simeon might show up at work and make good on all of his threats.

Once they entered the parking garage, Nedra put her car in park and let out the breath she had been holding for a long time. She scanned the garage and waited for Donovon to open her door. He looked so handsome in his black suit. His cologne clouded her thoughts for a moment as she reminisced about the love they'd made a few hours earlier.

"Hand me your briefcase, Nedra."

She climbed out of her car and pulled her purse onto her shoulder. Donovon scanned her body again. This was only the tenth time he'd done it since laying eyes on her that morning. Her long, shapely legs did the navy suit justice. No woman should look as sexy as Nedra did, and he was proud to have her by his side. A strand of her hair had worked its way out of place, and Donovon casually reached up to smooth it back into place as they walked to the elevator.

"Thanks. This hair—I can't do a thing with it. I'm thinking about cutting it."

Her hair was thick and he loved the way it felt in his hands.

"I like your hair the way it is, but if you want to cut it, that's your choice."

Nedra let out a long sigh as he pushed the button for the eighth floor. Once on their floor, Nedra felt 100 percent better. As they walked toward her office, they exchanged good morning pleasantries with various coworkers. It wasn't unusual to see Nedra and Donovon together like this. Most of the people in the office knew the history of their friendship, but they didn't know how deeply their feelings for each other really ran. Once they reached her office, she entered and Donovon closed the door behind them.

"Well, we made it in one piece. I told you there was nothing to worry about."

Scanning over her mail, she turned on her computer and looked up at him. "Sweetheart, thanks for keeping me safe. I owe you."

"All you owe me right now is a kiss so I can get to work."

Smiling, she came around her desk and cupped his face. He gripped her hips and savored the sweetness of her mouth.

"Now! Will that hold you for a while, Mr. Mc-Neil?"

"I guess it'll have to do, but just in case, don't go too far."

"I'm right down the hall if you need me."

"Yes. Now get to work, McNeil."

"Dang, you're bossy. I'll see you later."

She smiled as he exited her office. Her telephone buzzed as soon as she sat down.

"Miss Harris, I have a client on line one," her assistant said.

"Put it through, Vanessa."

"Right away."

Nedra waited for the call to be put through.

"Good morning. This is Nedra Harris."

"You thought you got rid of me, didn't you?"

It was Simeon and he wasn't happy.

"Why don't you just leave me alone, Simeon?"

Simeon laughed. "I can't. You're my fiancée now, so stop all this foolishness. I'm sorry about everything, and as far as that condom wrapper, well . . . that's over. She didn't mean anything to me."

Nedra slammed her fist on the desk. "I deserve to be treated better! If you don't leave me alone, I'm going to press charges against you for assault!"

Simeon gritted his teeth. "Are you threatening me? Do you know who you're messing with?"

"I'm not afraid of you, Simeon! Not anymore."

He laughed again.

"I don't want you to be afraid of me, baby. I want you to come back so we can work this out. We always work it out. I bought you a beautiful sapphire necklace and earrings to match. That's your birthstone, and it'll look beautiful on you."

Simeon was definitely out of touch with reality.

"Simeon! Listen to me carefully. It is over! Don't call me, don't come by, just leave me alone!"

"I'll see you dead first," he whispered coldly. "And tell your boy Donovon that he may have won the battle, but not the war. I will have you, or no one will. Have a good day, baby."

All Nedra heard was the dial tone. She knew now that Simeon's real reign of terror was not over. Once she hung up the telephone she called Donovon and told him about the phone call. Donovon made sure any future phone calls would be screened before they were transferred to Nedra's office.

Needing to lighten the mood, Donovon invited Lawrence and Ednita over to the house that evening for a game of cards.

"So, Nedra, are you still dating that fine attorney?" Ednita asked.

Her eyes met Donovon's before she responded.

"Not anymore. It didn't work out."

"Hmmm, I'm sorry to hear that. Girl, that man can wear a suit! No offense, guys."

Donovon and Lawrence just shook their heads in disgust. Lawrence's green eyes sparkled with laughter.

"Put me in a thousand dollar suit and I would look good too," Lawrence said. "All you women think about is looks. What about a man's intelligence?"

Ednita patted him on the shoulder and threw her card down on the table.

"Lawrence, I'm not saying that's all I look for in a man, but it helps."

"Women," Donovon mumbled.

Ednita laughed out loud.

"Men! Donovon McNeil."

Donovon threw his card on the table and added his two cents.

"Well, Miss Robertson, while we're on the subject, do you still have your hooks in that pro football player?"

She giggled.

"You'd better know it! He's really sweet, not like some of these athletes can be. Oddly enough, guys, when I met him, I didn't know he played pro football. By the time I found out, I was already emotionally involved. He's sweet like you, Donovon."

Lawrence took a sip of beer and shook his head.

"So, since I'm from Los Angeles, I guess I'm no good, huh?"

"Oh no! You're just from the land of playas, and I don't have time for no fast-talking playa."

The group laughed in unison, but Donovon still noticed Nedra's distance. Lawrence looked over at Nedra.

"It's your play, Nedra."

"Oh! Sorry, guys."

Nedra threw her card down on the table to keep the game going.

Lawrence looked up at everyone and revealed something that none of them could have ever imagined.

"I bet I can tell you guys something about me that you wouldn't believe."

"What?" Ednita asked as she turned up her beer.

"I used to be a gang banger," he announced as he stacked up the cards.

"No way!" Donovon yelled.

Shocked, Nedra looked over at him. "For real?" she asked.

"Yeah," he said as he stood up. "Check this out."

Lawrence pulled his shirt over his head and Ednita, Donovon, and Nedra watched in anticipation.

He turned his back to them and gave them a tour of his body. He had several tattoos on his back and arms, and then he started pointing out a couple of old bullet wounds. Everyone's eyes were on him as he put his shirt back on.

"I've done some foul things in my life, and hurt a lot of people. You don't know how much I regret getting caught up in that kind of lifestyle."

Donovon smiled and sipped his beer. "I bet you have some stories to tell."

He laughed and sat back down at the table. "Let's just say, I'm glad I got out of California when I did. I met my mentor at the Boys and Girls Club and he was the one who helped me get out. He got me to get serious about my life and I started studying very hard. My reward was a scholarship to Hampton University, which saved my life, because I know without college I would be dead or in jail by now. I owe everything to my mentor. He was the father I never had."

"Wow, Lawrence. That's a remarkable story. You need to write a book about your experience to help some of these other young men who are where you used to be."

He blushed and shuffled the cards.

"I thought about it. I've already started jotting down a few thoughts."

Donovon gathered his cards and smiled at Lawrence. "Where's your mentor now?"

"He's still working with the Boys and Girls Club. We stay in touch and we visit each other when we can."

Tears formed in Nedra's eyes. "That's beautiful, Lawrence. I'm proud of you."

"So am I," Ednita added.

Donovon raised his beer bottle. "I'd like to make a toast."

All of them raised their bottles as Donovon spoke.

"I would like to toast to good friends, new beginnings, and a life full of love and success for all of us. Lawrence, you're an inspiration to young people everywhere, and I pray that God guides your heart to share your story with the world. I'm proud of you and I'm glad to have you all as friends."

"Hear, hear," they all agreed as they clicked their bottles together.

After Donovon's toast, the group got back to playing some serious cards.

The next day came to an exhausting close. Nedra walked into Donovon's office to find him on the phone. He motioned for her to sit as he finished his conversation.

"Are you ready to go?" he asked as he hung up the telephone.

"Donovon, if you still have work to do, go ahead. I can get back to the house OK on my own."

He stood and put on his jacket.

"Tell that to someone who doesn't know you. I noticed you were a million miles away last night while we were playing cards."

Nedra walked over to the window and gazed out into rush hour traffic.

"He's not going to let me go, Donovon. He said he would see me dead first."

He walked over and embraced her from behind and kissed her neck.

"I won't let him hurt you, and just to be on the safe side, we're going downtown to get an official restraining order taken out against him. OK?"

She nodded and walked out of the office beside him.

Nedra and Donovon stood in the police station waiting to be helped. Donovon was livid that Simeon had reduced Nedra to the point of near depression.

Finally Nedra's name was called and the pair was ushered into a cubicle.

"How may I help you?" the clerk asked after they sat down.

"We're here to take out a restraining order against someone."

The clerk grabbed a stack of papers and held them out.

"Please fill out these papers."

Nedra took the papers out of her hand and slowly began to complete them. Occasionally, she would look up as if she expected to see Simeon walk by at any moment. Donovon patted her knee.

"Take your time, baby."

She kissed his cheek, finished with the papers, and handed them back to the clerk. The clerk's eyes widened as she scanned the papers.

"Simeon Mathews? You mean the lawyer, Simeon Mathews?" Donovon and Nedra both looked at the clerk when she questioned them.

"Yes. Is there a problem?" Nedra softly responded.

"No . . . I . . . I'm just a little surprised."

Clutching her purse, Nedra cleared her throat.

"How long will this take?" she asked.

"This order will be in effect as soon as the judge gives his stamp of approval. Mr. Mathews cannot come within one hundred feet of you or your property. Just so you know, he'll be served with a copy of the order.

Donovon leaned in and cautioned the clerk.

"Simeon Mathews is a violent man. I know he's well known down here, but I hope he doesn't receive any special treatment. He's a ticking time bomb whether you want to believe it or not. I expect the judge to have this paperwork on his desk within the hour, and if you can get it to him sooner, we would be even more grateful."

"I'll see to it, sir. Miss Harris, I'm sorry for your trouble."

Donovon and Nedra stood and walked out of the office, relieved.

Once they reached the house, Nedra told Donovon she was going to skip dinner and lay down. They went upstairs and he lovingly tucked her into bed.

Chapter Thirty-Eight

Someone To Watch Over Me

It had been a month since all the chaos had started, and Nedra was surprised that Simeon hadn't tried to call her or see her. Maybe the restraining order was all she needed to let him know she meant business. Simeon's face was all over the news. He was involved in a big case involving a local crime boss's son, and she was thankful he was occupied. She'd read about the case and couldn't understand how he could defend that terrible man. He'd worked for the Leonardo family for years, and would do whatever it took to keep their youngest son out of prison.

Nedra's head was pounding and her body felt detached. She had an important meeting first thing this morning, so she had to drag herself into the office whether she wanted to or not. Donovon was still trailing her to work in his car for safety reasons. He wanted to car pool, but she thought it was best this way in case they ran into Simeon. In a way, it was a comfort.

Donovon sipped his coffee as he wondered what was taking Nedra so long to get dressed. Upstairs Nedra was feeling terrible. She moved around the room in slow motion. After glancing at the clock, she realized she was going to cause them to be late. It was at that moment that her stomach gave way. She barely made it to the bathroom.

"Hey!! Are you OK in there?" Donovon yelled as he knocked on her bedroom door.

"Come in! I'll be out in a minute!"

Donovon entered her room as she exited the bathroom.

"You look terrible."

"Thanks a lot."

"No, I mean you don't look like you feel well. That flu is going around. You should stay home and get some rest. "

"I probably got it from Ednita. She had it last week."

Donovon walked over and placed his hand against her forehead.

"You don't have a fever, but you did toss and turn a lot last night."

"I'm sorry. Did I keep you up?"

"No. Besides I like sharing a bed with you."

She blushed.

"So do I."

He looked deeper into her eyes and looked at her with concern.

"You're not going in today. Get back into bed."

She walked away from him and picked up her blouse.

"I have to go in today because I have a meeting at ten."

"Reschedule it," he advised with compassion in his voice.

Silently she removed her blouse from the hanger. Even though he was concerned about her health, his body reminded him she was standing before him in only her bra and panties.

"I can't, Donovon. It's important."

"I'm sure it's not so important that you can't reschedule it, because you're not leaving this house."

She looked over at him. "Don't bully me."

He closed the distance between them and wrapped his arms around her waist.

"I care about you and I'm not bullying you. Look, do it for me. Would you please stay home and get some rest?"

"I care about you too, but . . ."

Her words were cut off as he took the blouse from her hand and proceeded to hang it up in the closet. Nedra had lost this battle, so she climbed back into the bed. She sat there watching his movements.

"I'm going to miss you today."

He came and sat down beside her on the bed.

"I'll stay home with you if you want me to. I really don't want you here by yourself anyway, especially if you're sick."

She placed her hand on his cheek.

"I'll be fine. Remember? Simeon doesn't have a clue where you live, and we have the alarm. I'll be OK. I'm not going to do anything but sleep anyway."

He leaned forward and kissed her gently on the lips.

"I'll call to check on you at lunch. Do you want me to fix you some breakfast before I leave?"

"No thanks. That's the last thing on my mind right now."

"Well, I'm off," he said as he tucked her back into bed. "Don't forget to call and cancel the meeting. I'll try to get home early."

"Bye, and have a nice day."

As she heard Donovon drive out of the garage, she picked up the phone to cancel her meeting. After she got off the telephone, she glanced at the calendar. She tried to dismiss it, but it was as plain as the writing on the wall. She had missed her period. She didn't want to face it, but the thought of her possibly carrying the child of Simeon Mathews terrified her. She knew that if he ever found out, he would try to take the baby away from her, and she would never let that happen. Her feelings toward him had nothing to do with the innocent life she possibly carried. Then, as if she had been hit with a lightning bolt, she sat straight up in bed.

Oh my God!!

Nedra's mind did a rewind. Simeon forced himself on her the day she left him. A week later, she remembered making love to Donovon. Hurriedly she slid into a pair of jeans and sweatshirt and drove down to the nearest pharmacy and purchased a home pregnancy test. Clutching it to her chest, she rushed back to the house and entered the bathroom. Minutes later she exited, sat on the bed, and sobbed. This time it wasn't stress, and she had known it. The test was positive. She crawled under the comforter and cried herself to sleep.

* * *

At the office Donovon tapped on his desk with a pencil. Something was going on with Nedra and he would find out what it was.

"Mr. McNeil? There's a gentlemen here to see you."

Donovon wasn't expecting anyone.

"Send him in," he answered anyway.

He put on his jacket and walked over to open his door. Simeon Mathews stood with his hand extended, looking like a million dollars.

"McNeil, thanks for seeing me on short notice."

Donovon frowned and made a fist with his hands. He was so angry he was trembling.

"How the hell did you get in here?"

"Security ain't worth a damn, is it?" Simeon said, smiling.

"What do you want?"

Simeon walked past Donovon with confidence as he looked around the office. He sat in a chair opposite Donovon's desk and crossed his legs. Donovon sat down in his chair in silence.

"McNeil, I'll get straight to the point. Where's Nedra? Her assistant said she called out sick today. I'm concerned about her. Tell me where she is and I'll forget about the ass kicking you put on me."

The nerve of this Wall Street pimp!

Donovon leaned back in his chair and smiled.

"You must think I'm a fool. I would never tell you where Nedra was, and second, I should've kicked your ass a long time ago."

Simeon laughed.

"You don't want to mess with me, McNeil. Nedra belongs to me. She always has and always will."

"She belongs to no one," Donovon replied calmly.

"I'm just concerned about her," Simeon lied.

"I heard the messages you left on her telephone. They were real caring!"

"Look, if Nedra's upset about that gun incident, I'm sorry."

"What gun incident?" Donovon asked as he sat straight up in his chair.

It was then that Simeon realized that Nedra must've kept that part of the story to herself.

"Look, McNeil, I know you and Nedra go way back, but you don't want to get in the middle of this."

"What gun incident? Did you pull a gun on her?"

"I guess Nedra doesn't tell you everything, huh?" He chuckled. "Look, I love Nedra, and I didn't mean to hurt her. Now tell me where she is so I can go get her."

"You're an idiot, Simeon. Nedra doesn't love you, and it would be in your best interest to move on."

Simeon stood and looked at his manicured nails.

"I get what I want, McNeil, and I *will* have Nedra one way or another. She just needs a little more taming."

Donovon was on Simeon before he realized it. Simeon's six foot, one inch stance was no match for Donovon's six feet, four inch frame. He had Simeon by the lapels of his jacket and had practically lifted him off the floor.

"Mathews, if you come near Nedra again, I will kill you. Do I make myself clear?"

Simeon was shaken, but kept his cool. He saw the fire in Donovon's eyes.

"Man, if you don't take your hands off of me . . ."

"What's wrong, Simeon? It's easy to smack women around, isn't it? Well, take a swing at me."

Donovon released him slowly. Simeon straightened his jacket and shook his head.

"You know, McNeil, you have a lot of balls, but you'd better watch your back."

Donovon picked up the telephone and called security to come escort Simeon from the building. They arrived quickly.

"Make sure I never seem him around here again," Donovon said as they led Simeon out.

"Yes, sir," the two officers replied.

"Have a good day, McNeil."

Lawrence entered Donovon's office just as Simeon was leaving. He pointed to Simeon.

"Was that who I think it was?" he asked.

Donovon walked back over to his desk.

"The devil himself," he answered.

"For real? What did he want?"

"He's lost his damn mind, coming up in here thinking I'm going to tell him where Nedra is."

Lawrence stood there in deep thought.

"Dude is crazy! I know it's exhausting protecting Nedra twenty-four, seven. All you have to do is say the word and I'll help you out."

"I appreciate it, Lawrence, but I got it," Donovon said as he picked up his keys.

"OK. I'll see you later."

Lawrence's heart accelerated at the sight of Simeon. He knew he had to help Donovon and Nedra, whether they wanted his help or not. Maybe this could help him right some of the wrongs he'd done in his past.

Chapter Thirty-Nine

Small Blessings

When Donovon got home, he found Nedra asleep. He started on dinner and caught up with some other household duties. He was still bothered by the comment Simeon made regarding a gun. Once Nedra was up, he was going to make her tell him everything once and for all.

Outside Donovon dumped the trash into the larger can. As he was about to pour more trash into the can, he noticed something from the corner of his eye. He reached into the wastebasket and pulled out the empty box.

Home pregnancy test? No wonder!

He finished dumping the rest of the trash into the can and ran up the stairs. He didn't knock when he reached the bedroom. When he entered, Nedra was sitting on the side of the bed with her head in her hands. His abrupt entry startled her.

"What's wrong?"

His eyes burned like coals.

"When were you going to tell me?"

"What?"

He held up the box and she dropped her head.

"I only found out today."

"You could've called."

"I didn't want to tell you over the phone."

"Is that why you're sick?"

"Probably, but Donovon, there's more."

He hadn't moved an inch since he entered the room.

"What?"

"Simeon forced himself on me the day I left him. He raped me."

Nedra noticed the muscles in Donovon's jar twitching.

He cleared his throat and asked the unthinkable.

"Did he use a gun to threaten you?"

Nedra nodded. "I was so scared."

Donovon didn't blink. It seemed as if his world had stopped revolving.

"Please say something, Donovon," she pleaded as she stood.

"You're having Mathews's baby?"

"I don't know, because it might be yours. I'm so sorry."

Donovon sat in a nearby chair and put his hands over his face. He was still holding the box. Nedra walked over and sat in his lap. He took a deep breath and put his arm around her waist.

"What are you going to do? Are you going to tell him?"

"If it's his, I'm sure he'll try to make my life even more miserable. He might even try to take the baby from me, but I'm having this baby, Donovon." She lay against his chest. "I pray to God this baby is yours," she whispered. "I'm so sorry for complicating your life even more."

He looked at her, surprised.

"You think I'm upset with you?"

"Well, yes."

"It's not your fault, Nedra."

She looked into his weary eyes.

"Yes, it is. I should've left Simeon a long time ago."

He kissed her forehead. "We need to focus on the here and now, Nedra, and forget about the past."

She lay against his warm chest in silence.

"Nedra?"

"Yes?"

"Simeon would have certain rights, but his abusive behavior could prevent him from having any contact with the child if it is his, and if this is *my* baby, I will promise to be the best father possible."

Tears dropped from her eyes.

"Nedra, we've wasted enough time. Marry me. Today!"

"Donovon, you can't do that."

"Why not?"

She lowered her eyes with shame.

"I don't want you to marry me because you feel like you have to."

He smiled down at her.

"I want to marry you because I love you. I've always loved you, Nedra."

"Are you sure about this? I mean, things are moving kind of fast."

"Actually, sweetheart, when you think about it, we've been moving pretty slowly."

"People will say we got married because I'm pregnant."

"Do you think I give a damn about what people think? This is our life and our love. We don't have to prove anything to anyone but each other."

She swallowed hard as she listened to him. He shouldn't have to convince her, but she didn't want him to feel obligated to her.

"This is crazy."

"What's crazy is that we've waited so long to do it. Our parents will be ecstatic, and so will everyone at work." Stroking her back, he kissed her lips. "So, are you going marry me or not?"

"Yes, Donovon, I'll marry you."

He smiled and pressed his mouth against her soft lips. To Donovon, this was the completion of a journey he thought he would never start. The kiss became more than just a seal of approval. It became the beginning of the rest of their lives. Overjoyed, Donovon's mouth was everywhere on her body. He ignited her with a fury of raw emotions. Her response to his pleasure startled him as she moaned out his name in a sultry, deep voice.

No man should be this good. God, please let this be Donovon's baby. Please!

"Donovon?"

"Uh huh?"

"If we're getting married today, we'd better stop."

He nodded in agreement.

"Nedra, this *is* our baby. I just want you to know that I'm not worried at all."

She raised his head to make eye contact.

"I believe you, and I'm not worried either."

* * *

The next morning Donovon and Nedra were married, but he promised her a real wedding whenever she wanted it. After they were married, Donovon and Nedra called their parents on three-way and decided to tell them the whole truth surrounding Simeon Mathews. It took the entire family hours to calm Nedra's father down. He told Donovon that he knew he would protect Nedra with his life, but that he shouldn't do anything that would put him in harm's way. Donovon's father reiterated Mr. Harris's statement.

"Donovon, call us if you have any problems or need anything. You take care of my daughter and grandchild."

"I will, sir, and thanks for everything. Daddy, I'll call you and Momma tomorrow. I love you."

When everyone hung up the phone, Austin Harris turned on the TV. The first face he saw was Simeon Mathews standing on the courthouse steps in an expensive suit. He was disgusted at his arrogant attitude as he explained the status of the mob case he was involved in. After listening to him, Austin cussed and shot the TV. Mrs. Harris came running into the family room in fear.

"Austin! What is wrong with you! Why did you shoot the TV?"

"That bastard Mathews was on it."

She removed her hand from her heart.

"Honey, you can't go around shooting out all the TVs. Donovon will take care of our baby. OK?"

"I'm sorry, Virginia. I'll buy another one tomorrow and try to get ahold on myself."

* * *

Later that night Nedra lay in Donovon's arms.

"What are you thinking about?" Donovon asked.

She kissed his neck.

"I'm thinking about how happy I am at this very moment."

"Same here, baby. Same here."

A couple of days later, Donovon and Nedra announced their marriage to their friends and coworkers. Their coworkers were shocked, but Lawrence and Ednita had been included in the private ceremony, and they couldn't have been happier for them.

Chapter Forty

Say It Isn't So

Approximately two months later the trial Simeon was involved in was the lead story in every newspaper and television station. His preoccupation with the trial made Nedra feel more at ease. The baby was also beginning to make his or her presence known physically. All of Nedra's clothes were becoming snug around the waist, so she decided to take the day off and go on a shopping spree and treat herself to some new outfits since she had a doctor's appointment in the afternoon.

Donovon had also become a little more relaxed since Simeon seemed to have moved on with his life. Maybe the meeting in Donovon's office was all the convincing Simeon needed. When Nedra told him she was going shopping, he was a little nervous, but he let her go with a warning to stay aware of her surroundings. They both knew Simeon was tied up during the day in court, so that was the best time for her to maneuver around alone.

* * *

After a couple of hours of shopping, Nedra made her way to the doctor's office. It didn't take long for the doctors to examine her and send her on her way. When she exited the examining room, she was in good spirits. At the receptionist's desk, the nurse spoke to her.

"Nedra, continue to take your prenatal vitamins and we'll do an ultrasound next time."

"Thank you. Good-bye."

She turned and walked out to the lobby at the same time a young couple exited another examining room. It was Simeon's friend, Raymond, and his wife. When he saw Nedra he did a double take.

"Wait here, honey. I'll be right back."

He went over to the sign-in sheet and scanned the signatures until he saw the name he was looking for,

Outside Raymond opened the car door for his wife and pulled out his cell phone.

"Hello?" Simeon answered.

"Hey, bro! You're on a break?"

"Something like that. What's up?"

"Why didn't you tell me Nedra was having a baby?"

"What did you say?"

"I just saw Nedra at the doctor's office. She didn't see me, and she left before I could get her attention. She's even showing a little. Why didn't you tell me you were going to be a daddy?"

Surprised, Simeon gripped the phone in anger.

"Look, Raymond, I can't talk right now, but I'll call you back later."

"Cool! Later, man, and congratulations."

Simeon hung up the phone and mumbled to himself.

"Well, well, well, I guess she didn't think I would find out." He pulled out his cell phone and dialed.

"Hey, man! I need a favor . . . a big favor."

Later that evening, Simeon went on one of his crazed rampages after learning of Nedra's pregnancy. He picked up one of his regulars and took her to a secluded cabin outside the city. The humiliation went on for hours and it didn't seem like it was going to stop anytime soon.

"Simeon, darling, can I at least get a drink of water?"

Simeon pointed his finger at her and yelled.

"You'll get a drink when I say you can have a drink, Nedra! Now get over here!"

"Who is Nedra?"

Simeon shook his head and laughed when he realized what he'd said. His behavior was erratic and he was nearing a complete mental breakdown. He pulled the woman into his arms and tilted her chin upward. His eyes were dark and glazy and it frightened her.

"She's just someone I used to hang out with, but she's dead now."

"Really? What happened to her?"

He slowly ran his hands down the woman's back and rested his hands on her backside.

"You don't want to know. Now come on, sweetheart. I want to feel your lips on me."

The woman did as she was told because she knew if she didn't, there would be hell to pay.

*   *   *

The following day the office gave Nedra and Donovon a surprise shower. They received gifts that would help decorating their new home much easier.

Ednita pulled Nedra to the side and smiled at her.

"Why are you smiling at me?" Nedra asked as she sipped her punch.

Ednita touched Nedra's stomach and smiled.

"It's just that I can't believe that you didn't tell me that you and Donovon were getting it on like that."

Nedra playfully slapped her hand.

"We didn't want to be the brunt of office gossip, so we kept our business on the down low."

"I understand, and I'm happy for you two. I hope you have a little girl."

"I'll be happy with either a boy or a girl, as long as it's healthy."

"I'll drink to that," Ednita said as she raised her glass in salute. "I can't wait to go baby shopping with you."

"I'd like that, Ednita."

Across the room, Lawrence patted Donovon on the shoulder.

"Man! You have got to be the luckiest man on earth!!"

"You're right," Donovon said as stared at Nedra from across the room.

"I just hope that lawyer guy has gone on about his business."

"You and me both," he said as he sipped his punch.

"I'm really happy for you guys. Nedra is a wonderful woman, and I know you two will be very happy together. Congratulations, man, and I still got your back just in case dude starts tripping again."

"Thanks, Lawrence. I'm really looking forward to holding my baby for the first time. I've loved Nedra for a long time."

"I knew it!"

Nedra and Donovon received so many gifts that they filled both of their vehicles. Back at the house, they enjoyed taking the time to look at each and every one of them. They knew the owners of the house they lived in would be returning from their trip the following week, so it would be the perfect time for them to purchase their own home. The three thousand square foot home they recently found would be plenty of room for them and the baby.

That night, as they boxed up their belongings, a breaking story came across the television.

"The case against Justin Leonardo has finally gone to the jury. Both the prosecution and the defense have rested their cases. Defense Attorney Simeon Mathews is confident that his client will be exonerated of all charges. The prosecution has a similar confidence in the justice system to prove that the Leonardo family will be recognized for what they are—criminals. The jury is not expected to return a speedy verdict. This could go on for days. Stay tuned for updates."

Donovon looked at Nedra's reaction to the news as he taped up a box.

"Don't let that upset you, Nedra. I'm sure that if Simeon had plans of causing any drama, he would've done it by now. OK?"

She smiled as she handed him another stack of baby items. "I'm kind of tired. Do you mind if we finish this tomorrow?"

"I'll take care of it because there's not much left to do anyway. Go on to bed. I have to pick up that new intern from the airport first thing in the morning. I'd feel better if you'd ride in with me."

She stood, stretched, and yawned.

"I'll be fine. I've been driving in without you for a while anyway."

She walked over to him and gave him a seductive kiss.

"You keep that up and you won't get any sleep tonight, Mrs. McNeil. Good night, and I'll be up in a minute."

"OK."

The work day was busy as usual. Nedra was handling her pregnancy well, and she was very excited about moving into their new home. She reached for the phone and dialed Donovon's extension.

"Donovon McNeil. How may I help you?"

"Well, for starters you can give me a hot bubble bath when you come home tonight."

He leaned back in his chair, enjoying the sensations running through his body at the thought of caressing Nedra's body in scented bath gel.

"Oh, Mrs. McNeil, I think I can handle that job with no problem. As a matter of fact, I think I'll come home early just to give you some special treatment."

Lawrence walked into the office, but when he realized Donovon was on a personal call, he started to back out the door.

"Hold on a second, Nedra. Lawrence, you can come on in and have a seat. I'm almost done."

Lawrence sat down in the chair opposite him and Donovon continued with his conversation.

"OK, Nedra, what were you saying?"

She giggled.

"I'm getting ready to go by the new house for a minute. I want to check some color swatches against the paint for the curtains in the baby's room."

"Can't that wait until I can go with you?"

"Donovon, I'm having the curtains made and the seamstress needs the information by tomorrow. I'll be fine. I'm only going to be out there for about thirty minutes."

Donovon tapped on his desk with concern.

"Be careful, Nedra. I don't have to tell you to watch your back."

"No doubt, baby. I'll see you in a few hours. I love you."

"I love you, too. Good-bye."

Donovon hung up the telephone and stared down at it. Lawrence snapped his fingers at him. "Hey, man, you look like you have a lot on your mind. Is Nedra OK?"

"Yeah, she's OK. I can't help but worry about her, you know?"

Lawrence laid some reports on Donovon's desk. "What is she up to?" he asked.

"She's headed out to the house to check some fabric or something for the baby's room," he said as he leaned back in his chair.

"Are you cool with it?"

"I'm cool. I just worry about her when she's traveling around town alone. Simeon's still out there, and you just never know what he might do. Luckily, he's in court most of the day."

"I don't blame you for worrying about her."

Donovon frowned and looked at his watch.

"Come take a ride with me, Lawrence. I have a few errands to run."

Their eyes met as if they were reading each other's minds. Donovon grabbed his jacket and Lawrence followed him out the door.

"Yeah, let's ride."

Nedra pulled into the three-car garage of their new home. She was anxious to move into their new home within the new subdivision still being developed. Their house was the only one near completion on their street, and they would be the first owners lucky enough to move in. She proceeded into the house and placed her purse on the kitchen counter. She rubbed her protruding stomach and smiled at the happiness filling her heart and her stomach. She pulled the color swatches from her purse and looked at them.

"OK, little baby, let's get this done so we can get home to your daddy."

She walked upstairs, leaving her purse and cell phone in the kitchen. She went into the baby's room and began to work with the swatches. Suddenly she heard a strange noise, but she couldn't tell where it had come from. Her heart started pounding when she realized she left her cell phone downstairs. Tiptoeing, she walked out into the hallway and listened for the noise again, but she didn't hear it.

She went back up to the baby's room and looked out the window. She noticed a large dog standing on a piece of aluminum siding. When it stepped off the piece of aluminum it made a loud popping noise. Nedra breathed a sigh of relief as she watched it turn the corner of the house.

When she turned around, Simeon grabbed her by the neck and pushed her hard against the wall. Stunned, she realized Simeon must have followed her and now she was at his mercy.

"Simeon! Please!!!

"Please what, Nedra? I told you, I would see you dead before I would let another man have you. First that big neck punk in college, now McNeil. Hell no!"

Nedra immediately noticed the gun in his hand and trembled in fear. Tears ran from her eyes as Simeon tightened his grip on her throat. She tried to remove his hand, but couldn't. She was starting to get lightheaded as she gasped for air. He noticed the wedding ring on her finger. He grabbed her hand and screamed at her.

"What the hell is this? You married him?"

Nedra knew she was in trouble when he started to cry.

"I've been nothing but good to you, Nedra, and look how you repay me. You have fought me the whole time, being so independent, arrogant, and stubborn. I'll be damned if I let someone else have you."

"Simeon, I'm pregnant, and it might be your child."

He looked at her in disbelief and started laughing hysterically. He kept his large hands around her neck and continued to laugh.

"That little bastard's not mine. I'm sterile, and have been for almost ten years thanks to an unfortunate motorcycle accident."

He reached down to caress her stomach and she flinched in fear. She had no idea what he was capable of at this point, especially since he was holding the gun close to her stomach.

"No, Nedra, there's no way that could be my baby. That means it must be McNeil's, but he'll never get to have you or this little bastard of his."

Shivering, she begged for her life and the life of her baby.

"Simeon, I'm sorry! Please don't do this!"

He leaned in and kissed her as she cried uncontrollably. Somehow she found the strength to raise her leg and knee him hard in the groin. He immediately released his grip and fell to the floor in pain. Nedra ran out of the room, stumbling in the hallway. She could hear him screaming her name.

"Nedra! Get back here!"

She practically fell down the stairs as she struggled to get away from him. She grabbed her purse, ran into the garage, and fell right into Donovon's arms.

"Help!!"

"Calm down, baby, it's me!"

"Donovon!!" she screamed. "Simeon's upstairs and he has a gun!"

"Get out of here, Nedra," he yelled before running inside the house.

"No, Donovon, don't go in there! Please!"

"Get out of here! Now!!"

Nedra drove her car out of the garage and down the street as fast as she could.

Lawrence was waiting in the car until he saw

Nedra back out of the garage at a high rate of speed. He jumped out of the car and ran toward the house to see what was going on. Inside the house, he found Donovon in the kitchen with his gun drawn.

"What's going on, Donovon? I saw Nedra hauling ass out of here."

"Nedra said Simeon's upstairs and he has a gun."

Upstairs they heard Simeon moaning and groaning.

"Hey, man, how do you want to do this?" Lawrence asked.

Donovon's eyes were red with anger.

"I'm going to go up the back steps and blow his ass away."

Lawrence thought about the risk Donovon was taking, and then he thought of another idea.

"Yo, Donovon, I know how much you want to kill him, but you're about to be a father. You have a lot at stake. Get in your car and get out of here."

"What?"

Lawrence repeated himself and held out his hand.

"Give me the gun and get out of here. You need to go see about Nedra. I can handle this."

Donovon was so angry he was about to explode.

"Hell, no," he whispered. "This doesn't concern you, Lawrence. Simeon is my problem. You're the one who needs to get out of here."

At that moment, they heard Simeon stumble out into the upstairs hallway cursing.

"Nedra! You bitch! You're dead!"

Lawrence looked around the kitchen and noticed some building supplies left by the contractors.

"I'm not going to tell you again, Donovon. Get

your ass out of here. Nedra could be hurt. She needs you. I got this."

"How are you going to get back to the office?"

"I'm not, and if anybody asks where I am, tell them I had to fly home unexpectedly to take care of some family business. Now go!"

He was worried about Nedra, but he wanted to be the one to confront Simeon, not Lawrence. Against his better judgment, he walked out of the kitchen, got into his car, and drove away, leaving Lawrence behind.

Nedra had driven a few miles when she pulled over into a mini-mall parking lot. The reality of what had just happened hit her as she laid her head against the steering wheel and sobbed. Her body was trembling like it never had before. She was so afraid that Simeon would hurt Donovon or worse. Her cell phone started ringing and she slowly pulled it from her purse.

"Hello?"

Donovon almost didn't recognize her voice.

"Nedra, where are you?"

"I'm in the parking lot of the Brenthaven Mall."

Within minutes, he came to a halt next to her car and jumped out. She was still clutching the cell phone with her head against the steering wheel. He knocked on the window and made her unlock the door. She practically dove into his arms. Donovon's heart was about to burst out of his chest with fear. He noticed the torn blouse and her bruised neck. He started inspecting her for more serious injuries.

"It's OK, baby. I'm here. Sh-h-h-h, I got you, sweetheart."

"I want to go home, Donovon. I just want to go home."

"Nedra, baby, I want to take you to the hospital to make sure you and the baby are OK."

She nodded in agreement as she wiped away her tears.

"What happened?"

He opened the door for her to climb into his car.

"Don't you worry about Simeon. I need to get you to the hospital."

Donovon drove her straight to the emergency room. After she checked out OK, they climbed back inside the car.

"I need to get you home."

She looked over at him curiously.

"What happened at the house?"

"I left Simeon there to come see about you. Are you up to going back out there to check on things?"

"I'm scared, Donovon," she whispered.

He caressed her face and kissed her cheek.

"Don't worry, Nedra. Everything will be OK. I'll make sure the house is secure and then we'll get your car so we can go home. "

It took Donovon about forty-five minutes to get back out to their house. When they arrived, they didn't see anything out of the ordinary. Donovon pulled in front of their house and opened the car door. Nedra nervously grabbed his arm.

"Donovon, I'm scared. What if he's still in there?"

He kissed her and smiled.

"I'll be fine. Sit tight. I'll be right back."

Nedra watched as Donovon cautiously walked toward their house. He took out his key and entered as quietly as possible. He searched each room and didn't find any sign of Simeon or Lawrence.

Donovon returned to his car and climbed in. He had no idea what happened between Simeon and Lawrence in the house, but he felt confident that Lawrence had everything under control.

"Is he gone?"

"Yes, he's gone. Let's get you home so we can call the police. Simeon has violated his restraining order and he needs to be locked up."

"It's my word against his, Donovon. Simeon is never going to give up until I'm dead."

"He will if I have anything to do with it. I want you on a plane in the morning to your parents' home until Mathews can be dealt with."

She looked over at him and shook her head. "I'm not leaving you."

"Yes, you are, and it's not up for discussion. I'm not going to let him get another chance to hurt you and our baby."

She lowered her eyes.

"Can we at least wait until morning to call the police? I can't deal with them tonight."

"Are you sure?" he asked.

"Yes, I'm sure."

"First thing in the morning, Nedra, we're calling the cops."

"OK."

*   *   *

Hours later Donovon gave Nedra the warm bubble bath he promised her. She lay back in the tub while he caressed her body with tenderness.

"Donovon?"

"Yes, sweetheart."

He gently rubbed the suds on her back.

"Simeon told me he was sterile."

Donovon stopped bathing her for a second and she turned to him.

"Are you serious?"

She smiled with relief. "He told me he had some type of motorcycle accident and had been sterile for over ten years."

He rubbed suds on her round stomach and sprinkled her neck with light kisses.

"Do you believe him?"

"Yes, because he was very upset with the fact that I was pregnant. He wouldn't have been upset if there was a chance that he was the father. That would've given him some leverage to make my life even more miserable."

Donovon continued to caress her stomach lovingly. She cupped his face and gave him a passionate kiss. He looked up at her with tearful eyes.

"Are you OK?"

"I couldn't be better," he said, smiling.

"Well, Daddy, in about seven months you will meet your son or daughter. Are you up to it?"

"I'm up to anything with you by my side. I love you, Nedra."

"I love you too, Donovon."

*   *   *

Late that night, as Nedra slept, Lawrence called Donovon from his California home.

"Hey, man. How are you two doing?"

Donovon quietly walked out of the bedroom so he could talk without disturbing Nedra.

"We're doing as well as can be expected. What happened?"

"You guys have nothing to worry about. Everything's cool. I just had to fly home to take care of a little business. I'll be back home in a few days."

Walking downstairs, Donovon made his way into the kitchen. As he listened to Lawrence, he realized he couldn't talk like he wanted.

"Thanks, Lawrence," Donovon said.

"No problem. I'll see you in a few days. Give Nedra my love."

"Will do, and have a safe flight back. I'll tell Nedra you called. Thanks for calling to check on us. Bye."

Lawrence hung up the telephone. "Lord, please forgive me," he whispered.

What he didn't reveal to Donovon was how he held a gun on Simeon as he tied him up. After putting a gag in his mouth, he took Simeon's car keys and wallet and forced him to tell him where his car was parked. Once Lawrence pulled Simeon's car into the garage of the vacant house, he was able to put Simeon in the trunk of the car and drive to his home. Once inside Simeon's garage, he opened the trunk, knocked Simeon unconscious, and put him behind the wheel of his car. After starting the engine, Lawrence slipped out of the garage unnoticed and walked until he got to a nearby train station. He hurried home, packed a few clothes and caught the next plane out of town to California.

He walked downstairs to continue visiting with his mother and some other members of his family. Donovon was relieved to finally hear from Lawrence. He didn't know what Lawrence meant by his comments, but he reassured Donovon that everything was under control. Donovon turned on the TV. He figured he would find out what had really happened as soon as Lawrence returned from California.

Donovon opened the refrigerator to search for a snack. He found some leftover lasagna, so he pulled it out and popped it in the microwave. The news was coming on. As Donovon pulled his dish out of the microwave, one name caught his attention.

"There has been a strange development in the case against the Leonardo crime family. Their long-time lawyer, Simeon Mathews, was found dead in his garage tonight by what appears to be suicide. Neighbors were drawn to his home after hearing his vehicle running in the garage. Detectives found Mathews slumped over behind the wheel of his car, apparently killed by carbon monoxide fumes. An autopsy will be performed to confirm the cause of death. As for the case he was defending, it had already gone to the jury, and a verdict is expected soon. We'll keep you posted on the outcome of the trial and the investigation surrounding Simeon Mathews's death."

Donovon nearly dropped his plate on the floor as he stood there mesmerized by the news report.

He decided right then that he wouldn't ask Lawrence anything about what had happened at the house today. Whatever went down, it was best he didn't know. The sad task would be telling Nedra what happened. While he knew she would be relieved, it would still hurt her knowing that Simeon's antics had brought him to an untimely end.

Epilogue

The following spring, Nedra gave birth to an eight-pound baby boy, whom they named Cameron Austin McNeil after both of their dads. They also chose a different house in a different neighborhood so Nedra wouldn't have to deal with the bad memories of Simeon Mathews.

Simeon's death was ruled a suicide, which detectives suspected was the result of stress brought on by the high profile trial of the Leonardo family. FBI sources also reported that Simeon had been under investigation for laundering money for the crime family; however, the investigation surrounding Simeon Mathews's death was closed forever.

Nedra was upset about Simeon's death, but as a child she was taught that if you lived by the sword, you would die by the sword. Her anguish was over, but she couldn't help but wonder if Simeon would still be alive if he had just left her alone and gone on with his life. He had some issues, and while she cared deeply for him at one time, something happened to him that put him on a destructive path.

Lawrence didn't miss a beat after returning back from California. He was back to being the office comedian, and neither he nor Donovon ever mentioned that one infamous day ever again.

Donovon never told Nedra about that day at the house, or how Lawrence was involved. He wanted her to focus on their future and not the drama of their past. After all, they had a son to raise, and hopefully a few more children in their future.

About the Author

Author Darrien Lee resides in Tennessee with her husband of fourteen years and two young daughters.

Darrien picked up her love for writing while attending Tennessee State University, and it was those experiences which inspired her debut novel, *All That and A Bag of Chips*, in 2001. She has published works by Strebor Books Int'l Inc. and a lot of new and exciting projects scheduled for future release.

Darrien's other literary accomplishments include *Been There Done That*, which made *Essence* Magazine's Bestseller's List in 2003 as the sequel to her debut novel. *What Goes Around Comes Around* followed up in July 2004 as part three of her series, and it was so successful it made *Essence* Magazine's Best-Seller's List on two separate occasions. The fourth novel in her series, titled *When Hell Freezes Over*, was released in September 2005 with hopes of following in the path of the two previous titles.

She is currently working on her teen series, Denim Diaries.

Darrien is a member of A Place Of Our Own On-line Reading Club as well as Authors Supporting Authors Positively Online Group. Darrien has been featured in several periodicals, which includes, *The City Paper* and the *Nashville Tennessean*. She was also a featured guest with popular Atlanta DJ Porsche Foxx on V103 Radio Station on her "Issues" segment in 2002.

See more information on Darrien at her website www. DarrienLeeAuthor.com.

PREVIEW

Someone Else's Puddin'

By Samuel L. Hair

When Melody entered room 222, Larry was lying naked across the bed, erect as penitentiary steel, and smoking a joint of chronic. She wasted no time getting naked and pouring herself a glass of vodka. As Larry relaxed, entertained by porn movies and her 38Ds, he smiled.

"You're my baby, Melody. Believe it or not, you're the best thing that has ever happened to me. I love you and I always will, no matter what."

She enjoyed hearing those words, especially coming from Larry, and not from her ghetto-fied, institutionalized husband who couldn't seem to stay out of prison for more than two months at a time.

Larry had stuffed his paraplegic wife, Pat, with tranquilizers, assuring she would remain asleep while he snuck out for his rendezvous with her beautician, Melody. Meanwhile, Melody had filled her teenage son's request for McDonald's and Taco Bell. Afterward, while watching BET, her son fell asleep. The secret lovers both had green lights. Luckily, the rich and ruthless Michelle, Melody's extremely jealous lesbian lover, had no knowledge of Melody's date with Larry. This was a good thing, since Michelle was known to kill when it came to someone messing around with her puddin'.

Larry had rented a suite at the Travelodge for the entire month—a luxury hideaway for himself and Melody to get away from life's issues, problems, and also from people who knew them and their spouses. It was a six-day-a-week ritual for the secret lovers to meet between two and six p.m. to socialize, have a couple drinks, and to have uncut, explicit sex.

They made each other feel needed and appreciated. Unfortunately, on this particular day, their date was delayed due to Pat's illness.

The fact that they were both married didn't matter to them. They had grown accustomed to fooling around with someone else's puddin'. They had kept their relationship a secret for over four years, and not once had Melody thought of saying no to Larry, dismissing him, or rejecting him for any reason, not even for her mother, who had advised her several times to break off her relationship with the married man. After all, he was the man who showered her with diamonds, gold, a variety of other expensive gifts, paid her house note, car note, dressed her son in name-brand tennis shoes and designer clothing, and gave her raw, pleasurable, uninhibited sex. Under no circumstances was she going to dismiss him out of her life. No way in hell.

After taking another long swallow of Popov vodka, she began showing her appreciation for all the things he had done for her. She fell to her knees like she was about to pray, while he sat comfortably at the edge of the bed sipping vodka. She then took his long, fat penis into her hands and began gently massaging and stroking it. Then she began sucking, licking, and slurping in exactly the way he had taught her.

"Uumhmm, yes, baby, yes. Damn, you make me feel so good," Larry moaned. Gradually, she sped up her rhythm, causing him to quiver and tremble, which is something his wife had never done. She thought about bringing him to a climax, but quickly dismissed the thought.

"No, baby, not now. I want to feel your hot, thick juice inside me," Melody said.

She brought her lips and tongue to a halt and quickly exchanged positions with him. It was now her turn. He ran his snake-like tongue up and down her legs while twirling three long, fat fingers in and out of her hot, juicy womb. He then began licking her clitoris, causing her to move rhythmically and have tremors that triggered breathtaking multiple orgasms. They had been sexing one another for so long that they had mastered each other's bodies and knew when the other was about to climax.

"I want it, baby. Now." Melody moaned, giving him the signal to immediately enter her. Suddenly he flipped her like a pancake, and she dutifully bent over and grabbed the edge of the bed. Impatiently, he thrust his rock hard penis inside her hot, wet, trembling tunnel of passion. His strokes were slow and deep and his penis touched all the right spots.

"Ooh, yes, give it to me, Big Daddy. Yes, damn, I

want it all," Melody begged. At that moment he pulled out, flipped her on her back as if he was angry, and she instinctively placed her legs over his shoulders. He thrust his hard, throbbing penis inside her, plunging into the depths of her womb, riding her with rough passion, pounding like a jackhammer, just the way she enjoyed it. Her cries of pleasure filled the room and caused a crazed, wild look to develop in his eyes. He plunged harder, deeper, and faster, and then suddenly, simultaneously, they exploded like volcanoes in full eruption. Afterward, they lay side by side totally spent, but relieved of all stress and daily pressures.

Mission accomplished. And so they returned to their spouses.